THE VOICES

F. R. TALLIS is a writer and clinical psychologist. He has written self-help manuals, non-fiction for the general reader, academic textbooks, over thirty academic papers in international journals and several novels. Between 1999 and 2012 he received or was shortlisted for numerous awards, including the New London Writers' Award, the Ellis Peters Historical Dagger, the Grand Prix des Lectrices de Elle and two Edgars. His critically acclaimed Liebermann series (written as Frank Tallis) has been translated into fourteen languages and optioned for TV adaptation. His most recent books are *The Forbidden*, a horror story set in nineteenth-century Paris, *The Sleep Room*, about a pioneering, controversial sleep therapy, and this, *The Voices*, which is his latest.

For more on Frank Tallis, visit his website
www.franktallis.com
or follow him on Twitter @FrankTallis

BY F. R. TALLIS

The Forbidden

The Sleep Room

The Voices

Writing as Frank Tallis

FICTION

Killing Time

Sensing Others

Mortal Mischief

Vienna Blood

Fatal Lies

Darkness Rising

Deadly Communion

Death and the Maiden

NON-FICTION

Changing Minds

Hidden Minds

Love Sick

F. R. TALLIS

THE VOICES

PAN BOOKS

First published 2014 by Pan Books
an imprint of Pan Macmillan, a division of Macmillan Publishers Limited
Pan Macmillan, 20 New Wharf Road, London N1 9RR
Basingstoke and Oxford
Associated companies throughout the world
www.panmacmillan.com

ISBN 978-1-4472-3602-3

1 3 5 7 9 8 6 4 2

A CIP catalogue record for this book is available from the British Library.

Typeset by Ellipsis Digital Limited, Glasgow
Printed and bound by CPI Group (UK) Ltd, Croydon, CR0 4YY

THE VOICES

November 1974

The newsreader's voice was solemn, his delivery self-consciously measured. Two bombs had exploded in Birmingham the previous evening. They had been left in pubs: the Mulberry Bush and the nearby Tavern in the Town. Nineteen people had been killed and over one hundred and eighty injured. Most of the casualties were teenagers and police believed that the Provisional IRA was responsible.

Christopher Norton glanced at Laura, his wife. He knew what she was thinking. *What a world. What a world to bring a child into.* They spoke for a while about how terrible it was, bandied around words like 'atrocious' and 'horrific', but neither of them confessed their deepest fear. The baby – nameless, unborn – was already arousing their protective instincts.

The road ahead was dappled with shadow like a country lane. It penetrated the southern edge of Hampstead Heath and led down to a collection of villas nestled at the foot of a wooded slope: a hidden village, concealed in a pocket of London's complex topography. The houses were clean, well maintained, and produced a typically English impression of quaint gentility. Even the lamp posts were old-fashioned and resembled gaslights.

Christopher stopped the car and peered through the windscreen. Set apart from the other dwellings was a substantial Victorian edifice. It had bay windows decorated with stone tracery, a magnificent porch and tall, ornate chimneys. Laura unfastened her handbag, removed a powder compact, and studied her face in the small, circular mirror. A swarthy man wearing a bright blue suit was approaching. The collar of his shirt was dark and projected out onto the broad lapels of his jacket.

'Mr Petrakis,' said Christopher.

Laura looked up and snapped the powder compact shut.

They got out of the car and Christopher introduced his wife. The estate agent commented on the bombings and added that a member of his family lived in Birmingham: a cousin studying to be a dentist at the university.

'Is he all right?' Laura asked.

'*She*,' Petrakis corrected. 'Yes, she's fine. But we were very worried, as you can imagine.' Petrakis led them up a path and pushed open an iron gate. The hinges squeaked. 'Be careful now. Don't trip.' Tiles had fallen from the roof and shattered pieces of slate lay on the ground. The garden was wild and full of litter. Mr Petrakis produced a bunch of keys and unlocked the front door. 'After you,' he said, ushering them into the hallway.

The house smelt of damp. All the carpets were rotten and upstairs one of the ceilings sagged ominously. Nevertheless, the stately grandeur of the original features was redeeming. There were marble fireplaces, carved banisters and exquisitely moulded cornices; four bedrooms, two bathrooms, a drawing room and a vast kitchen.

When Christopher had viewed the property for the first time, he had appreciated its possibilities, but was disinclined to commit himself to such a major restoration project. The house needed a lot of work to make it habitable. Even though the investment would probably pay off in the long term, he had realized the initial outlay would be punitive. His reservations, however, had been mitigated by the airy room on the top floor that he instantly recognized as a potential studio. It was perfect. He had seen, at once, where everything would fit: the guts of an old piano, the mixing desk, the VCS3, the tape recorders. He had imagined himself seated within a horseshoe arrangement of equipment, working on new compositions and pausing to enjoy the view over the treetops.

After Petrakis had finished showing them around,

Christopher asked him why the house was in such a dilapidated state.

'It hasn't been lived in for years,' Petrakis replied. 'Developers acquired the property in the sixties. They wanted to knock it down and build a block of flats, but the local residents objected and planning permission was refused. The company had a large portfolio – too large, actually – and they forgot about this place. As you know, many businesses have been struggling. The company went bankrupt in January. There was a lot of legal wrangling and eventually the receivers were called in.'

Christopher and the estate agent talked for a little while longer but eventually their conversation stalled. 'I'm just going outside for a cigarette,' said Petrakis. He had sensed that the couple wanted to be alone. 'Have another look around. Take your time. I'm in no hurry.'

Laura was standing by the French windows, leaning backwards and pushing the tight, unusually rounded bulge of her stomach forward. She pressed the base of her spine with both hands. It was curious, Christopher thought, how pregnancy hadn't really affected her figure. She was just the same as before, lithe, supple, the only difference being the odd, ball-like distension. Christopher walked over to her and kissed her on the lips.

'Well?' he asked. 'What do you think?'

Laura smiled. 'It's amazing, but . . .'

'What?'

'How long would it be before we could move in?'

'I don't know. A while.'

'Six months?'

'I don't know. Maybe more. We can manage until then, can't we?'

'Yes. I suppose so.'

Laura turned away from him and looked through the grimy French windows into the rear garden, which was a jungle of apple trees, bushes and weeds encircled by a high wall. The original landscaping was buried beneath the overgrowth, but an open space – roughly in the middle – might have once been a lawn. At the far end of the garden was a dilapidated gazebo.

'I expect you've already chosen the nursery,' said Christopher.

Laura glanced over her shoulder. 'Of course. The room with the striped wallpaper.'

Christopher went over to the fireplace and examined the maculated red marble surround. Even the corbels had been carefully crafted. They were shaped like waves and decorated with a scallop shell relief. Many of Christopher's friends had had their old fireplaces ripped out, because they considered them to be too fussy, too ugly, too ostentatious. Victorian excesses didn't go well with plain brown walls, white curtains, and the compulsory acreage of shagpile carpet. Christopher's modernism rarely accompanied him out of the studio. He didn't like the cold uniformity of contemporary design. He found it soulless.

Suddenly, his thoughts were interrupted by the sound of Laura gasping – an intake of breath that signalled surprise. He looked across the room and saw her cautiously approaching the French windows.

'What is it?' he asked.

Laura removed a layer of dirt from the glass with her sleeve, creating an arc of improved visibility.

'Laura? What is it?' Christopher repeated.

She met his concerned gaze with a puzzled expression. 'I thought I saw something.'

'What? An animal?'

'No. It was nothing.' She suddenly appeared embarrassed. 'I was mistaken.'

'Shall I get Petrakis?'

'Whatever for?'

Christopher realized he was still reacting to her initial alarm. He moved to her side and surveyed the green expanse. 'It could have been a fox.'

'No. It wasn't anything. Really.' Laura smiled and

promptly changed the subject. 'I've always wanted to live in a house like this.'

'It'll look great. When everything's done. And so much space. More space than we're ever going to need. Even if we decide to expand. Plenty of room for brothers and sisters.' Christopher rested his hand on Laura's stomach. He felt the impact of a small heel in his palm and Laura raised her eyebrows, smiling at him.

'Did you feel it?'

'Yes. I felt it.' He kissed her again. 'Of course, we're not near any shops here.'

'That's OK.'

'Pushing a pram up and down the hill isn't going to be easy.'

'It'll keep me fit.'

Christopher took Laura's hand, and together they walked out into the hallway and up the stairs.

'A lot of famous people have lived in the Vale,' said Christopher.

'And now you,' said Laura, playfully.

Christopher ignored the compliment. Or at least he pretended to ignore it. In fact, he found his wife's loyalty and support deeply satisfying. He continued: 'D. H. Lawrence, Compton Mackenzie . . .'

'D. H. Lawrence?'

'Yes.'

'I read *Women in Love* when I was at school. It felt like I was reading something completely wicked. I thought I'd be arrested if anyone found out.'

'Who gave it to you?'

'One of my friends – Imelda Cartwright. Her parents were old-fashioned intellectuals and quite eccentric. They didn't mind her reading Lawrence.' Laura frowned. 'Not like my parents. Sanctimonious prigs.'

'Forget them.'

'I have. Though . . .' Laura paused and it seemed to Christopher that she wasn't sure whether to express what she was thinking. 'Though it's a shame the baby won't have grandparents.'

'Oh, I don't know,' said Christopher, remembering his own mother and father – a rather stiff and undemonstrative pair. Even if they had survived their respective illnesses, he didn't think they'd have been very interested in a grandchild: hospital visits and ongoing treatment had become an almost exclusive preoccupation. Towards the end of their lives, there hadn't been much room for anything else.

After reaching the first-floor landing, Christopher and Laura entered the room with striped wallpaper. Laura let go of Christopher's hand and walked over to the sash window. She looked down into the garden, albeit briefly, but Christopher noticed the casual glance. He couldn't help but think she was, in some sense, checking.

'The cot will go here,' said Laura, approaching a corner. 'And the chest of drawers over there.' She pointed at the opposite wall.

Christopher tried to imagine how the room would look after it had been redecorated. Pink for a girl, blue for a boy? Laura occasionally held a pin on a thread above her bump and observed its movements; however, she had never been inclined to share the results of her divinatory experiments. Christopher found it easier to picture pink surfaces rather than blue, and this, perhaps, reflected a slight gender preference on his part, although the idea of producing a daughter aroused many anxieties. Little girls grew up; they became interested in boys and stayed out late. The sexual threat that inevitably attaches itself to an attractive young woman (and Christopher had no doubt that his daughter would be attractive, if only because of her mother) touched the rawest of parental nerves. A daughter would mean many sleepless nights.

When Laura had finished planning the nursery, she walked briskly out onto the landing and then into an adjacent bedroom.

'I'm just going to the top floor,' said Christopher. 'OK?' He wanted to look at his studio again.

'OK,' Laura replied. 'When you're done, maybe we should let Mr Petrakis get back to his office?'

'Sure.'

Christopher climbed the stairs, eager and excited.

That night, they made love. The bedroom curtains were only half drawn and admitted a haze of neon luminescence: a jaundiced city light that transformed objects into floating, pale grey forms. Christopher and his wife lay side by side, both facing the same way, their movements eliciting a slow metallic accompaniment from the mattress springs, a rhythmic see-sawing of pitches. Paradoxically, Christopher's pleasure was amplified by Laura's condition, because it necessitated restraint. Frustration seemed to make him exquisitely sensitive.

Laura curled around her swollen stomach and raised her knees.

'I love you.'

It was said with unusual force, as though she were making a demand rather than a declaration. Christopher embraced the taught, hard surface, the curved drum of skin. Their hands slid together and locked tightly.

Sex had never felt so strange: so carnal, and yet so exalted.

Laura began to breath faster and lowered her knees. The upper half of her body twisted away and she buried her face in a pillow. She emitted a low moan. He raised himself on an elbow in order to watch her climax. In everyday life, she was so careful about her appearance. Her make-up was always applied with fastidious precision, her hair reinforced with lacquer and cunningly trained into a semblance of felicitous neglect. To see her like this – febrile, dishevelled, beaded with perspiration, and lost in abandonment – was unbearably exciting. She closed her eyes and Christopher felt her shudder. He could no longer hold himself back and his explosive release left him feeling deliciously spent.

The room smelt of joss sticks and fresh linen. Christopher traced a line down his wife's spine and she acknowledged the contact with a soft sigh. His mind was pleasantly vacant, but it soon filled with recollections of the day: the house, the room he had chosen as his studio, and Petrakis. He needed to get a surveyor, an architect and a reliable builder. The garden could wait.

This last thought reminded him of Laura, standing by the French windows. The memory reconstructed itself in the soft pastels of his imagination. He saw her once again leaning back and pressing the base of her spine. He remembered her gasping, her agitation as she looked through the glass.

'Laura?'

'Yes.'

'When we were at the house today . . .'

'Yes.'

'What was it that you saw in the garden?'

'I told you. It was nothing.'

'All right, what did you *think* you saw?'

'A man. A man coming out of the gazebo.' She paused. 'But there was no one there. Not really.'

'What did he look like?'

Laura showed her irritation by striking the duvet. 'There was no one there.'

'What are you saying? That you were hallucinating?'

'Maybe.'

'Maybe?' Dismay made his voice climb to a falsetto.

'It happens,' Laura replied, unperturbed by her husband's reaction. 'It's not uncommon during pregnancy.'

'Since when?'

'Lots of women see things. Dots, shapes . . .'

'You've never mentioned that before.'

'Would you have been interested?'

'Yes. How many times has it happened?'

'Only once or twice. I've seen the dots – out of the corner of my eye. They move very fast.' She replicated their trajectory with her hand.

'What's the cause?'

'Hormones, I suppose. They seem to account for everything.'

Christopher was silent for a few moments. Then he said: 'Seeing dots is one thing. But a man? Seeing a man—'

'Hormones,' Laura cut in. 'Chris, it doesn't matter. He wasn't there.' She turned to face Christopher. The change of position was difficult for her to accomplish and the effort made her slightly breathless. 'Why are you going on about this?'

'I'm not going on about it.'

'Yes, you are.'

'All right. What if you weren't hallucinating? What if there's a tramp living in the garden?'

'There was no one there,' Laura said firmly.

'But what if there was?'

'He'll move on. That's what tramps do. As soon as the builders turn up.' A car passed and Laura yawned. 'Besides, I didn't see a tramp.'

'What did you see?'

'A man wearing an old-fashioned coat. A frock coat. I blinked – and he wasn't there anymore. OK?'

Christopher stroked Laura's hair. 'OK.'

'Can we go to sleep now?'

'Yes.'

Christopher closed his eyes and entered a state that was neither wakefulness nor dreaming, but somewhere in between. He heard fragments of conversation and saw flickering images of red double-decker buses, but he remained tethered to reality. He knew all along that he was still in his bed.

'Oh my God!' Laura screeched.

Christopher was wide awake in an instant. 'What? What is it?'

Laura sat up and put her hand between her thighs.

'Oh my God,' she repeated, this time less hysterically. 'I think my waters have broken.'

'Jesus Christ,' said Christopher. 'What do we do now?'

A West Indian nurse, smiling broadly, was standing in front of him, holding out a bundle of terry cloth. Buried in a loop of towelling was a tiny pink face: eyes, nose, lips and ears, compressed into an unfeasibly small space. Christopher took his daughter and sat down on an orange plastic chair. Without breaking the spell of this first, special communion, the nurse repositioned his elbow so that the baby's head was better supported. Her ministrations were performed with such sensitivity that Christopher was completely unaware that she had intervened. Time became meaningless. Each subjective moment stretched beyond the arbitrary limits of measurement. Christopher, entranced, stunned, placed his index finger into the palm of his daughter's hand. She opened her mouth and emitted a small cry. Her vulnerability was simply too much to bear. Something seemed to rupture in his chest, the world blurred and tears began to stream down his cheeks. 'Faye,' he said very softly, struggling to control himself. 'Hello, Faye.'

March 1975

Four months later

The door of the house was wide open. Christopher could hear the sound of hammering and loud, distorted music. He locked the car and made his way through the front garden between a yellow skip and piles of stacked timber. After entering the hallway, he turned into the drawing room, where he found two carpenters replacing floor-boards. The air was opaque with cigarette smoke. One of the men noticed Christopher and nodded.

'Where's Mr Ellis?' Christopher shouted above the din.

'The governor's upstairs,' the man hollered back.

Christopher climbed to the top of the house where he found a ladder angled into the attic. Footsteps crossed the ceiling and Mr Ellis's face appeared in the square outline of the hatch. He had long, greasy hair and uncultivated sideburns that grew down to his jawline. 'Ah, Mr Norton. How are you?'

'Very well, thanks. And you?'

'Not so bad. I've been taking a look at the roof.' The builder paused and his expression became sombre.

'Bad news?' asked Christopher.

'Why don't you come up here and have a look for yourself?' Christopher climbed the ladder and joined his builder. The attic was much brighter than Christopher had expected. 'Just walk on the beams, yeah?' said Ellis. 'If you put your feet anywhere else, you'll go straight through.' He chopped the air to make sure that his companion understood what would happen. Christopher followed Ellis like a tightrope walker, his arms extended, carefully placing one foot in front of the other. The two men arrived beneath a gaping hole through which slow-moving clouds were visible.

'Jesus,' said Christopher.

'You need a new roof, really,' said Ellis. 'But I can patch it up if you want.'

Christopher thought about his mortgage, his bank loans and the number of HP agreements he had signed recently. 'Patch it up.'

'All right,' said Ellis. The builder pointed at an assortment of objects in a shadowy recess. 'Do you want me to take this stuff down to the skip?'

'What is it?'

'Junk.'

'What kind of junk?'

'Old junk.'

'I'll take a look at it first.'

'Fair enough.' Ellis returned to the ladder. 'I'm going to see how they're getting on downstairs. Don't forget to walk on the beams, eh?'

'I won't.' The builder paused to have one more look at the roof, before vanishing through the floor.

Christopher went to examine the discarded items. At first it was difficult to determine what he was looking at, because everything was covered in a thick layer of dust. The most conspicuous objects were four large boards lying on their sides. They were decorated with faded Chinese dragons. Christopher thought that they were probably the remains of an oriental screen, and wondered whether it could be reassembled. When he examined the panels more closely, he discovered numerous scratches and cracks. The screen – if it was a screen – was obviously beyond repair.

In a cardboard box he found a collection of 78 rpm shellac records. None of the artists were significant and many of the discs were in fragments. He held one up to the light and read the label: *The International Zonophone Company. Death of Nelson, sung by Mr Ernest Pike with orchestral accompaniment, London*. The formality of the language amused him. There were some large mirrors –

once again, broken – some thin wire on a reel and a lampshade. Another cardboard box contained a vintage camera. It was made from mahogany and brass but its bellows were torn. When Christopher turned the camera over some of the parts fell away. He didn't bother to pick them up. By his feet, Christopher saw what looked like a framed theatre handbill. He crouched to take a look. A web of cracks obscured most of the text, but he was able to make out a few details: *Mr Edward Maybury . . . secrets of the ancient world . . . automatons . . . manifestations and vanishings.* At the bottom of the bill was some practical information: *Every day from 3 till 5 and 8 till 10. Carriages at 5 and 10. Fauteuils, 5 shillings; Stalls, 3 shillings; Balcony, 1 shilling.* Turning his attention to a heap of floral curtains, he tugged them aside. The action was excessively violent and he had to wait for the dust to settle before he could identify what he had uncovered. It was a traveller's trunk made from brown leather and reinforced with metal trim. A tarnished nameplate near the lock had been engraved with the initials 'E.S.M.' *Edward Maybury?* Christopher lifted the lid and found himself looking down at a clock-work monkey, a spinning top, some lead soldiers and a mangy teddy bear, but the trunk was otherwise disappointingly empty. Ellis had been right. There was nothing here of value. It really was 'old junk'.

Christopher was about to close the lid, but hesitated. He picked up the clockwork monkey, half expecting it to fall apart like the camera. In spite of its advanced age – Victorian, Christopher supposed – the toy was in relatively good condition. The monkey was dressed in a military uniform and held two cymbals in front of its chest. Christopher turned the key and felt the mechanism engage; the mainspring tightened, and when he let go the key spun around and the monkey crashed the cymbals together with manic enthusiasm. The burst of activity was brief, but curiously engaging, if only for its freakish intensity. Stroking the creature's nose, Christopher imagined the monkey, shiny and new, on a table in the drawing room downstairs, surrounded by girls in long bulky frocks and boys in sailor suits. He could almost hear their cries of wonder and delight.

Would Faye find the monkey interesting?

The idea of continuity appealed to Christopher. It was somehow pleasing to think of Faye having a connection with the children who had lived in the house before. Christopher closed the lid of the trunk and returned to the ladder, clutching the clockwork monkey and mindful of Mr Ellis's advice with respect to the beams.

May 1975

Two vans were parked outside the house and men in blue boiler suits were unloading heavy packing cases. They worked in a leisurely fashion, often stopping to smoke or read the *Daily Mirror*. Consequently, everything was taking much longer than anticipated. Laura had positioned herself by the front door and she was directing each man as he came through the porch. She looked quite commanding, her expression made more severe by an Alice band that exposed her brow. When she wasn't issuing instructions, she adopted a distinctive posture: hand on hip, lips pursed – almost belligerent.

Christopher had moved his electrical equipment into the house the previous day. Now he was feeling somewhat redundant. Laura had already decided where everything should go and the final destination of the linen or the china didn't really concern him.

As Laura checked labels and directed the flow of traffic, Christopher wandered into the drawing room. He negotiated a low maze of cardboard boxes and proceeded to the French windows. After opening one of them, he stepped out onto the flagstone terrace and, surveying the overgrown garden, inhaled the cool air. It was suffused with fragrances that reminded him of vanilla and honeysuckle. For a moment his worries, most of which were financial, receded and he allowed his chest to swell with proprietorial satisfaction. He had purchased a substantial property in a very desirable part of London. It was a milestone, a reckoning point, something to be proud of. He could hear the removal men's banter – the occasional expletive – and a car coming down the hill. The pitch of the engine changed and then fell silent.

When Christopher turned to go back inside he was arrested by his own reflection. As far as he could tell, he could still be legitimately described as handsome (albeit in a lean, world-weary way) and the streaks of grey above his ears created an impression of mature distinction. He was tall and the passage of time hadn't made him stoop. Through the transparency of his own image he saw Laura enter the drawing room. 'Chris? Ah, there you are. Look who's here.' She swept an arm back to indicate a man clutching a champagne bottle and a woman wearing a short denim jacket and jeans.

'Simon!' Christopher cried. He advanced and welcomed his friend with a firm handshake. Then, turning to face Simon's wife, Amanda, he added, 'Good to see you. What a pleasant surprise.'

Amanda tilted her head to one side, then the other, to accommodate the double peck of Norton's continental kiss. 'I hope we're not intruding,' she said apologetically. 'It was *his* idea, not mine.' Her eyes slid sideways towards her husband.

'Of course you're not intruding!' Christopher laughed. 'Although I'm afraid there's nowhere for you to sit yet.'

The four friends joked and talked over each other's sentences. They were excitable and the tone of their conversation was resolutely skittish.

Simon Ogilvy had been one of Christopher's contemporaries at Oxford. His hair was thick and brushed back off the forehead, his nose large and aquiline. Like Christopher, Simon had also married a conspicuously younger woman. Amanda was fifteen years his junior, striking rather than beautiful: dark, full-figured and husky-voiced. She taught English at a further education college and also wrote poetry. Two collections of her sardonic verses had been published by Anvil, *The Resourceful Goddess* and *The Hostile Mother.*

Drawing attention to the bottle he was holding, Simon addressed Laura. 'Would it be possible to dig out some glasses?'

'Certainly,' Laura replied.

'She's been very organized,' said Christopher.

'I can't promise champagne flutes,' said Laura, as she glided to the door, 'but I'll be able to find something.' She returned, triumphant, holding up four wine glasses as if they were trophies.

'Oh, well done,' said Christopher. Then, pointing towards the French windows, he said, 'Let's do this on the terrace.'

They went outside and Simon whistled when he saw the wildly abundant vegetation. 'Extraordinary. Like deepest Borneo.'

'It's going to be a massive job cutting that lot back,' said Christopher.

'I rather like it as it is,' said Amanda.

'Not very practical, though.' Christopher sighed.

Simon peeled the foil away from the neck of the champagne bottle and loosened the wire cage underneath. Amanda and Laura winced, tensely awaiting the 'pop'. Holding the bottle at arm's length, Simon waited. After a few seconds the cork shot over the bushes and a frothy discharge splashed onto the flagstones. When all the glasses had been filled, Simon proposed a toast: 'To Chris and Laura.'

As they sipped their champagne, Amanda, frowning slightly, said, 'Where's . . .'

'Faye?' Laura repositioned her Alice band. 'Oh, don't worry, we haven't mislaid her.'

'She's with a babysitter,' Christopher added. 'I'm collecting her later this afternoon.'

'How is she?' asked Amanda.

'Fine,' said Laura. The word came out rather clipped.

'Delightful,' said Christopher, 'particularly when she laughs.'

Amanda raised her eyebrows. 'She's laughing already?'

'Oh yes,' continued Christopher proudly, 'she's been doing it for months – terribly cute.'

A removal man entered the garden through the side entrance. 'Mrs Norton?'

Laura, her face suddenly flushed – perhaps it was the champagne? – excused herself and went to see what he wanted.

'Such a big house,' said Simon.

'Yes,' Christopher agreed. 'You should see the studio.'

'It's already set up?'

'Yes. Come on, I'll show you.'

Amanda pouted. 'What about me?'

'You can come too,' said Christopher. He guided them through the drawing room and they ascended the stairs together. On the first floor he showed them some of the finished rooms. 'I've had the place virtually rebuilt. It was in a terrible state.'

'Must have cost a fortune,' said Simon.

'Don't ask,' Christopher groaned.

Eventually, they reached their destination and Christopher ushered Simon and Amanda into his studio.

'Most impressive,' said Simon, gazing at a wall of switches and loosely hanging wires.

'Are you working on anything?' Amanda enquired.

'My agent called last week,' said Christopher. 'There could be a new project coming my way soon. A Mike Judd film – maybe . . .'

'Mike Judd,' Amanda repeated, uncertain. 'I don't think I've seen a Mike Judd film.'

'There's no reason you should have,' said Christopher. 'It's not really your thing – dystopian futures—'

'Dystopian futures? Isn't the present bad enough?'

Simon coughed, a little disconcerted by his wife's directness, and raised his glass as if he intended to propose a second toast. The gesture proved to be merely ornamental. 'I'm sure you'll produce some very fine work here.'

'Thank you,' Christopher replied, but he was troubled for a moment by Simon's smile, which lacked sincerity, and he disliked the substitution of the word 'work' for 'music'. A general feeling of unease was clarified by an inner voice that declared: *He doesn't think you're any good. Not really. Not anymore.*

'Are you OK?' Amanda asked. Her eyes were searching.

'Sure,' Christopher improvised. 'I just remembered another thing that I've got to do later.' He made a concerted effort to conceal his discomfort and marched over to the window. 'Come over here. Take a look. The view's great.'

April 1976

Eleven months later

Christopher was seated in his studio listening to a short piece of unfinished music. When completed, it would be incorporated into the soundtrack of the latest Mike Judd film: a low-budget space opera called *Android Insurrection*.

An oscillator throbbed at a very low frequency below intermittent clicks and whirring sounds that suggested the operation of mechanical devices. A pure, inhuman soprano made a slow, steady ascent, and a ring modulator, shaped and filtered to sound like bells, supplied a celestial accompaniment. The music was clearly intended to evoke the future. But it was the future as imagined by a person living in the past, someone with a 1950s comic-book vision of life in the twenty-first century. Christopher favoured primitive, rather outmoded methods of sound production. Many of his most interesting effects were still achieved by playing tape recordings backwards and at different speeds, or by playing several loops of tape simultaneously. Although he owned three synthesizers – a VCS3, a Minimoog and an ARP 2600 – he hardly ever used them.

After graduating, Christopher had received a bursary to visit the NWDR studio in Cologne and it was there that he came under the influence of Stockhausen: a cerebral, charismatic man, who even then was clearly destined to become the most controversial composer of his generation. When Christopher returned to England, he was fêted by the avant-garde. His uncompromising pieces were rarely broadcast, but he was a frequent guest on radio discussion programmes. He could always be relied upon to deliver a spirited defence of new music.

There was only one electronic music studio in Great Britain – the BBC Radiophonic Workshop – and Christopher managed to get a job there. He spent the next few years writing theme tunes and incidental music for science documentaries and experimental plays. After everyone else had gone home, he would stay behind in order to work on his own pieces, and colleagues would often find him the following morning, slumped over the OBA/8 mixing desk, fast asleep.

His music came to the attention of a young American director and he was commissioned to compose the soundtrack for a B-movie called *Parasite*, which, surprisingly, became an international box-office hit. More film work followed and as soon as he could afford oscillators, modulators and recording devices in sufficient number to equip a modest home studio, Christopher left the BBC. The demand for his services increased and he was invited to LA. He acquired an agent who negotiated higher fees and Christopher enjoyed a corresponding improvement in his standard of living. The pieces he had been working on while he was at the BBC were never finished. His old tapes, neatly packed and labelled, were forgotten, and nobody referred to him anymore as the 'English Stockhausen'.

The oscillator faded and a beat of silence was succeeded by a delicate, high-pitched thrumming. This transparent, tonal haze was sustained for several seconds before the effect was spoiled by an intrusive knocking. The same noise had occurred in the middle of another piece he had been working on the day before but he had been able to salvage most of the material with some judicious cutting and splicing. *Android Insurrection* was a different matter. It was more densely textured and he suspected that he might have to scrap everything after the beat of silence.

Christopher rewound the tape and replayed the offending passage. The knocking seemed to become louder as he listened more intently. It could only have been caused by a technical fault; however, the 'strikes' were resonant, as if they had been recorded in a natural setting with a microphone, and there was something about the regularity of the rhythm that suggested human agency. Christopher jabbed the 'stop' button and got up from his seat. There was no point in continuing.

On his way down to the ground floor he discovered Laura in their bedroom, her body half concealed by the soft, snowy cloudscape of a continental quilt. She was wearing a loose cheesecloth smock, baggy cotton trousers and a flimsy pair of leather sandals. Her eyes were open but she was so deep in thought that she did not realize her husband was standing in the doorway.

'Where's Faye?' Christopher asked.

Laura's head rolled slowly to the side. She looked at him for a moment as though he were a stranger.

'Where's Faye?' Christopher repeated, a little irritated by her failure to answer the first time.

'Asleep,' Laura replied.

'I've got a problem,' said Christopher. 'I'm going to call Roger.'

'OK.'

Christopher went down another flight of stairs, picked up the telephone, and dialled Roger Kaminsky's number.

The engineer wasn't very busy and said he could come straight over. Forty-five minutes later a dented Ford Capri pulled up outside the house and a young man wearing a Led Zeppelin T-shirt and patched blue jeans jumped out. Christopher greeted Kaminsky at the door and showed him up to the studio. He pressed the 'play' button and described the problem. After the beat of silence the thrumming began and the knocking followed. Kaminsky didn't react.

'There,' said Christopher, pointing at one of the speaker cabinets. 'Do you hear it?'

Kaminsky tilted his head. 'Knocking, you say?'

'Yes,' said Christopher. 'Rat-a-tat-tat.' He turned up the volume and rapped the mixing desk when the rhythm next occurred.

'I think I can hear something,' said Kaminsky. 'Yeah.'

'Jesus, Roger,' said Christopher. 'What do you mean, you *think* you can hear something?'

'Well, there's definitely some stuff going on in the background. I just can't tell what. Got any cans, Chris?' Christopher handed the engineer a pair of headphones and pushed the jack plug into a socket on the tape machine.

Rewind. Stop. Play.

Kaminsky closed his eyes and after a few moments he said, 'Yeah, yeah. I see what you mean.'

'Do you?' Christopher could still detect uncertainty in Kaminsky's voice.

The engineer dislodged the headphones. They fell to his shoulders and the metal arch closed around his neck. 'Cool piece. What is it?'

'The soundtrack for a film called *Android Insurrection.*'

'A bit like Tangerine Dream.'

'Maybe,' said Christopher. He didn't like the comparison.

Kaminsky opened his toolbox and said, 'I'll give you a shout when I'm done.'

In the kitchen, Faye was crawling on the floor playing with her dolls. She looked up when Christopher entered and produced a squeal of pleasure. Laura was seated at the kitchen table reading a book that Christopher had vaguely heard of: *The Feminine Mystique.* He didn't know what it was about and didn't care to ask, but he quite liked the title. He crouched beside Faye and with the aid of two dolls, one small and the other large, enacted a conversation in correspondingly high and low voices. Faye was, for a few seconds, a little alarmed by their sudden animation. When Christopher laughed at her surprise, she laughed too. He handed her the dolls and she clutched them to her chest.

'This is so annoying,' Christopher said. 'I'd had a good morning too. It was coming along nicely.'

Laura looked over the top of her book. 'I'm sorry?'

'There's this knocking sound. I'm sure Roger will get to the bottom of it, but it might take him a while. I was hoping to get the whole sequence done by the end of the week.'

Laura put her book down, leaving the pages open to keep her place.

'Chris, would you mind if I went out tonight?'

'Where are you going?'

'A bookshop in Islington. There's a young writer I'm interested in. She's giving a talk about her new novel.'

'OK.' He was expecting Laura to elaborate, but instead she picked up her mug and blew across the surface of her tea. Ripples appeared very briefly and then vanished.

The conversation that followed was fragmented and it was only when they talked about mundane necessities that they seemed to find a common purpose. Laura took to removing the dead leaves from a spider plant and Christopher reached for *The Times*. He found nothing pleasantly diverting in its pages. Only the usual depressing copy: the threat of terrorism, industrial action, the failing economy. It was the same every day. Politicians seemed completely unable to stop the nation's decline, a problem compounded by an apathetic silent majority addicted to light entertainment, gassy beer and greasy food.

An hour elapsed and Christopher sank into a state of despondency, after which he heard Kaminsky calling. Christopher made his way into the hallway and shouted, 'All right. I'm coming up.'

When he entered the studio he found the engineer looking out of the window across Hampstead Heath.

'Well?' Christopher asked.

Kaminsky turned to address him: 'There's nothing wrong with your machine.'

'But there must be.'

'Everything's fine. I checked.'

'Then what caused that noise?'

The engineer raised his hands, offering his ignorance to the heavens as well as his employer. 'I have no idea.'

Although Christopher went to bed early he didn't fall asleep. The heat of the day seemed to be trapped in the house and he could not make himself comfortable. Timbers creaked and the baby monitor hissed in the darkness. Very occasionally Faye would snuffle or cough, but she didn't wake. When Christopher heard the sound of an approaching vehicle he hoped that it was Laura returning from the talk she'd attended in Islington. The engine fell silent and a car door slammed shut. *Good,* Christopher thought. *It's her.* The wideness of the bed had unsettled him. Other sounds preceded her arrival: her key in the lock, the latch chain being secured, her footsteps on the stairs; a toilet flushing and then water flowing through the pipes. The door opened and Laura crept in.

'It's all right,' Christopher said. 'I'm still awake.' Laura slipped beneath the quilt and Christopher embraced her naked body. 'How was it?'

'Interesting,' she replied. She spoke a little about a couple of the women she had met. One of them was a psychotherapist, the other a garden designer.

'Did you get the designer's number?' Christopher asked. 'We've got to do something about the garden soon. It's getting like a wilderness.'

'Yes,' said Laura, 'I got her number.' And then, after a lengthy pause, she added, 'I might join a readers' group. The shop has one that meets every fortnight.'

'OK,' Christopher replied, laying his palm on her stomach. She had put on a little more weight recently. Not much, but enough to cause a revision of the contents of her wardrobe. She used to wear tight jumpers and T-shirts, garments that emphasized her slender form, but she was now much more likely to throw on a smock. Christopher supposed that she had become self-conscious, which was ridiculous, he thought, because it would take more than a few additional pounds to ruin her figure. Her graceful transit across a room never failed to stop conversations and attract interest.

Laura's body seemed to be giving up its scents to the night: the lavender of her soap, the lacquer in her hair, the musk of her perfume, all of the sweet-smelling lotions and creams that she assiduously rubbed into her skin. Christopher's hand moved over the fleshy contours of Laura's abdomen and it came to rest between her thighs. His index finger curled into her and he began a gentle oscillation that eventually elicited a moan of pleasure.

Their lovemaking was slow, not merely because of the heat, but because slowness (a slowness close to lethargy) had become almost second nature. A miscarriage following Laura's first pregnancy had made them overly cautious when making love and the habit had stuck. Although Laura responded to Christopher's initial caresses, she quickly lost interest. She became inert, detached. There was no mutuality or reciprocation. It made Christopher feel as if he were pursuing his pleasure alone. When it was over, Christopher extricated himself, somewhat inelegantly, and rolled over onto his back.

A police siren sounded in the distance.

Christopher felt disappointed. It hadn't always been like this. Sex used to be meaningful, imaginative and fulfilling. Since Faye's birth, however, Laura's desire for intimacy had dwindled. Where there had once been a great torrent of libidinous energy, there was now only a thin, miserly trickle. She never showed any enthusiasm. Their infrequent couplings were rarely protracted and Laura's forbearance was clearly dutiful, a spousal obligation that could be discharged along with the childcare, cooking and cleaning. Laura's sexual disengagement was only one part of a general torpor that made her seem distant. When Christopher spoke to her, he was never quite sure that she was listening.

It was all so ironic, because Laura had built her modelling career on a sexually confident persona. Around the house there were cupboards filled with old editions of magazines with Laura posing on the covers: auburn hair disproportionately thick and styled; her eyes, a pale, delicate brown – so pale, in fact, that they turned gold in a certain light. Lips parted, glossed, glistening.

Christopher missed her – that woman. The woman he had married.

They had met six years earlier at a party, a glitzy affair attended mostly by people in film. Laura was there because, at that point in her life, she was getting bored with modelling and wanted to become an actress. Christopher couldn't remember their conversation, but he could remember Laura's eyes, the way that her irises changed colour, from brown, through amber, to gold.

Two weeks later she was sitting, cross-legged, on the floor of his little mews house in Maida Vale and looking through his LP collection. She was curious about his musical tastes. Remarkably, she had heard of Stockhausen and appeared to be impressed when Christopher mentioned that he and Stockhausen had once been acquaintances. They made love for the first time that afternoon. There was no shyness or anxiety, no awkward fumbling. It felt entirely natural – the removal of clothes, the stroking and the kissing, everything flowing inexorably towards a rapturous climax and the mute tranquillity of post-coital exhaustion. Christopher had wondered if their physical compatibility wasn't, in some abstruse way, significant? He asked himself if it wasn't just chance that had brought them together, but a loftier intercessional power – destiny, fate? He had been forty-two and she had been twenty-four. The neat symmetry of this numerical reversal, with its suggestion of arcane influence, had played on his mind. The idea that their union might be preordained was one that, until very recently, had occupied a central position in his personal mythology: the story he told himself, about himself.

Laura went to the bathroom. When she returned, she climbed back into bed and lay on her side, facing away from Christopher. He edged across the mattress and wrapped an arm around her waist.

Before long, he was thinking about *Android Insurrection,* a particular scene in which an army of humanoid robots goose-stepped down an enormous ramp. Christopher knew what was required: an accompaniment made from percussive tape loops. He possessed a very vivid, auditory imagination, and his tired brain, without much effort, invented effects that he hoped to reproduce in the studio the following day.

Christopher slipped in and out of consciousness. Just as he was about to make what felt like a final descent into oblivion, he heard a knocking sound coming from the baby monitor: a distant *rat-a-tat-tat* through the hiss. It delivered him back again to wakefulness.

'Did you hear that?' he said.

'Hear what?' Laura replied.

'The monitor. I thought I heard something.'

'I didn't hear anything.'

'Are you sure?'

Her voice hardened. 'You were dropping off – I could tell from your breathing.'

'OK.' Christopher rested his cheek against his wife's shoulder blade. He had intended to go back to sleep but he was soon agitated by a growing sense of unease. Faye. He should check on Faye, just in case. A question arose in his mind: *in case of what, exactly?* His unease was not connected with any readily identifiable threat but he found himself motivated to get out of bed.

'What are you doing?' Laura asked.

'I'll be back in a second,' he answered, unwilling to justify his behaviour. He pressed the light switch on the landing wall and entered the nursery. Leaning over the cot, he studied his daughter. She seemed to coalesce out of the darkness, gradually acquiring shape and substance. Her face was the last thing to clarify. Christopher listened for the reassuring rhythm of her respiration and relaxed. He felt somewhat self-conscious, even a little embarrassed.

When he got back into bed, Laura turned over and said, 'Is she all right?'

'Yes. She's fine.'

'Why did you get up? Did you hear something else?'

'No,' Christopher yawned. 'I just thought I'd check, that's all.' He shifted position so that his wife could lay her head on his chest. 'Goodnight,' he whispered.

Early May 1976

'I won't be long, love,' said Christopher. 'A couple of hours, maybe.'

'Where are you going?' Laura asked. She was perched on a high stool by the kettle.

'Only the village. Le Cellier du Midi – lunch with Henry. I did say . . .'

'Has he got you some work?'

'I don't know. He mentioned a new Peter Cushing film on the phone. We'll see.'

Christopher lifted a pale linen jacket off a coat hook and rifled through the contents of a drawer. His movements were abrupt and hurried.

'Next one down,' said Laura.

'Right.' Christopher followed his wife's advice and there were the car keys he had been looking for. He picked them up and went over to his wife, loose change jangling in his trouser pockets. 'Thanks.' He gave her a perfunctory kiss on the forehead, pulled on his jacket, and said, 'See you later.'

Laura listened to his footsteps receding down the hallway, the loud crash of the slammed front door. The house shook and when the reverberation faded the ensuing silence filled her with cold dread. Suddenly, she felt entombed. Her heart thumped in her chest and she struggled to draw air into her lungs. She gripped the edge of the worktop and waited. 'It's OK,' she said out loud. 'Nothing's going to happen.' Gradually, the panic subsided and she began to feel normal again.

Laura made herself a camomile tea. *Good for the nerves.* She took a tin of biscuits down from a shelf and prised the lid off with a butter knife. The chocolate digestives and bourbons were gone. She had eaten them the day before. It wasn't that she had been hungry, but rather that she had found the sweetness of the chocolate comforting. She grabbed a handful of shortbread cookies and pushed the tin away.

What was happening to her?

She had consulted her doctor – a jolly, avuncular type with half-moon spectacles and a suspiciously florid complexion – earlier in the year, and he had said that it was common for women to get emotional after childbirth. Even as he was saying these words, she was thinking, *but that was fourteen months ago now*. He mumbled something about chemical imbalances and appeared uncomfortable when she tried to articulate her feelings. He interrupted her tentative disclosures with bland reassurances. His heedless manner made her feel stupid, as though she was making a fuss about nothing. She felt like a child, sitting with her knees pressed together and her feet wide apart. He surprised her at the end of the consultation by scribbling out a prescription. 'To be taken three times a day,' he said, without looking up. 'You may feel a little drowsy, so be careful when you're driving.'

The pills made her feel less tense and agitated, but when she was alone, she still felt panicky for no good reason, and she still cried without knowing why. She was unable to talk to her husband about what she was going through. Christopher was a sympathetic man; she knew that he would be concerned and try his best to help her, but she doubted that he could. Indeed, she doubted that anyone possessed the means of restoring her former happiness and self-confidence – except perhaps herself. She was hoping for an epiphany, after which everything would click back into place.

Sometimes, she felt as though she was no longer one person, but two. There was the Laura who looked after Faye and went about her daily routine, and then there was another Laura who critically observed the first. She was familiar with the term schizophrenia and knew that the condition had something to do with split personalities, but she was sure that she wasn't going mad. At least, not like that. She felt like she was watching herself in a film. A woman, just turned thirty, with uncombed hair and a blank expression, sitting by the kettle eating chocolate biscuits, or staring out of the window into the garden, or lying on the bed waiting for Faye to wake up – and she didn't know who that woman was. She had become a stranger to herself, and when she was alone, this self-estrangement became frightening.

Laura drank her tea. She tidied the kitchen, painted her nails, and then wandered into the drawing room, where she sat in an armchair and began reading a novel: *The Waterfall* by Margaret Drabble. The psychotherapist she'd met in the bookshop in Islington had recommended it. There wasn't much of a story and the tone was bleak, but occasionally the heroine described feelings that Laura recognized. Although Laura wasn't really enjoying the novel, she persevered, because it was short, and because she thought that it might contain answers. She had only managed to read ten more pages before she was disturbed by the sound of Faye crying. Laura placed the book on the chair arm and went upstairs.

Faye was standing up in her cot, gripping the rail, red-faced and angry. She was trying to get out, hopelessly attempting to get some traction on the bars with her feet. Clearly, she was finding the absence of progress extremely frustrating. 'Hush now,' said Laura. She picked up her daughter, comforted her and then changed her nappy, after which she carried the child down to the kitchen and fed her some tomato pasta out of a jar. When Faye had had enough, Laura took her to the drawing room and placed her at the centre of a circle of toys. Laura wanted to read some more of her novel, but Faye kept on distracting her, so she had to lay it aside once again.

The days were so long.

Faye ran around the room on short, fat legs. Her balance was precarious and every step seemed to flirt with disaster. Eventually, she ran into the side of the sofa, banged her head, and more comforting was required.

'Let's go upstairs,' said Laura, wiping away Faye's tears. 'You can help Mummy sort her things out.' She took Faye's pudgy hand in her own and they ascended the stairs.

On the top floor was a room full of cardboard boxes and packing cases. They contained old clothes, shoes and miscellaneous items of no great value. Laura hadn't had enough time to go through all of her possessions before moving. It had seemed too much, too effortful, having to care for a newborn baby and make decisions about what to keep and what to throw away. But things had changed. Laura wasn't feeling quite so tired and she couldn't justify putting the task off any longer. She bolted the stair gate, an original fixture decorated with carved roundels, and set to work. *Three piles: Keep. Not sure. Oxfam.* She tried to engage Faye and pretended that emptying the boxes was a kind of game. Despite her efforts the child soon lost interest and wandered onto the landing.

As she sorted her clothes, Laura was reminded of particular photo shoots, parties and people. She should have felt nostalgic remembering those times, when London seemed like the centre of the universe and she was young enough to enjoy it. But not all of her memories were good. There had been significant lapses of judgement. The see-through blouse that she threw onto the Oxfam pile had once been too easily removed, with her full consent, by an Italian couturier she had not known very well, or liked very much, but who had made plain his willingness to advance her career if they became better acquainted. Laura fought to dispel an image of an expensive hotel interior: black leather furniture, modern art, champagne on ice, and the slow, hypnotic movement of luminous forms in a lava lamp. She persevered with her task, detaching memories from garments like price tags.

Laura discovered that she was capable of being quite ruthless and that disowning tokens of her former existence was curiously liberating. This sartorial exorcism, this casting out, made her feel less encumbered by the past. She was embarrassed by her old wardrobe: her buckskin jacket with tassels, her Mary Quant hot pants, her gold lamé boob tube. It all seemed so tawdry.

Up until that moment, she had been dimly aware of Faye making noises outside, a constant babble of laughter and baby talk. Now there was silence. Laura stopped what she was doing, listened, and waited for Faye to resume her play. The house was strangely becalmed.

'Faye?' Laura raised her head and looked through the architrave. 'Faye? Where are you, darling?' She could hear her own pulse, which began to quicken slightly. 'Faye?'

Laura tossed aside the hot pants she was holding and walked out onto the landing. It was empty. A mental picture sprung unbidden into her mind: her unconscious child, sprawled at the bottom of the stairs. The image possessed the startling clarity of a scene illuminated by a flashbulb. Laura ran to the stair gate and looked down to the next landing. After a moment's reflection, she realized that her premonition could never have become a reality.

Faye didn't have the ability to release the bolt. Her fingers were too small and she didn't have the strength.

So where was she?

The door of the studio was closed, as was the door to the box room where Christopher stored his records and tapes. Another door, which led to an as yet undecorated and empty bedroom, was also closed.

'Faye?'

Laura was sure that all of the doors had been closed when she and Faye had come up the stairs. Faye couldn't have reached and turned the handles, so one of them must have been left slightly open. The toddler would have pushed the door open, stepped inside one of the rooms, and then shut the door behind her – which was odd, because Faye didn't like to be on her own and Laura hadn't heard a thing.

She checked the studio first.

'Faye? Where are you?'

Laura walked past banks of tape recorders and speakers, around the central horseshoe of equipment and Christopher's office chair, but Faye was nowhere to be seen. She then poked her head into the box room. The tiny floor space was littered with cassettes and tangled leads. But no Faye. Laura crossed the landing to the empty bedroom, grasped the door handle, turned it to the right and pushed. The door didn't open. She then tried turning the handle to the left. Still the door didn't open.

'Faye? Are you in there?'

Laura listened. She couldn't hear anything apart from her own heavy breathing.

'Faye? Faye!'

She looked around the landing. Faye could only be in the empty bedroom. There was nowhere else she could have gone. In which case, why wasn't she making any noise or crying? Laura rattled the handle and leaned against the door. It didn't budge. Somehow, the door had become stuck. Laura clenched her fist and struck the paintwork several times. Some flakes fell to the floor and it seemed to Laura that their descent was unnaturally prolonged.

'Faye? It's all right – don't be frightened. It's only Mummy.'

Why wasn't she making any noise? Why wasn't she crying?

Two more flashbulb images made Laura freeze: an open window, Faye standing on a chair and leaning out; Faye's face, turning bright red, her windpipe blocked by some small and inconsequential object that she had just picked up and innocently pressed into her mouth. The terror that seized Laura was fierce and explosive.

She mounted a ferocious attack on the obstinate door. Eventually, the futility of her violence made her stop and she paced backwards and forwards, running her hands through her hair.

'God!' Fear had made her throat dry. *What do I do? What do I do?* She turned to face the door again and gave it another kick. 'Faye! Oh God, honey, please say something, please, please say something!'

A few moments earlier, when Laura had been in the studio, she had registered a framed poster leaning against a wall. It was for a film called *Night Carrier* and showed a silhouetted figure standing in front of a taxi with blazing headlights. Why was she thinking of that poster? Christopher had been intending to hang it up after breakfast and Laura had offered to help, but for some reason he hadn't got round to it. Then it came to her. She wasn't really remembering the poster at all; she was remembering what she had noticed on the mat beside it. A hammer. Laura dashed to the studio, picked up the heavy tool and charged back to the empty bedroom. Raising her arm, she hit one of the door panels with the flat end. The blow created a dent. She raised her arm again and continued hitting until the wood began to crack and splinter. 'Hold on, Faye,' she cried. 'Mummy's coming.' The head of the hammer smashed through the panel and Laura struggled to pull it out again. Another blow created a hole big enough to see through. Laura closed one eye and looked through the hole with the other. She couldn't see her daughter. 'Faye? Where are you?' Laura stepped back and used the claw to tear away more loose wood. She thrust her arm through the opening and felt blindly for the latch. It was an old-fashioned mechanism and her fingers closed around a metal bar. She pulled it up and the door moved forward. Jagged points of wood tore her smock and pierced her skin but she was beyond feeling pain. Ahead of her, she could see the window that she had imagined Faye leaning out of. It was closed. An empty expanse of bare floorboards stretched between herself and the motionless net curtains. There were some rolls of wallpaper, a tin of paint and a wicker chair. She registered each of these and withdrew her arm from the ragged hole in the door. Where was Faye? Laura's legs weakened and she thought they might give way. She reached for the door jamb. As she turned, an alcove came into view, and in that alcove she saw her daughter, standing still, swaying slightly, and totally oblivious to her mother's violent entry. Laura couldn't see Faye's face, because Faye was standing with her back to her, transfixed by the wall.

'Faye?'

Laura's instinct was to run forward and scoop Faye up, to cuddle her and smother her with kisses. But the peculiarity of the situation caused Laura to check her initial impulse and hold back. The atmosphere felt brittle, as though a wrong move might cause irreparable harm. She noted the normality of her daughter's appearance – the large nappy, the white cotton vest, the sparse blonde curls – and felt less wary, less confused. Even so, the unusual stillness of the child prevented Laura from experiencing relief.

'Faye?' Laura whispered. 'What are you doing, honey?' Faye didn't respond and Laura stepped closer. 'Faye, darling. What's the matter?'

There was a metallic clap. It made Laura jump and she spun round in surprise. On the other side of the room was a clockwork monkey, an ugly thing that Christopher had found in the attic. The cymbals that the animal held in its paws had been brought together.

'Jesus,' said Laura. She turned her attention back to Faye. It was as though the child was sleepwalking or in a trance. Laura tiptoed into the alcove and knelt down in front of her daughter. 'Faye, darling, what's the matter?' The child's eyes were open but glassy. 'What are you looking at?' She stroked her daughter's forehead, laid a hand on her shoulder, and gave her a little shake. Faye's gaze became more focused and her expression showed surprise. She blinked a few times and then started to cry. Laura wrapped her arms around Faye and drew her close. 'There, there. Don't cry, honey. Everything's fine.' It was only then that Laura noticed the blood seeping through her smock and felt the pain in her arm.

Henry Baylis was a stout man with a jowly face and undisciplined, fly-away hair. The temperature had climbed into the mid-seventies but he had chosen to wear a three-piece pinstriped suit. Prior to setting up his agency, he had worked in orchestral management, and before that as a barrister. Although his legal career had been short-lived, he hadn't forsaken the habit of formal dress.

The two men were sitting at their preferred table in Le Cellier du Midi, a dark, subterranean restaurant in Hampstead village favoured particularly by local residents connected with the arts and television. Christopher and Baylis had finished their *filets de boeuf dijonnaise* and were now waiting, respectively, for a *crème brûlée* and a *mousse au chocolat*. A bottle, their second, contained only an inch of burgundy. Baylis had been gossiping throughout the meal and they had only just started to discuss prospective commissions.

'If they can get Cushing,' said Baylis, 'then they'll go ahead. Almost certainly. But he's a bit tied up at the moment.'

'What with?'

'Oh, a rather silly American film. Well, I say American, but they're making it over here to save money.'

'What's it called?'

'*Star Wars.* Dreadful nonsense, apparently. Cushing thinks it's utter twaddle.'

'*Star Wars*? That sounds . . .' Christopher cleared his throat. 'That sounds like something I might have been interested in.'

'Oh, no, Christopher, really.' Baylis produced a handkerchief and mopped his glistening brow. 'You wouldn't have wanted anything to do with this one. I'm hearing very bad things. The director's young and doesn't see eye to eye with his cinematographer. The actors think it's rubbish . . .' Baylis indicated that he could go on.

'So, Henry, what do you think? Is it going to happen?'

'I beg your pardon?' Baylis poured the last dregs of their burgundy.

'*The Warlock.*'

'Well, if Marcus and Diane can get Cushing on side, I'm sure they'll be able to raise the capital. And the script is very good. A nice meaty part for Peter to get his teeth into. He'll want to do it, I'm sure. Especially after this *Star Wars* fiasco.'

Christopher folded and unfolded his napkin. 'It's just . . .' He paused before adding, 'I've had a lot of outgoings lately. You know, what with the house and the baby.'

Baylis offered him a sympathetic and slightly pained expression. 'Yes, yes. Of course.'

'And . . .'

The agent nodded. 'Things could be better, certainly. But I have every confidence in Marcus and Diane. They make a great team and they absolutely love your work. Ah, here comes pudding!'

Thirty minutes later, they climbed the stairs and emerged into brilliant sunlight. They shook hands and went their different ways. Christopher walked up to the tube station and turned right onto the High Street. As he approached Flask Walk, he couldn't stifle his disappointment. He had been expecting more from Baylis. Much more.

Christopher closed the front door and put the keys in his pocket.

'Laura?' He looked in the kitchen first and then the

drawing room, but his wife and daughter were absent. He knew that they must be somewhere in the house, because he had noticed the pushchair and Faye's shoes beneath the stairs. He glanced at his wristwatch. 'Laura? I'm home.'

His call disturbed the stillness and he observed a flurry of motes in the air. He was about to call again when Laura's voice filtered down from above.

'I'm up here.' There was no gladness in her voice, no warmth, merely a flat statement of fact concerning her location.

Christopher found the stairs surprisingly difficult to negotiate. His legs felt heavy and the large amount of burgundy he'd drunk was starting to make his head ache. He had expected to find Laura in the bedroom, but when he craned his neck around the door jamb he discovered that she wasn't there. He saw her on the upper landing leaning over the banisters.

'Where's Faye?' he called up.

'In the nursery.'

'Asleep?'

'Yes.'

He tilted his arm and looked at his wristwatch again. 'At this time?'

'Yes. I'm not sure but I think she might be unwell.'

Christopher continued his ascent.

'What are you doing up there?'

'I . . .' She seemed confused. 'Something happened. I damaged one of the doors.' He detected a certain strained quality in her voice and made an effort to climb faster. On arriving on the landing he paused to take in the scene: Laura, the right sleeve of her smock stained with blood; the door of the empty bedroom, smashed; wood splinters on the carpet.

'Jesus. What happened?'

'The door got stuck. Faye was on the other side.'

He noticed the hammer. 'So you took a hammer to it?'

'Yes.'

'Laura,' he said in disbelief. 'We were going to have it stripped and revarnished.'

'I was sorting out my old clothes and she was playing out here. The latch got stuck. What was I supposed to do?'

'You didn't have to do this,' he said, pointing at the damaged panel, 'surely.'

'What if the window had been open? Faye could have fallen out.'

'We don't use this room. Why would the window have been open?'

'Chris, I wasn't prepared to take the risk, OK?'

Christopher crossed the landing and examined the

door. He ran his finger around the jagged hole. 'We won't be able to get this repaired.' He took a step back. 'And look, there's a crack that runs right down to the lower panel. We'll have to get a new one.' *More expense*. Christopher supposed that a Victorian door wouldn't cost very much, but it would have to be restored and fitted. 'What happened to your arm? Is that blood?'

'I cut myself trying to get the door open.'

Christopher scratched his head. 'I don't understand. It's never got stuck before.' He opened the door, pushed it shut, and repeated the action several times.

'It was stuck.' Laura's tone was tetchy. 'The metal bar thing on the back got jammed.' Christopher continued to demonstrate the ease with which the door could be opened and closed. 'Chris, stop doing that. What are you trying to prove? It doesn't change anything. I'm telling you, the door was stuck.'

Christopher let the door close one last time and they stood, very still, staring at each other. Eventually, Christopher asked: 'What's wrong with Faye?'

'I don't know,' Laura replied.

'You said she was unwell.'

'When I got the door open I found her gazing at the wall.'

'That doesn't sound so bad.'

'It was like she was in a trance or something – a world of her own. You'd have thought the noise I was making would have frightened her. She should have been upset, crying.' Laura's hair had fallen in front of her face and she pushed it aside. 'She was all right for a bit but then she got really tired and fractious so I put her to bed.'

Christopher sighed. 'She's probably coming down with something.'

'She hasn't got a temperature. Maybe I should take her to the doctor's.'

'If you want.' Christopher shrugged. 'No harm.'

The atmosphere was suddenly less tense. Christopher took off his jacket. 'It's hot, isn't it?'

'Yes,' said Laura. 'How was Henry?'

'Fine.'

'Any luck?'

'Nothing concrete. There's a film called *The Warlock* that might be coming my way.'

'When will you know?'

'Henry didn't say.'

Laura nodded and indicated the splinters on the carpet. 'I'll clean this up.'

*

The doctor completed his examination of Faye and smiled. 'She's fine.'

Laura picked up her daughter and gave her a plastic hoop to play with. 'Then what happened?'

'Nothing that you need to be worried about,' said the doctor, permitting himself a reassuring chuckle. 'Look at her! I've never seen a healthier child.'

'I thought she was having a fit or something.'

The doctor drew his head back sharply and adopted an expression that declared his amusement and incredulity. 'No. I think not.'

'Then what was it? What happened?'

'A little *absence*, that's all.'

'An absence?'

The doctor's eyebrows drew closer together. 'Mrs Norton,' he continued with weary forbearance, 'I could refer your daughter to a specialist, but it would serve no purpose, save, perhaps, that of easing *your* anxiety.' Laura felt a creeping sense of shame. Yet again she had wasted his time. The hiatus that followed made her feel uncomfortably exposed. She was desperate for the doctor to say something else, to end the silence and, with it, her humiliation; however, he remained impassive and she was forced to mutter, 'Yes, yes. I'm sorry.'

The doctor shook his head. 'Oh, good heavens, Mrs Norton, please. You've no need to apologize. Motherhood is a demanding occupation.' He stood up and extended his hand. 'Your daughter's fine.'

Mid-May

Christopher was so engrossed in his work that he'd lost track of time. It was probably two o'clock in the morning, or thereabouts. He could only estimate the hour because he'd left his wristwatch on the kitchen table. Christopher liked working late – the absence of distraction. It reminded him of his years spent at the BBC when he would stay behind to use the equipment for his own compositions and musical experiments. He felt a twinge of sadness, a nostalgic yearning for his younger days – the solitude and cigarettes, the sleepless nights and grey, autumn mornings. Just before sunrise, he would leave the BBC studios in Maida Vale and walk up and down Elgin Avenue. There was usually no one about, apart from the occasional prostitute dressed in a raincoat and high heels. Of course, there was something contrived about his behaviour. Even then he knew that he was adopting an attitude, a posture, but the romance of it all was so very seductive, and the excitement of being part of something entirely new was a powerful drug. The fact that he was able to create music from sounds that had never before been heard by the human ear was, as far as he was concerned, utterly miraculous.

The music coming through the headphones dispelled Christopher's reminiscences and brought him firmly back into the present. His 'score' was marked with circular coffee stains and looked more architectural than musical. The system of notation he employed was a haphazard combination of borrowed symbols and his own idiosyncratic shorthand – angled lines, filled-in oblongs and a range of invented hieroglyphs. When a melodic fragment did appear it was accompanied by a general indication of the desired effect: *reed, carillon, theremin.*

Pitches fell at different rates, their descent finding chance harmonies that quickly dissolved again into discord. A throbbing bass note, deeper than the lowest church organ pedal, provided a fundamental that helped the listener to appreciate these moments of transparency. The music suggested slow disintegration and reminded Christopher of a painting by Salvador Dalí showing a landscape draped in wilting clock faces. It was a beguiling sound and Christopher was pleased with what he had accomplished, but at the same time he regretted that this artful composition would be largely wasted on an audience whose attention, at this particular juncture in the film, would be wholly directed at the screen and an action sequence involving a perilous escape from an exploding space station. He imagined teenage boys sitting in half-empty cinemas, their eyes flickering in the darkness, their hands transferring popcorn from big cardboard buckets into their wide-open mouths.

Christopher had been finding that he was increasingly envious of those Oxford peers of his who had continued to compose serious music. When their pieces were praised by critics in the broadsheets he felt strangely desolate. He had begun to think much more about posterity. In the past he had accepted his loss of 'reputation' with stoic indifference. It would have been churlish to complain as he had been amply compensated. His association with the film industry had allowed him to enjoy London throughout its decade of swinging pre-eminence. But now that his fiftieth birthday was only a few years away, things had changed. The world was a gloomier place and getting lucrative commissions wasn't quite so easy. These days, he found it harder to be 'philosophical' and his expulsion from the ranks of the avant-garde rankled.

Christopher had become so preoccupied that when the music faded he forgot to turn the tape machine off. The reels turned and the headphones hissed. He had followed his train of thought as he might a clue in a labyrinth, and he had discovered hitherto unsuspected dead ends of bitterness and envy. A noise roused him. He had been too self-obsessed to do much more than register that an event had occurred; however, a disquieting after-impression lingered. What had he heard, exactly? It had been buried in the tape hiss, a rhythmic inflection, something that, by rights, shouldn't really have been there.

He rewound the tape and watched the digits on the counter revolving backwards. After a few moments he pressed 'stop' and 'play' and turned up the volume. The hiss in the headphones sounded like a cataract. Christopher listened, and then he started when he heard a voice speaking over the roar. Even though it was loud, he couldn't make out what was being said. He tried again. This time, he was able to determine the gender of the speaker, a woman with an unusually deep voice, and she was speaking in German.

Christopher replayed the phrase several times and found that with each repetition he was able to hear what was being said a little better.

'Wie heilig für uns Toten.'

Christopher's German was good enough to translate what she was saying: *How sacred for us dead.*

It sounded like a fragment of something larger, an

excerpt from a sermon or poem. Was there any more? He let the tape run on. After five or six seconds of tape hiss, the deep, female voice returned. *'Lange sollen diese Mauern Zeuge unserer Arbeit sein.'* Once again, Christopher had to replay the phrase several times before he was able to translate it: *Long shall these walls be witness to our work.* After another short interval, Christopher heard a man's voice – much clearer than the woman's – saying, *'Die Sonne sinkt.' The sun is sinking.* Nothing else followed.

Christopher spoke out loud the phrases he had listened to: 'How sacred for us dead . . . Long shall these walls be witness to our work . . . The sun is sinking.'

He did not puzzle over the significance of these cryptic utterances, but rather he wondered how it was that two voices (and two German voices at that) had come to appear on what should have been a completely blank part of the tape.

Christopher and Laura were sitting at their dining-room table with their guests, Simon and Amanda Ogilvy. The starter course had already been served – an Alsatian fondue made from Munster cheese – along with a flowery Riesling. It was a tricky operation, spearing the pieces of wholemeal bread, rotating the skewers in the molten cheese, and preventing any excess from dribbling onto the tablecloth, but frequent practice had made them all expert. Candles flickered, joss sticks burned and an unobtrusive Mozart string quartet played in the background.

After the fondue, Christopher went to the kitchen and returned with a wide earthenware pot brimming with spaghetti bolognese. The Mozart quartet had come to an end but the 'automatic arm' on the turntable hadn't lifted. A regular, muffled pulse was coming through the speakers. Christopher told his guests to help themselves and went to change the record. He replaced Mozart with Bach: Glenn Gould playing the two- and three-part inventions. Simon was talking about a programme he had heard on the radio in which several politicians had been attempting to predict the outcome of the current economic crisis. As Christopher sat down, his friend said, 'We've been living well beyond our means and we can't go on like this.'

'What if the money does run out?' asked Laura innocently. 'What will happen? I mean, I know this sounds selfish, but how will it affect people like us?'

'I don't know,' Simon replied. 'You hear different things. The Americans already think we're a Third World country. Shanty towns on the heath – it isn't inconceivable – no food in the shops. God knows. The real issue, of course, is whether democracy can survive if things get any worse. There are a lot of people out there,' he said, pointing at the window, inviting his companions to imagine an unthinking multitude beyond the glass, 'who want somebody strong to take over and sort it all out.'

'We're not going down that road,' said Christopher. 'I don't think our military have the stomach for it. If they had, they would have acted by now. No.' He twisted his fork into the mountain of spaghetti and minced beef piled on his plate. 'It isn't going to happen, whatever the scare-mongers say.'

'Who would want a dictatorship?' asked Laura. 'It's ridiculous.'

'David Bowie,' Amanda replied.

Christopher stopped eating. 'What?'

'He said some very odd things last year,' Amanda continued, 'about wanting the army to take over.'

'Jesus,' Christopher growled. 'What was he thinking?'

'It just goes to show how frustrated people are,' said Simon. 'A sign of the times.'

'My students found his position very confusing,' Amanda continued. 'You know, for a man who used to wear make-up and a quilted body stocking.'

'Who cares what David Bowie thinks?' said Christopher, more vehemently than he had intended.

'He's very influential,' Amanda replied.

'He's a pop singer,' said Christopher, enunciating the word 'pop' with scornful emphasis.

'Yes. But people like him matter now,' said Amanda. Then, turning to Laura, she said, 'Are we speaking too loudly?'

Laura indicated the baby monitor. 'We'd know if there was a problem. I think she'll sleep through.'

'What time will she wake up?'

'Six if we're lucky.'

'Christ.'

Simon was still thinking about the economy. 'The unions demand more money, profits go down, and the cost of goods goes up. I hope to God Callaghan doesn't repeat Wilson's mistakes.'

In due course, the table was cleared, and Laura retreated to the kitchen. A few minutes later she returned pushing a trolley, on top of which was a Black Forest gateau. 'I took it out of the freezer an hour ago. I hope it's properly defrosted.' She cut the cake into thick slices and circulated the plates. Addressing Simon, she said, 'I understand you're having something performed at the proms this year.'

'Not in the Albert Hall, though. They're putting all us *living* composers in the Roundhouse. I know it's petty, but

I'm a bit irritated by their decision. When you get a prom, you expect the Albert Hall, not a train shed.'

Laura took her place at the table. 'Is it a new piece?'

'*Nyx*,' said Simon, 'for chamber orchestra and tape.'

'*Nyx*?' Laura repeated.

'Night,' said Amanda. 'In Greek myth, she was one of the earliest deities, the daughter of Chaos.'

Simon smiled at his wife. 'Amanda suggested the title.'

Christopher asked his friend some questions about the new work and their talk soon became more technical and exclusive. Laura and Amanda lost interest and began a conversation of their own. By the time coffee was being served, the women were speaking in low, confidential tones about a common acquaintance, and Christopher inferred that it was acceptable to invite Simon upstairs to the studio. 'I'd like you to hear something,' he said.

It was not uncommon for the men and women to separate at this point in the evening. Consequently, Laura and Amanda barely acknowledged their husbands' departure. The two friends climbed the stairs, but on the way up Christopher entered the nursery to check on Faye. He could smell her – a curious blend of animal fragrances and talcum powder. Christopher looked through the bars of the cot. Faye had her eyes closed and was sucking her thumb in her sleep. She had kicked off her blanket but Christopher didn't bother covering her again. The room was warm and slightly stuffy, even though the upper sash window had been left open a fraction to let in fresh air.

'She's very beautiful,' whispered Simon.

Christopher nodded. 'Like her mother.' They tiptoed out of the room and continued their ascent.

In the studio, Christopher played his friend the music he had composed to accompany the escape sequence in *Android Insurrection*. Simon stood listening, clasping his chin, his brow furrowed with concentration. The pitches began to descend and his expression showed surprise when the notes suddenly constellated to produce recognizable harmonies.

'That's rather good,' said Simon. 'Quite unexpected.'

Christopher felt a sense of relief. He wanted Simon's approval.

A decade earlier, Simon had been struggling to get commissions. He had been living in a cramped, rather shabby hovel overlooking the bleak scrubland of Wanstead Flats. At that time, Christopher was doing exceptionally well – parties, fast cars, women. Back then, he didn't care what Simon thought. Now that Simon's music was being performed by the world's leading orchestras, Christopher cared very much. The two men seemed to have gone through a reversal of fortunes. Or, at least, that was how Christopher perceived the situation. He played Simon a few more pieces, although none had the same effect as the first, and Christopher's sense of accomplishment gradually ebbed away. Moreover, he found himself feeling slightly resentful towards his friend. Simon could have been a little more fulsome, he thought, less reserved in his praise. Christopher maintained a show of conviviality, and later, when Simon and Amanda were leaving, he shook Simon's hand and wished him well.

'Let's leave the washing-up,' said Christopher.

'I don't mind doing it,' said Laura.

Christopher dismissed her offer. 'I'll help tomorrow morning.'

Laura went to collect the baby monitor and when she returned, she switched off the ground-floor lights and they went straight to bed.

Christopher had been admiring his wife over the course of the evening. She had forsaken her loose tops and pyjama-style trousers for a stylish blouse and tight jeans. At some point, possibly when she had made her entrance with the Black Forest gateau, he had decided that later they would make love, and he had been quietly looking forward to it. The prospect had added a register of pleasant expectation to his otherwise despondent mental state. Christopher signalled his intent with touches and kisses, and Laura, reliably willing, allowed him to continue. She was not properly aroused, but Christopher knew that his persistence would eventually be rewarded. Just as a mutually satisfying rhythm had been established, the steady hiss of the baby monitor was disturbed by a snuffling sound. He could feel Laura tensing beneath him.

'It's all right,' Christopher whispered. 'She's fine.'

But the snuffling didn't stop, and then there was movement – rustles, creaks, knocks – and then whimpering.

'Stop,' said Laura. Christopher pressed his hands flat against the mattress, raised the upper half of his body and listened. The whimpering was becoming more and more like crying. 'I'd better go,' said Laura, rocking her hips from side to side.

'Maybe she'll settle down,' Christopher ventured hopefully.

'I don't think so.'

'OK.'

Christopher flopped onto his back. Laura swung her legs off the side of the bed, stood up, and left the room. He heard her entering the nursery, picking up Faye, and cooing. 'There, there. What's the matter?' Laura's attempts to settle the child were not entirely successful, and Faye continued to grizzle. Christopher was impatient for his wife's return. He felt wound up and irritable. He closed his eyes, took a deep breath, and tried to transcend his emotions. But Faye was inconsolable. It took more than thirty minutes before she fell silent, and Christopher's discomfort was extended further when Laura chose to spend an additional fifteen minutes waiting to see if Faye would wake up again.

When Laura finally returned, Christopher was anxious to resume their lovemaking; however, Laura disappointed him by removing his hand from her breast.

'No,' she said. 'I'm sorry. I'm really very tired.'

'OK,' he said. She turned her back on him but he continued to stroke her spine. 'OK,' he repeated.

The next day, Christopher was in the studio creating effects with an archaic piece of equipment known (to a small number of former Radiophonic Workshop initiates) as a 'wobbulator'. It was a large metal box with a few switches and a centrally placed rotating knob. The device produced a raw, atavistic sound, to which varying amounts of pitch wobble could be added. The sequence

Christopher was working on involved throbbing bursts of output from the wobbulator, followed by long pauses, and it was during one of these pauses that Christopher detected, once again, the sound of a human voice. He rewound and replayed the tape. There were, in fact, unwanted intrusions in almost every interval of silence. Six altogether. Christopher set about saving the effects he had already recorded by cutting and splicing the tape, and in no time he had removed the spoiled sections and completely restored the soundtrack. He then telephoned Roger Kaminsky, who agreed to pay Christopher a visit later that afternoon.

On returning to his studio, Christopher did a little tidying, examined one or two scores, and then found that he was bored. The excised pieces of tape, which were still hanging from hooks above the splicing table, caught his attention. He had plenty of time to kill, and for want of anything better to do, he decided to join the pieces together so that he could play them to Kaminsky. When Christopher had accomplished his task, he listened to the voices through headphones. None of the utterances were very clear, so he used filters to attenuate some frequencies and strengthen others.

The first voice was female and spoke in French: *'Désolée. Elle est morte la nuit dernière.' I'm sorry, she died last night*. The second voice was male, and spoke two phrases in German: *'Ich bin hier fremd'* and *'Wo treffen wir uns?' I am a stranger here* and *Where shall we meet?* There was then a faint whisper in a Slavic language that Christopher was unable to translate, then a phrase spoken by a woman in what Christopher guessed to be Hungarian. The final voice spoke in declamatory English: 'Come, Tommy. Fate! Come, Tommy. Fate!' The speaker was male and he pronounced his words like a drunken aristocrat.

It was all very curious.

By manipulating frequency levels, Christopher was able to produce an engineered version of the tape that, although still lacking definition, was much 'cleaner' than the original.

When Kaminsky arrived, Christopher explained how voices had started to appear on his recordings.

'No more knocks?' asked Kaminsky.

'No,' Christopher replied. 'But this is just as bad.' He pressed 'play'. 'Listen. The first voice says, *"Désolée. Elle est morte la nuit dernière."*'

Kaminsky tilted his head and asked: 'What does it mean?'

Christopher stopped the tape. 'I'm sorry, she died last night.'

'Weird. Do you mind if I smoke?'

'Providing it's legal. The next voice is German. *"Ich bin hier fremd."* It means I am a stranger here.' Christopher started the tape again.

When the Slavic whispering came through the speakers Kaminsky guessed that it might be Polish.

'Do you speak Polish?' Christopher asked.

'My dad never bothered to teach me,' Kaminsky replied, his admission tinged with regret.

They listened to the Hungarian and English voices, before Christopher rewound the tape and played it a second time from the beginning. 'Well, Roger, what do you think?'

'Have you been using old tape?'

'No.'

'If the record and erasing heads aren't exactly aligned, some of the things you thought you'd wiped can still be there, albeit faintly. Sure it's not old tape?'

'Positive. Besides, I wouldn't have forgotten making recordings like these, would I?'

The young man exhaled a cloud of smoke. 'Could be radio interference – something here acting as an aerial.'

'Why now?'

'Change of weather conditions. A new transmitter, maybe. My old guitar amp picks up radio signals.'

'But there's nothing here that would do that.'

'I don't know. A mate of mine swears that his dental fillings pick up radio programmes. When he clenches his teeth together, he can hear voices, like vibrations in his skull.'

'Then we must suppose that this friend of yours has smoked one joint too many.'

Kaminsky drew on his cigarette. 'I'll take another look at your set-up, but I was pretty thorough last time and—'

'You might have missed something,' Christopher cut in.

'We'll see. Give me a couple of hours.'

Christopher went downstairs and began reading a book in the drawing room. Laura had gone out with Faye, so there was little to distract him. He became absorbed by the narrative and when two hours had elapsed he returned to the studio. Kaminsky was sitting next to the mixing desk, deep in thought and massaging his chin.

'Roger?'

Kaminsky stirred from his reverie. 'Chris.'

'Well?'

The engineer shook his head. 'Nothing.'

'What do you mean, nothing?'

'I couldn't find anything wrong.'

'But the voices . . .'

'Yeah,' said Kaminsky. 'The voices.' He lit a cigarette and nodded silently to himself. 'I've been listening to them, and if you think about it . . .' He hesitated and seemed uncertain as to whether to proceed or not.

'Yes?'

Kaminsky continued. 'They don't sound anything like radio broadcasts, do they? *She died last night; I'm a stranger here; Come, Tommy. Fate.* In French, German, English. I mean, what sort of stations are we picking up here?' It was true. The voices didn't appear in an ongoing stream of interference, and it was difficult to imagine them in the context of an ordinary radio programme. 'And why no music?' Kaminsky added, foreshadowing Christopher's own thoughts. 'No records, no jingles, nothing.'

'What are you suggesting?' Christopher asked.

The engineer studied the smoke rising from his cigarette. 'I don't think these voices are radio transmissions.'

'Then what are they?'

'I don't know, but . . .'

'But what?'

'You'll just say I smoke too much Mary Jane.'

'If you think you know what's going on, say.'

'I don't know what's going on. Not really. It's just a thought.'

'Tell me.'

'I don't think they're transmissions. I think they're communications.'

The two men looked at each other and the quiet seemed to congeal around them. Christopher was surprised to discover that he felt uneasy. With cautious deliberation, he said, 'You think these voices are ghosts?'

'Well, they aren't radio interference, that's for sure.'

'When you say *communications*, what do you mean precisely?'

'Look, Chris, I don't want to get into some big, heavy scene here. I was just saying, that's all. My wife's into all sorts of stuff. You know, spiritualism, auras, meditation . . .' The engineer's sentence trailed off.

'And . . .' Christopher rotated his hand in the air.

'There's a professor,' Kaminsky began again, haltingly, 'who's written a book about voices that appear on tape. You know, a serious book. Scientific.'

'And he thinks they're the dead trying to communicate with us?'

'Yeah.'

'I've worked with tape all my life and the dead have never shown any interest in me or my compositions before.'

'Could be the house.'

Christopher scowled. 'So what am I supposed to do now?'

'I don't know, Chris,' said Kaminsky. 'But I promise you, there's nothing wrong with your gear.'

That night, Christopher found it difficult to concentrate on his work. He kept on thinking about Kaminsky. It seemed a ludicrous idea, the dead communicating with the living through the medium of magnetic tape, but at the same time Christopher's mind was not entirely closed to extraordinary possibilities. During the late sixties, under the influence of a lover who had travelled around India, he had developed a voguish interest in eastern mysticism, and he was not opposed, as a matter of principle, to belief in the supernatural. The voices *were* very strange. Their presence on the tape was inexplicable. Furthermore, Christopher was now obliged to reconsider the very first instance of the phenomenon, which had been a German speaker intoning the words *How sacred for us dead*. This otherwise obscure phrase was now loaded with new significance.

There was a knock on the door.

He called out, 'Come in,' and Laura entered carrying a mug of tea.

'How's it going?' she asked.

'OK.'

Laura placed the mug on the splicing table. 'I made you some tea.'

'Thanks.'

'Will you be working late?'

'I don't think so.'

She turned to leave, but Christopher called out: 'Wait a minute. I want to play you something.' Laura looked at him quizzically. He had stopped playing her his compositions a long time ago. Christopher read her expression and said, 'No, it's not a piece of music. Take a seat.' He offered her his chair and found the spool labelled 'voices'. As he threaded the tape around the tension pulleys, he said, 'You'll hear people speaking – a French woman, a German man—'

'Who are they?' Laura interrupted.

'I don't know. They just appeared. I've manipulated the recordings a little to improve the sound quality, but it's still quite difficult to make out what they're saying.'

'What do you mean, they just appeared?'

'Exactly that. One minute the tape was blank, then a few minutes later it had voices on it.'

'How could that happen?'

'I don't know. Nor does Roger. There's nothing wrong with the equipment, no faults. Just listen. The first voice says *I'm sorry, she died last night* in French. The second says *I'm a stranger here* and *Where shall we meet?* in German. Then there are some east European speakers before someone says *Come, Tommy. Fate!*'

'It's gibberish.'

'Just listen, OK?'

Christopher pressed 'play'. The spools revolved, the slack tape became taut and the voices began their odd recitation. Christopher couldn't see his wife's face, because her head was bowed. When the Englishman's inebriate drawl filled the room, Christopher noticed her shoulders tensing. She leaned forward in her chair. It was as though she had recognized the speaker.

'Laura?'

'Play that last one again.'

'Why?'

'Just play it again, will you.' An increase in volume betrayed her impatience.

Observing the counter, Christopher rewound the tape. The wheels ran backwards and the number in the perspex window got smaller. After a beat of silence, the English voice repeated its demand, 'Come, Tommy. Fate! Come, Tommy. Fate!'

'Jesus,' Laura hissed.

'What?'

'Can't you . . .' She looked up and raked her hair back. Her eyes narrowed.

'What?' Christopher asked again.

'Who are these people?'

'I don't understand. Why are you getting so agitated?'

'What did you say you thought he said? Tommy . . . what?'

'Come, Tommy. Fate!'

'Well, he isn't saying that, is he?'

'Yes, he is.'

'No, he's not. He's saying . . .' Laura paused for a moment before continuing: 'Come to me, Faye.'

Christopher shook his head. 'No, no, no.'

'Come to me, Faye. That's what he's saying. Who is he?'

'Just a second.' Christopher rewound the tape and put the headphones on. 'Let me hear it again through these.' He was sure that his wife was mistaken. Even so, he decided that he should at least appear to be taking her assertion seriously. The voice started and Christopher listened. He closed his eyes and was surprised to discover that he was now less sure about what he was hearing. Simply knowing that the speech could be interpreted differently seemed to introduce a subtle shift of emphasis. The consonants softened as he strained to clarify the words. Another replay failed to resolve ambiguities. Christopher realized that he hadn't cleaned the tape up quite as much as he'd thought. There was still a lot of hiss and rumble to confuse matters. He opened his eyes. 'Yes, I see what you mean.'

Laura's stare was accusatory. 'What's going on, Chris?'

He slipped off the headphones and gestured at the tape machine. 'Roger thinks that these people are dead.'

'I don't understand.'

'Neither do I. Not yet.'

Christopher parked his car on the Archway Road and walked a short distance, over cracked paving slabs, to The Earth Exchange. Massive lorries and double-decker buses laboured their way towards Finchley, belching black smoke from shaking exhaust pipes. He turned into an open yard and approached an imposing brown-brick house ahead. Some of the windows were decorated with colourful transfers and the front door had been left half open. Christopher ascended the stairs and stepped inside. Immediately, the smell of diesel was replaced by wholesome fragrances wafting up from the vegetarian cafe below. He advanced down the shabby hallway, his heels banging loudly on the exposed floorboards, and turned into a large, brightly lit room. He saw baskets full of pulses and grains, fruit and vegetables, and shelves stacked with cartons of tofu, soya chunks and bottles of sarsaparilla. Sitting by the till was a young woman with straggly black hair. She was wearing a skimpy white vest through which Christopher could see the shape of her small breasts and the raised dark outlines of her nipples.

'Hi,' she said, smiling. There wasn't a trace of make-up on her face.

'Hello,' Christopher replied.

'Nice day.'

'Yes. It is very nice.'

He went over to a tall bookcase and glanced through the titles. They were just as he had remembered: books on Buddhism, hypnosis, tarot cards, telepathy, stone circles, astrology and ghosts. He picked up a volume by two authors who were identified on the cover as 'professional ghost hunters', and then consulted the index for any mention of tape machines or tape recordings, but he couldn't find anything relevant. He continued his search, inspecting the contents pages of other books without success.

'Can I help you?' The young woman had emerged from behind the till. He could now see that she was wearing a long, rustic skirt, the embroidered hem of which stopped short of her bare feet.

'I'm looking for a book,' Christopher replied, 'by a professor who claims to have made tape recordings of spirits.' He felt slightly embarrassed by this admission and gave a nervous laugh.

'Yeah, yeah,' said the young woman, 'I know the one.' When she moved, tiny bells attached to an ankle bracelet jingled. She stopped next to a carousel of books and spun it around. Standing at her side, Christopher could smell patchouli and a slight undertow of musky perspiration. 'You must mean this.' She handed Christopher a thick hardback.

He took it from her and momentarily their hands touched. 'Thank you.'

She turned and sashayed back towards the till. Christopher found that her slender figure held his attention and he had to force himself to avert his gaze. He bowed his head and studied the book. The author's name was Konstantin Raudive. There was no professorial prefix. Beneath the title, *Breakthrough,* Christopher read: 'An Amazing Experiment in Electronic Communication with the Dead'. Inside, he discovered some drawings of tape recorders and circuit diagrams. This was surely the book that Kaminsky had referred to.

Christopher took the book to the till. 'Looks interesting.'

The young woman nodded. He gave her a ten-pound note and asked her if she'd read it.

'No,' she replied, 'but it's supposed to be really good. I'm more into past lives. You know, hypnosis, regression . . .'

She was obviously bored and wanted to talk, but Christopher recognized that if he delayed his departure, he would be committing himself to an entirely fraudulent conversation. His inclination to tarry had much more to do with the transparency of the young woman's clothing than any interest he might have in her views on reincarnation. He felt annoyed with himself, guilty, but within seconds something like an alchemical process had transmuted all of his guilt into blame. If Laura had been more sexually responsive of late, then the shaded circles that showed through the young woman's thin cotton vest wouldn't have been nearly so distracting.

Christopher took his change and said, 'Thanks for your help.'

'See you around,' the young woman replied.

He flattered himself that a fleeting shadow of disappointment had passed across her face. With his book tucked under his arm, Christopher made his way down to the vegetarian cafe in the basement. It was entirely empty but for a hairy individual, probably no more than nineteen years of age, standing behind a serving bay of heated metal trays. Christopher bought himself a flapjack and a cup of tea, pulled a chair from beneath one of the old wooden tables and sat down to examine his purchase.

The bulk of the book consisted of transcripts. Obscure, telegraphic communications that didn't make much sense without the explanatory notes that the author had provided. They were presented in a variety of languages with English translations. An introductory chapter detailed a range of recording techniques involving microphones, radios and diodes. Christopher read these sections with considerable interest. They were quite technical but not beyond his understanding. He then looked at the photographic plates. Dr Raudive, a balding gentleman with glasses, was shown operating tape machines, conversing with engineers or posing with his scientific collaborators. One of these was described as 'Germany's leading parapsychologist'. Another was a Swiss physicist. Christopher had half expected *Breakthrough* to be a sensational polemic, full of outrageous claims, but it was nothing of the sort. It was more like a treatise, restrained, meticulous and endorsed by respected members of the international academic community. Clearly, in certain circles, the appearance of spirit voices on tape was an accepted phenomenon.

Christopher closed the book and tasted his flapjack. It was extremely good, a weighty agglomeration of oats and raisins, bound together with honey. As he chewed, his mouth filled with sweetness. He thought about the voices that he had recorded. If it were true that the speakers were spirits trying to communicate with the living, then how utterly extraordinary it was that they should have chosen to make their existence known by interfering with *his* tape machines. An alternative possibility was that the recordings were simply opportunistic: that the conditions in his studio were, for whatever reason, favourable and that the spirits had no special interest in him or his family. Or perhaps choice and intention were entirely irrelevant in this context? Perhaps the tape machine had simply captured random phrases floating in the ether?

Just thinking about these questions made him feel light-headed.

Yet, he had to concede, there was nothing random about the phrase 'Come to me, Faye'. If, as Christopher was slowly coming to accept, this was what the English voice had actually said, then quite clearly he, the spirit, had demonstrated knowledge of at least one of the house's occupants.

Christopher thought about Laura. She had perceived the communication as sinister. Indeed, she had become quite upset. When he had challenged her, she hadn't been very forthcoming. 'I don't like it,' was all that she had had to say. Later, that night, she had been distinctly moody, and when they were in bed together, and Christopher had tried to reach out to her, she had turned her back on him.

The basement door opened and two people entered – a couple, dressed identically in flared maroon trousers and yellow T-shirts. They were evidently regulars and engaged the youth in a conversation about the food in the heated trays. It was a curiously solemn exchange.

Christopher noticed a discarded newspaper on an adjacent table. A partially exposed headline piqued his curiosity, but when he investigated further he found that the story was, in fact, quite dull, so he turned to the arts pages. The name Simon Ogilvy seemed to leap out at him. His friend was mentioned, along with Oliver Knussen and Peter Maxwell Davies, in an article on 'highlights to look out for' in the coming prom season.

A distinctive voice . . . innovative harmonies . . . exceptional command of orchestral resources.

Every compliment Simon collected seemed to bespatter Christopher's own achievements with ordure. Christopher yearned for such praise, intelligent audiences and meaningful plaudits. But it would never happen. Not now. Christopher cast the newspaper aside and picked up *Breakthrough*. The dust jacket was silver and decorated with a stylized wave pattern. He stared at the pattern for so long he experienced the illusion of movement. An idea had been taking shape in his mind, its constituent elements emerging from an inner vacancy and gradually coalescing into something concrete and intelligible. The voices of the dead could be incorporated into a piece of electronic music. Instantly, the scope and structure of the work were revealed to him: a major undertaking, with extended movements, a kind of anti-requiem, in which instead of the living addressing the dead, their roles would be reversed and the dead would address the living. The boldness of the concept made his heart quicken. He hadn't felt so inspired in years and he imagined his composition provoking controversy, heated debate. He would be invited to speak on radio programmes, just as he had in the past, and the music critics would refer to him once more as the 'English Stockhausen'. It was such a good idea, and bound to attract interest from all quarters. He could barely contain his excitement.

*

On returning home, Christopher marched down the hallway and into the kitchen. Faye was in her highchair, foraging through raisins piled on a saucer. When she saw her father enter, she rocked backwards and forwards, pointed and said, 'Da-da.' Christopher turned to share the child's reaction with his wife and froze. Laura was perched on a stool, reading a magazine and about to bite into a chocolate biscuit. What *had* she done to herself? Their eyes met and her expression darkened. 'You don't like it,' she said tersely.

Her hair, with its glossy waves and carefully positioned curls, had been shorn off, leaving only a short, spiky fleece that made her face seem much larger.

'It's not that I don't like it,' said Christopher, attempting to conceal his true feelings. 'It's just . . . I really liked your hair the way it was.'

Laura bit a corner off her biscuit. 'I felt like a change. It's been so hot lately, and I was getting fed up with having to fiddle around with the tongs every morning. Chris, *do* stop looking at me like that!'

'I'm sorry.'

'It'll grow back, you know.'

'Yes, I know.'

Laura put her magazine down next to the biscuit tin. Christopher registered the title – *Spare Rib*. On the cover was a black-and-white photograph of two women holding guitars. One of them had her hair completely hidden beneath an elaborate headscarf and the other wore her hair very short – like Laura's. A green banner that sliced diagonally across the lower right-hand corner of the page announced: 'Rape Crisis Centre Opens – *Spare Rib* Special Report'. When Laura realized that her husband was studying the cover of her magazine, she pushed it beneath a copy of the *Listener*. After swallowing the remains of her biscuit, she said, 'Henry called.'

'What did he want?'

'He didn't say.'

Christopher went over to Faye, bent down and kissed her on the head. She offered him a raisin, holding it up with her chubby hand. Christopher took it from her and said, 'Ta.' The child repeated the syllable, extending the vowel, and then adopted a curiously coy expression. 'What?' Christopher asked. 'What's the matter?' She clapped her hands and started to rock backwards and forwards again.

Laura sighed and slid off the stool. She picked up her empty mug and carried it over to the sink, the loose heels of her sandals slapping against the floor tiles. After turning the tap on she rinsed the mug in a stream of water and placed it upside down on the draining board. Looking out of the window, she said, 'More good weather. We must get the garden done.'

'Yes.'

Laura turned the tap off and dried her hands on a tea towel. 'I'll talk to Sue.'

'Who?'

'Sue. The garden designer I met. Remember?'

'You could get an estimate, I suppose. I'm not sure it would be wise to start another big project. Not just yet.'

'Why not?'

'We're not exactly flush at the moment.'

'She won't be expensive.'

'OK. See what she thinks. I'm going upstairs.'

'OK. Don't forget to call Henry.'

'No. I won't.'

Christopher was breathless by the time he reached the second-floor landing. It was hotter at the top of the house, and as soon as he got into the studio he opened one of the double-glazed windows. The air, which should have been fresh, carried with it a whiff of stagnant water from the Vale of Health pond. He sat down in his swivel chair, opened *Breakthrough* and began to read, although on this occasion with greater care.

One of the recording techniques that appealed to Christopher involved making use of radio noise. A radio could be tuned between stations and the static – the crackling rush of electrical interference found between broadcasting frequencies – could be fed directly into a tape machine. When played back, such recordings were often found to contain voices. The procedure struck Christopher as interesting, because the voices he had already recorded seemed to actually arise out of the background hiss of the tape. Perhaps tape hiss and radio noise, two very similar sounds, possessed common elements that could be used by spirits as the raw material for the construction of their messages. Raudive advised that each experimental session should commence with the investigator using a microphone to record the time and date, his or her name and an invitation for 'unseen friends' to manifest on the tape. Questions could be asked, providing each question was followed by a pause for answers. Tape speed could be set at either three and three-quarter or seven and a half inches per second, although some researchers (the name Friedrich Jürgenson was cited) favoured seven and a half inches per second for 'faster' voices. Much was made of the unusual rapidity of spirit speech, a phenomenon that Christopher had not, as yet, encountered. Rerecording communications at least five times was recommended to improve clarity. Christopher thought that he could achieve superior results using filters.

As soon as he had digested the technical pages, Christopher was eager to try out what he had learned. He opened a brand new tape box and removed the spool from its transparent cellophane wrapping, before pressing it onto the vacant spindle of his Akai. He threaded the tape through the guides and poked the laminated end into the hub slot of the empty reel. He then set up the microphone and radio connections as described by Raudive. After turning the dial of the radio so that the needle occupied a position between stations and the speaker was emitting nothing but noise, he tapped the microphone and adjusted the recording levels. Feeling somewhat self-conscious, he said: 'Two fifteen p.m., Tuesday the eighteenth of May, 1976. This is Christopher Norton. Is there anybody there?' He paused before continuing: 'Who are you?' And after another pause he asked, 'What do you want?' He then repeated his questions, rewound the tape and listened to the recording. His voice entered above the radio static, but in the gaps between his questions there were no responses. He made another ten-minute recording, but when he played it back there were still no voices, only lengthy intervals of frothy interference.

Christopher felt deflated. The idea of using the voices of the dead in a serious musical work had offered him a tantalizing prospect of professional redemption. But now, his vision of concert halls, ovations and interviews had begun to shimmer like a mirage – the light of hope refracting through layers of disappointment. He could not abandon his fantasy of rehabilitation, his return to the intellectual fold, and he consoled himself with the thought that his expectations had very probably been too high. It had been unrealistic to suppose that the dead would communicate at his convenience. Raudive hadn't achieved instant success, he had applied himself over a period of many years. Moreover, identifying spirits on tape was evidently a skill that developed over time. Investigators became more 'attuned' with continued practice. No, he wouldn't give up. He would persevere. The idea for the new work was simply too good to discard, especially at this early stage. Perhaps the 'unseen friends' would be more talkative later on. In the meantime, he would continue composing the next section of *Android Insurrection.*

The three hours that followed were spent recording the sound of piano strings being hit with a small mallet. These recordings were then played backwards, at different speeds, and rerecorded onto a master tape. When he had finished, Christopher went downstairs to join his wife and daughter for dinner.

'I was just about to call you,' said Laura.

She was serving moussaka from a baking dish with a large spoon. As she broke the cheese topping, the fragrances of cinnamon, oregano and thyme were released into the air. Laura mentioned, in passing, a news item that she had heard on the radio concerning the new Concorde service to Washington. 'Three and a half hours,' she said. 'Amazing.'

They both sat down to eat. Faye was in her highchair, attempting to impale pasta shells on the tines of a plastic fork.

'Shame the Americans won't let the thing land in New York,' said Christopher. 'People – well, rich people at any rate – would start going to New York for the weekend. When's the first flight?'

'Next week, I think.'

The conversation that followed was fitful. Something of their earlier difference of opinion over Laura's hairstyle still lingered, creating a distance between them that seemed to augment the width of the kitchen table. Laura pushed some food around the rim of her plate. 'I'd like to go out this evening. If you don't mind.'

Christopher looked up. He really didn't like her hair. 'Sorry?'

'There's a speaker appearing at that bookshop in

Islington – you know, where the readers' group meets. I wasn't going to go, but I saw something about her today in a magazine and I've changed my mind.'

'OK.'

'You can carry on working. I'll put Faye to bed. It doesn't start until eight.'

'OK.'

Laura took Faye's fork and scooped a pasta shell into the child's mouth. Most of the pasta had been removed from the bowl and dropped onto the highchair tray. The white Formica was smeared with tomato sauce.

'Sue will be there tonight,' said Laura.

'Who?'

'The garden designer.'

'OK. We only want an estimate.'

'I know.'

Faye struck the Formica, demanding to be fed.

'You're a big girl now,' said Laura. 'You've got to learn how to do it yourself.'

The child opened her mouth like a gannet.

Christopher returned to the studio and pressed the 'on' button of the radio. He rotated the tuning dial this way and that, listening to brief snatches of incomprehensible speech and bursts of pop music. In the perspex window that covered the frequency markings he noticed a reflection of his eyes: resolute, focused. When the needle was positioned at the midpoint between two stations separated by a broad band of static, he started recording. Taking the microphone, he said, 'Seven twenty-five p.m., Tuesday the eighteenth of May, 1976. This is Christopher Norton. Is there anybody there? Any unseen friends? Or enemies? Talk to me. I'd really like you to say something.'

He let the tape run for twenty minutes, then rewound it and listened. Soon after his introductory comments he heard something faint, like the rustling of dry autumn leaves in the static. He stopped the tape, listened and made a note of the number displayed on the rev counter. He then let the tape continue. There were some more indistinct murmurings, and then a female voice said, 'Do not continue.' It was very clear and Christopher was so surprised he let out a nervous laugh. A few seconds later, the woman repeated this firm injunction. Christopher made another rev counter note and continued listening. After a minute or so, a man with a distinct Scottish accent said, 'We cannot intercede and the light is failing.' This was followed by a French woman, who, after several replays, Christopher understood to be saying, '*Quels que soient les mots . . . les laisser couler.*' *Whatever the words . . . let them flow.* Then the first voice returned: 'Leave them alone, I implore you. Leave them alone.' A crackling within the static seemed to come forward, becoming more sharply defined as laughter. After a few moments it receded, before being lost in the seething effervescence of the radio noise. There were no more communications on the tape.

Christopher stopped the Akai and sat back in his chair.

'Jesus,' he said aloud. 'That's incredible.'

First week in June

Where was Faye?

She had lost her daughter and was searching for the child on the ground floor. But everything was different. Out of the window she could see a neatly cut lawn, a small orchard and the gazebo, the woodwork of which was painted bright red. Laura ran into the hallway and was confused by the number of doors. There were many more than she remembered. She ran from room to room and discovered more doors and more rooms. The house was like a honeycomb. Gilt mirrors, brocade curtains and benighted oil paintings, yards of intricately patterned carpet, chandeliers and classical figures on columns, deeper and deeper, the rooms went on and on. When Laura tried to call Faye's name, she produced a sound like a tape recording played at half-speed, a kind of bellow – like a cow. Without having ascended any stairs, she suddenly found herself on the top floor of the house, standing in the unused room opposite the studio. She was facing the empty alcove. Once again, she tried to call

Faye's name, but her mouth wouldn't open. The best she could accomplish was a low, prolonged moan.

Mummy. Mummy, help me.

Faye wasn't old enough to speak properly. But it was definitely Faye, and her voice was coming from the other side of the wall.

Mummy – please. Please help.

Laura stepped forward and reached out to touch the floral wallpaper. Her fingertips met no resistance, and, as her arm extended, her hand vanished up to the wrist.

Mummy. You must help me.

She advanced, passing through the wall and into a windowless cell. Edges hardened, as if everything had been brought into sharper focus. A paraffin lamp hung from a ceiling lagged with cobwebs, and water dripped down into puddles on a concrete floor. She saw exposed brickwork splattered with ochre stains and the carcass of a rat. The creature's head had been crushed and the contents of its shattered skull had sprayed some distance from its body. She was surrounded by rusty chains of varying lengths and sizes and attached to many of them were hooks or manacles. The latter were very small. One row of chains was swinging gently, as if they had been recently disturbed. Their frequent collisions created a constant *clink-clink-clink.* Laura brushed the nearest curtain of hooks and restraints aside and discovered a large wooden table. Some tools had been laid out: a hacksaw with blackened teeth, a hand drill and several instruments with opening bills that Laura couldn't identify but guessed might have some surgical use. A set of meat cleavers were attached to a carousel. Next to the table was a tiny chair, a spinning top and an empty champagne bucket filled with ice.

Faye, for God's sake, where are you?

She could hear her own breathing – quick and shallow. The dank, cold air seemed to insinuate itself into her bones. She heard a key turn in a lock, hinges groaned and, behind her, a metal door opened and closed. It produced a resonant clang and the flame in the oil lamp trembled. She tried to turn round to see who had arrived, but she found that she was paralysed.

Slow footsteps, the tip of a cane tapping on concrete. Chains collected together and released – *clink-clink-clink* – loud at first, then becoming softer and less resonant, until all that remained was a sound like the dry click of billiard balls.

Somebody was standing behind her. She screamed, but her throat muscles contracted and she could only produce a lengthy exhalation. Her mouth remained open, wide open, fixed in an attitude of mute terror. The threat that she sensed was not merely physical: any pain that she was forced to endure would be a mere preamble to something far worse, a violation so profound that it would leave an indelible stain on her soul. Already she felt breached, undone, from the trespass of another mind probing her own. She looked at the surgical instruments again, imagined their forceful insertion into her body, the bills drawing apart, the stretching of flesh to its limit, the slow tearing of skin and dribbles of blood . . .

Laura woke up. She could hear her heart pounding: a rapid, irregular beat, like the footfall of a cripple attempting to escape mortal danger.

Little by little, familiar impressions returned – the pressure of the mattress against her back, warmth, Chris snoring. She sighed and raised the upper half of her body on her elbows. Her eyes adapted to the darkness and the light-polluted sky made the windows glow. She got out of bed and shuffled to the bathroom, where she studied her face in the mirror. Her hair had clumped together in places and her skin looked dry. She was about to apply some moisturizer, but she stopped herself. Instead, she opened the medicine cabinet and took out a plastic container full of pills. She tipped a couple onto her palm and swallowed them with some water that she scooped up to her mouth from the tap.

The dream had been so vivid. She wondered if nightmares were a side effect of the medication. Perhaps she had been taking the pills for too long.

She put the container back in the medicine cabinet and crossed the landing. Her failure to find Faye in the dream had left Laura with a strong desire to see her daughter again, to know, without doubt, that she was safe. She recognized that this impulse was irrational, but it was something she felt compelled to act on. Standing next to the cot, Laura wanted to lift the child over the bars and hold her close, but she resisted the urge. It would be selfish to disturb Faye's sleep just so that she, Laura, could allay her irrational fears. She had to content herself with touching Faye's cheek and inhaling her distinctive baby smell. The drone of an aeroplane became louder and then faded into the night. Silence flooded the house like black water.

When Laura climbed back into bed, Christopher stirred and said in slurred, thickened speech, 'What's the matter?'

'Nothing,' Laura replied. 'Go back to sleep.'

The telephone was ringing. Christopher entered the drawing room and picked up the receiver. It was Henry

Baylis: 'Bloody hell, Chris, have you stopped returning calls?'

'I'm sorry, Laura did remind me. I forgot.'

'You forgot?'

'Yes, I've been preoccupied with something . . .'

'What?'

'A project. Nothing to do with films.'

'You do realize that Dan and Mike will be wanting to meet up soon. How is *Alien* . . .'

'*Android Insurrection*.'

'How is *Android Insurrection* coming along?'

'All right. I'm pleased with what I've done – so far.'

'Good. Now, I hope you haven't got anything special planned this week.'

'Why?'

'Fabrice Ancel wants to meet you.' Baylis hesitated before adding, 'In Paris'.

'Fabrice Ancel?'

'He caused something of a stir last year at Cannes with a film called *Autodestruction*? Violent but fiendishly clever. The critics compared it to *A Clockwork Orange*. Turns out he's a great fan of yours.'

'Really?'

'Oh yes.'

'Paris . . .'

'Yes. He's getting ready to shoot a psychological thriller called *Le Jardin des Reflets*. Sounds very interesting. What do you think? I know it's short notice but I don't think we should dither.'

'Did Marcus and Diane get back to you?'

'What about?'

'*The Warlock*.'

'Oh yes, that. Cushing said no, I'm afraid, which means that it probably won't happen. So, as things stand, Ancel's approach is very timely.' Baylis paused for a few seconds, and when he spoke again his voice was less robust. 'There's just *one* thing . . .'

'What?'

'I don't think there's going to be a great deal of money in this. One of the backers dropped out a few weeks ago.'

'Oh? Why was that?'

'God knows. Anyway, Ancel's decided to push on regardless – still thinks he can get the film made with a few cuts and a bit of recasting. Look, Chris, I know all this doesn't sound very promising, but I've been hearing good things about Fabrice Ancel. He's a young man who's going places. Katie and Brad think it's only a matter of time before he wins the Palme d'Or. If *Le Jardin des Reflets* turns out to be the one, and you've written the score, well, imagine what a big difference that'll make.'

'When you say that you don't think there's going to be a great deal of money . . .'

'It was only a preliminary conversation and the production team are an extremely pretentious lot – art for art's sake and all that. They would have considered any horse-trading at this stage very bad form. You know what the French are like. Well, what do you say?'

Their conversation lasted for another ten minutes, and at its conclusion Christopher found that (perhaps against his better judgement) he had agreed to fly to Paris at the end of the week. Somehow, in spite of being disconcertingly vague, Baylis had managed to persuade Christopher that *Le Jardin des Reflets* was a prestigious undertaking and that his involvement would lead to many more commissions in the future.

Christopher sauntered into the kitchen. Faye was running around the table, her curious elastic step producing an exceptional degree of buoyancy. Laura was watching her with detached interest. Christopher caught his daughter, tickled her and said, 'Slow down, honey, or you'll fall over.'

'No, she won't,' said Laura.

'She might.'

'She does this every day. She's fine.'

'I wasn't being critical.'

'What do you mean by that?'

Christopher dismissed Laura's question with a frown. He released Faye and the child continued circling the table.

'I've got to fly to Paris on Friday.'

'Why?'

'Henry wants me to meet a director.' The muscles around Laura's mouth tightened. She raised her hand and touched a finger to her lips. Suddenly she looked confused, vulnerable. 'What is it?' Christopher asked.

'Nothing,' she replied.

'It's all right, isn't it? There's no reason why I shouldn't go this Friday, is there?' She shook her head. 'Well then . . .'

Christopher and Simon Ogilvy had arranged to meet at Jack Straw's Castle – a large pub with a slatted, timber exterior that overlooked the western extremity of the heath. They conversed as equals on most subjects, but when it came to music and especially their own compositions, a precedent favouring Simon's eminence had been firmly established. This inequality was, so Christopher thought, acceptable under the circumstances as his friend's music was serious and merited extended discussion, and although Simon might not have starved for his art, he had certainly struggled and made significant personal sacrifices. Simon had earned the right to talk at length about his musical development, his clever conceits and artistic goals, even if his rhetoric often became immoderate and close to self-indulgence. That evening, however, Christopher was less content in his listening role. He found it difficult to permit his friend the customary laxities; he was impatient and fidgety, eager to tell Simon about his own extraordinary undertaking.

Simon was in full spate. 'It's a rather interesting harmonic device. The listener experiences the illusion of movement – a musical paradox, where journey and stasis coexist without contradiction.'

'I'm working on something too,' said Christopher, clumsily interrupting Simon's train of thought. He couldn't contain himself a moment longer. 'Something I'm really excited about.'

Simon made an inadequate attempt to conceal his irritation and, feigning curiosity, asked, 'What's the film called?'

'No,' Christopher responded. 'No, it's not a film score.'

'What then? A new . . .' Simon hesitated.

'Piece,' Christopher said. 'Yes, a new *piece*.'

One of Simon's eyebrows ascended a fraction. 'Really?'

'Yes, an electronic work. Like I used to write, you know, back in Cologne, and when I was at the BBC. Let me tell you about it.'

Simon raised his hand. 'Can I get you a drink first?' He indicated Christopher's empty glass. 'Same again?'

'All right. Thanks.'

Christopher watched Simon cross the patterned carpet and lean against the bar. The atmosphere was smoky and created a glowing halo around every light. A strikingly handsome young man, perhaps in his early twenties, came and stood next to Simon. He was wearing a short black leather jacket and jeans. They started talking and Christopher noticed that Simon was shaking his head. The drinks arrived, Simon paid for them, and he was about to leave the bar when the young man said something else and tapped his wristwatch. Once again, Simon shook his head. Although Simon appeared to be refusing a request, he was smiling, and the exchange seemed to be good-humoured. The young man nodded, walked off, and vanished into a crowd at the back of the pub.

Simon placed the drinks on the table.

'What did that boy want?' Christopher asked.

'Oh, nothing,' Simon shrugged, seeming a little flustered. 'He asked me for some money, actually.'

'Why? What did he want it for?'

'Oh, I don't know. He didn't say. He was here a couple of weeks ago and he did exactly the same thing.'

'I wonder why he chooses to bother you.'

'Perhaps I look gullible.' Simon pushed a pint glass in Christopher's direction. 'So, this new piece of yours. I'm intrigued.'

Christopher took a deep breath. 'You're going to have to keep an open mind, OK? Because what I'm about to tell you will sound, at least initially, very peculiar indeed; however, I'm convinced there's something in it – well, more than that really.' Simon's brow furrowed as Christopher continued. 'Have you ever heard of electronic voices before? Or voice phenomena?'

'Electronic voices? No, I haven't.'

'The name Konstantin Raudive?'

'No.'

'Right.' Christopher proceeded to give an account of how voices had, quite inexplicably, begun to appear on his recordings, and how he had subsequently learned that the phenomenon was recognized by scientists. He braced himself before saying, 'It's controversial, of course. But there seems to be an emerging consensus that these voices are spirit communications.' He was conscious throughout that he was in danger of sounding a little unhinged, and made every effort to maintain a level delivery in spite of his excitement. He told his friend about the drawling, aristocratic voice that had called his daughter's name, and then explained how he intended to incorporate these 'communications' into an original work. As he spoke, he was encouraged by Simon's expression, which gradually changed from sceptical dismissal to rapt interest. When Christopher had finished, Simon leaned forward and said, 'That is . . . fascinating. But how can you be sure that these voices don't have a terrestrial origin?'

'They don't sound like any broadcast you've ever heard. They speak in many different languages. And the voice that called out to Faye is surely pretty convincing, isn't it?'

'Yes. That is very odd.' Simon drained his glass and looked across the pub. He seemed distracted for a moment but when he fixed his eyes on Christopher again, he repeated the word 'Fascinating.'

'Look,' said Christopher. 'Why don't you come and hear what I've done.'

'Now?'

'Yes. I've only got a few minutes of material. It won't take long.'

Simon shrugged. 'All right. Why not?'

They went to the car park, got into Simon's Austin 1800

and drove the very short distance along East Heath Road and down into the Vale of Health.

Christopher unlocked the front door of the house and ushered Simon into the hallway.

'I'm home,' Christopher called.

Laura stepped out of the drawing room. She was wearing a baggy green T-shirt and a pair of flared slacks. Under her arm was a paperback book with a creased spine.

'Simon,' she said, surprised.

He advanced and gave her a peck on both cheeks. 'You've had your hair cut.'

'Yes,' Laura replied. 'Chris doesn't like it.'

'I didn't say that,' Christopher protested. 'I've never said that.'

'But you don't,' Laura said. 'Not really.'

Christopher looked at Simon and sighed. 'I can't win.'

'It looks rather good,' said Simon. He glanced at Christopher. 'No? I like it. Honestly, I do.'

'Thank you,' said Laura, inclining her head.

'We're going upstairs,' said Christopher.

'OK,' said Laura. 'Do you want some tea, coffee?'

'Not for me,' Christopher replied.

'Nor me,' said Simon. 'But thanks for offering.'

The two men ascended the stairs and entered the

studio. Christopher switched on a lamp and offered his friend a seat. Around the horseshoe arrangement of electrical equipment an array of dials emitted a soft yellow glow. Christopher approached a large, centrally positioned tape recorder and pressed the 'play' button. 'Listen to this.' The sound of two oscillators floated out of the silence. They were so widely separated that the listener could not escape an impression of a void or chasm opening up between them. A whispering began to infiltrate the emptiness, first one voice, then another, until the cumulative chatter produced a sustained chaos. The overall effect was vaguely avian and evoked images of mobbing birds and beating wings, or something more elevated, a host of angels, perhaps, cherubim and seraphim. The texture was enriched by an exquisite rippling, like a thousand harpists producing circular glissandi. Brassy Doppler effects receded into an imaginary distance, suggesting boundless space. Occasionally, a word or phrase seemed to escape from the polyglot maelstrom. Quite suddenly, the music came to an end and all that remained was the hiss of blank tape. Christopher pressed a button and the reels stopped revolving.

He looked at his friend. 'Well?'

'Those voices . . .'

'Yes.'

'They're dead people?'

'Yes.'

'That's what the dead sound like?'

'Not exactly. I use filters to clean the sound up. They don't always come through clearly.'

'I see.'

'Well, what do you think?'

Simon inflated his cheeks and let the air out slowly. 'I don't know what to say.'

That night, lying in bed, Christopher couldn't stop thinking. Simon's reaction had been at best lukewarm, and at worst perfunctory. He had made some comments concerning the 'ingenuity' of 'the concept', but at the same time, Christopher had detected an underlying reticence, an unwillingness to commit himself to a straightforward compliment. After a very brief technical discussion, Simon had wanted to hear the original unadulterated recordings of the voices, and he had sat very still, his elbow on the chair arm, the weight of his head supported on the heel of his palm, listening intently, his expression slightly troubled. Christopher had asked his friend if he knew any producers at the BBC who would be willing to programme the work when it was completed. 'Perhaps you could put in a good word?' But Simon had only responded with vague, empty remarks, and when pressed, he became downright evasive. By the time Simon left, Christopher was simmering with resentment – a resentment that had failed to dissipate and was now keeping him awake.

The bed felt uncomfortable, the sheets clammy. Laura's body seemed to be generating an intolerable amount of heat and he could hear Faye's distracting snore over the baby monitor. It was pointless trying to sleep, so he got out of bed, put on a dressing gown and crept up the stairs to his studio. Christopher plugged in a pair of headphones and prepared to listen again to the music that had so obviously failed to impress his friend. Simon's cool reception had planted niggling doubts in Christopher's mind (perhaps it wasn't as good as he had thought?) and he was a little apprehensive as he waited for the piece to begin. But as the vast emptiness – defined by the oscillators – began to fill with voices, Christopher felt calmer, more confident that his prior estimation of the work's value was accurate. This was fine music, possibly great music. He even allowed himself to think that Simon might have been threatened by what he had heard.

Christopher didn't want to go back to bed. Nor did he

feel like composing, so he decided that he would attempt to record more voices.

'One twenty a.m., Wednesday the second of June, 1976. This is Christopher Norton calling any unseen friends – is anybody there?' He paused. 'Would you care to introduce yourself?' Again he paused. 'It would be helpful if you spoke loudly and clearly. Could you do that?' His mind emptied and a few seconds passed before he added, 'Any special messages?' And so he continued improvising questions in this manner until the background monotony of the static made him feel sleepy. He sat back in the chair and closed his eyes. When he looked at the tape machine again, the spool that had previously been full was now almost empty. He had obviously been dozing. Christopher switched off the radio, stopped the tape, then pressed 'rewind' and 'play'. He listened to his introductory remarks and his first question, 'Anybody there?' Almost immediately a familiar drawling voice responded, 'I am here.' Christopher leaned forward. 'Would you care to introduce yourself?' The static continued for a few moments before the same voice, with slow, effortful deliberation, replied, 'Edward Stokes Maybury.' Christopher pressed the 'stop' button, rewound the tape and played the recording again. 'Edward Stokes Maybury.'

Where had he heard that name before?

Christopher strained to remember. Suddenly, his hitherto opaque memory became perfectly clear.

Mr Edward Maybury . . . secrets of the ancient world . . .

The name had appeared on the framed theatre bill that he had discovered in the attic. Carriages had been mentioned and seats priced at only one shilling.

Automatons . . . manifestations and vanishings.

Maybury must have been an Edwardian or Victorian stage magician. Christopher remembered the broken Chinese screen, the large mirrors and the traveller's trunk engraved with the initials 'E.S.M.' Had Maybury been a former occupant of the house? Christopher remembered seeing other discarded items in the attic: a camera, some broken records, a reel of thin wire, toys. Everything – apart from the clockwork monkey that he had rescued for Faye – had been thrown away. Christopher now wished that he had kept more of it, especially the theatre bill. He pressed 'play' again and listened to the rest of the tape. There were no further communications, although somewhere in the middle of the static that had been recorded while he had been dozing there were a few Russian phrases. They were very faint and not worth cleaning up. Christopher turned the radio on, pressed 'record' and spoke into the microphone. 'Maybury? Are you still there? Did you once live in this house?' Christopher left enough time for an answer and continued, 'What do you want?'

When he played the tape back, he could hear only his own voice against the steady rush of radio noise. Maybury had gone.

The following morning Christopher telephoned the estate agent. He didn't expect Mr Petrakis to remember him, but he did, and evidently very well. 'Your wife was pregnant? What did she have in the end, a boy or a girl?' They made polite, inconsequential conversation for a few minutes before Christopher broached the subject of former occupants. 'I was wondering, Mr Petrakis, do you have any idea who lived in this house before us? Would you have anything in your files – a list of prior owners, perhaps?'

'Nobody lived there before you. It was owned by developers and was empty for years. Didn't I mention that? I'm sure I did.'

'But people must have lived in the house before the developers acquired it.'

'Of course. Many people – probably. It's an old house. Mr Norton, the person you need to talk to is your solicitor. He would have contacted the land registry and authorized a search for title. I don't know how far back he went, but if he's still got your particulars, he might be able to give you some answers. Why do you want to know who lived in your house?'

'I think someone quite famous might have lived here once. A stage performer.'

'Really?'

'Yes.' Christopher heard the ringing of a telephone in the earpiece.

'I'm sorry, Mr Norton. The other phone's going. I'm in the office on my own today. I'm afraid I've got to pick it up.'

'That's fine. Thank you for your help.'

Christopher put the telephone down and flicked through his address book. He found his solicitor's number and was about to call him, but hesitated. Perhaps it would be better if he put his question in a letter. Yes, that was probably a better way to proceed. He put the phone down once again, crossed the room and searched in the bureau for a writing pad. At that moment, Laura entered. Their eyes met and she said, 'Middle drawer.'

'You don't know what I'm looking for.'

She frowned and bit her lower lip. 'Paper?'

Christopher raised his eyebrows. 'How did you know that?'

'Just a hunch.'

*

Simon and Amanda Ogilvy were sitting opposite each other at the breakfast table. They had risen late. The radio was on, but set at a very low volume. Strains of a Rachmaninoff piano prelude could be heard intermittently, the swell of luscious harmonies, sparkling technique. When the fortissimo passages subsided, only a barely detectable background jingling persisted. Amanda was wearing a gauzy orange negligee decorated with flounces and dangling ribbons. Her dark hair was in a wild state of disarray and her eyes were slightly bloodshot. Traces of yesterday's mascara, now a granular black residue, still clung to her eyelashes. Her large, olive breasts were almost fully exposed by a capricious neckline. Simon, unlike his wife, had already had a shower. He had shaved with an electric razor and the astringency of his cologne had brought colour to his cheeks. His brown paisley dressing gown made him look rather foppish.

'I believe in ghosts. Don't you?' Amanda's husky voice was almost gruff. She had been to a student party the night before and had smoked excessively. This degree of overindulgence reliably extended her vocal range downwards and she rarely missed an opportunity to exploit it.

'Well, yes,' Simon replied, 'in so far as I believe that people sometimes see things that can't be explained. Places have atmospheres, certainly, and I suppose that powerful, emotionally charged events might leave some kind of impression – a kind of memory. But as for the dead coming back to meddle with the affairs of the living? I'm not sure I believe in that sort of thing.'

'When I was at university we had a séance. A spirit came through with a message for me. He said that my Aunt Lucy, who had just died, was happy, and she wanted to know if I liked her necklace.'

'Had she left you a necklace?'

'Yes.'

'Do you still have it?

'I don't wear it so much these days. It doesn't seem to go with anything.' Amanda leaned forward, placing her elbows on the table. She raised the cup of coffee she was holding with both hands and took a sip. 'I hadn't told anyone in the room about Aunt Lucy dying, or the necklace. So nobody taking part in the séance could have faked that message.'

'Perhaps *you* did. Not consciously, of course. But unconsciously.'

Amanda shrugged. 'Perhaps.'

Simon spread marmalade over his buttered toast. It was almost the same colour as Amanda's negligee. 'I'll definitely get a copy of Raudive's book. His work *does* sound interesting, although I'm really not sure that Chris knows what he's doing. It's a great idea, a piece of music incorporating spirit communications, the sort of idea that would certainly attract public interest. You can just imagine the newspapers: composer writes oratorio for the dead! Journalists would love it, like they loved Rosemary Brown. Remember? The medium who wrote music dictated by Bach and Beethoven.' Simon cut the toast in half and balanced the knife across his plate. 'The thing is . . . when I listened to Chris's original recordings, I can't say I was very impressed. The voices, if they were voices, weren't terribly clear. I heard *something,* but I'm not sure what, just something tinny in the static. Chris said that the more you listen to the tapes, the better you get at interpreting what's being said. But if you listen hard to anything long enough, you'll start to hear things. I imagine it works like those inkblots that psychiatrists use.'

'The Rorschach test.'

'Yes. They're just shapes – smudges – but people see all sorts of things in them, don't they? Chris edits his recordings. And I think he does so in accordance with his expectations. In the end, he gets what he wants. I doubt that it's conscious – same as your séance.'

Amanda returned her coffee cup to its saucer. 'Was the music any good?'

'All right, I suppose.' He sounded grudging, insincere. 'It was very similar to his film scores. Although Chris seems to think that he's writing something far superior. He wants me to help him get it broadcast on Radio 3. But it's difficult enough getting my own work programmed.' Simon picked up his toast and took a large bite. As he was chewing, he studied his wife. His expression changed, the wrinkling of his nose suggesting mild distaste. It was as though he had suddenly noticed her dishevelled appearance. 'What time did you get back last night?'

'Late. I don't know.'

'I hope you got a cab.'

'Someone gave me a lift.'

'Oh? Who was that?'

'Penelope.'

'Penelope?'

'A new lecturer. Liberal Studies. Lives in Golders Green.'

'I hope she didn't drink too much.'

'She doesn't drink. And you?'

'What?'

'What time did *you* get back?'

'Early,' said Simon. 'I came home after leaving Chris's.' He pushed the marmalade jar across the table. 'Aren't you going to eat anything?'

'No,' said Amanda. 'I don't feel like it. Can't you help him?'

'What?'

'Chris. Can't you speak to someone at the BBC?'

'He's only written a few minutes of music. And besides, it's all a bit passé now, that particular sound. Things have moved on.'

Amanda nodded. 'Shame.' She rotated her shoulders and repositioned her breasts. An asymmetry in their prior arrangement had evidently been causing her some discomfort.

'Yes,' said Simon. 'It is a shame. But what can I do?'

Laura was lying on a sofa in the drawing room reading *The Bell Jar* by Sylvia Plath – another book recommended by the psychotherapist she'd met at the Islington bookshop. The writing struck a sympathetic chord, particularly the author's description of being depressed, which, with poetic genius, Plath had likened to being trapped beneath a bell jar and starved of air.

Faye was playing with some wooden blocks, quietly amusing herself on the other side of the room. The hollow sound of their collisions was accompanied by the occasional twitter of birds.

Laura put the book down on her stomach with its pages spread out so as to keep her place. It was a powerful image, the bell jar, because it was so truthful. Emotion often weighed heavily on Laura's chest, preventing her lungs from expanding, and depression was so very isolating. When she got depressed, everything in the world seemed to exist behind thick glass.

She had only intended to stop reading for a few seconds to rest her eyes, but she found herself thinking about the past. It was happening more and more – memories would detach themselves from some deep, murky place of concealment and rise into her awareness. An image of the Italian couturier formed in her mind. She had thought about him a lot since being reminded of his existence by her old see-through blouse (which she had now given to Oxfam). Once again, it all came flooding back. The hotel, the black leather furniture and the floating forms in the lava lamp. She had absorbed enough pop psychology from magazine articles to know that the insistent return of these memories was symptomatic. It meant something.

In fact, there had been many hotel rooms in which a similar transaction had taken place, in which the boundary between business and pleasure had been blurred. Some of these rooms she could only dimly recollect, because at the time she had been plied with obscene quantities of champagne and, occasionally, drugs. Another memory surfaced: a four-poster bed, a latex hood with a zipped mouth and handcuffs. She had always thought of them, these men, as former lovers, but that was no longer possible.

The word 'rape' was similar to the word 'cancer'. People instinctively lowered their voices when they said either. That is how it had always been, that is how Laura had always remembered it. But in the bookshop in Islington women used the word 'rape' freely, without shame or inhibition, some casually accusing all men of being rapists – or at least of having the potential. It was not an opinion that Laura shared, but hearing the word spoken so frequently had, without doubt, altered her perception of those youthful indiscretions, and of those men of influence, with their bouquets, champagne and promises. They had not forced themselves upon her, but they had been devious and manipulative. What had happened in those plush hotel rooms had never been truly consensual, which was why, in the past perhaps, she had always shied away from those memories. They had always made her feel ashamed, soiled.

Once, when she was trying to become an actress, she had been summoned to do a 'screen test' for a director in

LA. She had been told by her agent that she was a very 'lucky girl' and that this might be her 'big break'. 'Make the most of it,' her agent had counselled. Under pressure, Laura had agreed to perform a nude scene with an aging actor who she remembered as having been famous when she was still at school. The result was mildly pornographic. She wasn't offered the role and the film was never made.

Why had she been so easily persuaded? Why had she been so malleable, yielding and submissive? Why had she been so willing to please? Part of the explanation was ambition – she wanted everything back then – but there was a much deeper and more significant reason: she didn't want to be alone. Going along with what other people wanted ensured acceptance and popularity – or so she thought at the time.

When Laura had given up modelling, she had assumed that the mainstays of conventionality – a big house, a loving husband and a baby – would bring her contentment. But she had all of those things now and she was still unfulfilled and dissatisfied. She felt trapped by the necessities of her daily routine – preparing food, changing nappies, doing the washing-up – and even more so by the truly inescapable impositions of the body – eating, sleeping, expelling waste. Endlessly repeating cycles. The atmosphere became thinner just thinking about it. She seemed to have exchanged one bell jar for another. And more importantly, she still felt horribly alone.

What, then, did she want? What would make her happy? She didn't really know. Moreover, she had a fearful premonition that personal fulfilment was not compatible with her current situation. There might be difficult choices to make in the future – angry scenes, threats, hurt, probably lawyers – and if that ever happened, she suspected that she would still be riddled with doubts, seized by a profound dread that she was simply repeating her mistakes and that she was merely exchanging her second bell jar for her third.

The flow of her thoughts was interrupted by the sound of breaking glass and a scream.

Laura looked across the room. Faye was no longer there. All that she could see was a pile of wooden bricks.

The scream continued.

Laura threw the book aside and it fluttered across the rug like a wounded bird. Launching herself off the sofa, she ran into the hall, where she skidded on the polished floorboards and hit her shoulder against the banisters. Pain radiated through her body. She regained her balance and sprinted towards the open door ahead.

'Faye!'

When Laura entered the kitchen she saw her daughter standing by the oven. The child's face was dark red, and getting darker – so much so that it was almost purple. Her mouth was stretched wide open to allow her shrill cry to escape. Faye was wearing a tiny cotton vest, the bottom of which stopped short of her bulky nappy. Her legs were bare and she was shifting her weight from one foot to the other as if dancing. The tiles were smeared with blood. Laura leapt to her aid, scooping her up and enfolding her in her arms. 'There, there. It's all right. Mummy's here.' The child was inconsolable. Laura stepped away from the oven, glass crunching unpleasantly beneath her sandals. 'There, there . . .'

The rumble of Christopher's descent of the stairs heralded his appearance in the doorway. He glanced at the blood stains on the tiles.

'Jesus. What happened?'

'She knocked over a glass.'

'Her feet are bleeding.' He had to shout to be heard over Faye's bawling.

'She stepped on the pieces,' Laura shouted back.

'Weren't you watching her?'

'What?' Laura couldn't hear him.

Christopher stepped into the kitchen. 'I said, weren't you watching her?'

Laura looked at him angrily. 'Instead of standing there criticizing, why don't you make yourself useful?'

'What do you want me to do?'

'Well, you could sweep up that glass for a start.'

Laura hurried past Christopher and back into the drawing room, where she walked around the sofa, jiggling Faye up and down and stroking her hair. She cooed and made other soothing noises. Outside, the fevered garden was awash with colour – peonies, sweet William, dandelions. The light was so bright Laura had to turn away from the window. She looked at Faye's blood-covered toes and felt remorseful. Chris was right. She should have been paying more attention. She should have been watching Faye more closely. Nevertheless, she still felt irritated by the tone he had chosen to adopt, his blunt questions, the ease with which he had accused her. When he finally appeared she felt like picking up a vase and hurling it at him. She struggled to control her anger.

Christopher strode up to Laura and stood squarely in front of her.

'Stop moving a second.' He lifted Faye's right foot, looked at it and then inspected the left. He pinched a splinter of glass from her heel and brushed it into an ashtray. 'There's another piece.' After a few unsuccessful attempts he said, 'No. It's too small. I can't do it.'

'Here. Take her,' said Laura, holding Faye out. 'I'll get some tweezers.'

She went to the bathroom, and when she returned she found Chris sitting on the sofa, Faye on his knee, not screaming or sobbing, but whimpering like a puppy. Christopher gripped the child's ankle. 'See – there.' The splinter was quite conspicuous and glinted in the sunlight. Laura removed it without any difficulty. She held the tweezers over the ashtray and the splinter fell soundlessly. It was practically invisible when not lit directly.

'Can you see any more of them?' Christopher asked.

'No,' Laura replied.

'I can't understand how she reached the glass.'

'She probably used something.'

'What?'

'I don't know.'

'We must be more careful.' He had used the word 'we' but it was obvious that he had meant 'you'.

Laura took a handkerchief from her pocket and wiped the blood off Faye's feet. 'I'll give her a bath – make sure she's clean.'

'OK.' Christopher kissed the child's head and handed her back to Laura. 'I'm going back upstairs. I was in the middle of something.'

'OK.' At the door, Christopher hesitated, and Laura saw that he was uncomfortable, troubled by the tension that had arisen between them. She sensed that he wanted to resolve it, to dispel the oppressive atmosphere, but she doubted his sincerity. She suspected an ulterior motive. He wanted them to part on good terms, Laura supposed, so that he could go back and concentrate on his work without being distracted by the prospect of a deferred confrontation. 'What?' asked Laura.

'I'm sorry,' he said. 'I shouldn't have—'

Laura waved him away. 'It's all right. Really. It doesn't matter.'

'Good.' Christopher offered his wife a weak, apologetic smile and left the room. Laura stared at the empty doorway, listening to his nimble, eager ascent of the stairs.

When Christopher returned to the studio, the first thing he noticed was that the tape machine he'd been using was still going. He had heard Faye's scream and run onto the landing without pausing to turn it off. The spools were still revolving. He had been recording the sound of a coin being dragged along piano strings, which he knew would produce a particularly interesting effect, especially when played back at half-speed. The metal piano frame (salvaged from a defunct Weber he had once discovered, by chance, abandoned in a skip) was propped up near the window. Two microphones were attached to stands, their insulated diaphragms angled close to the longest and thickest strings. Christopher stopped the machine, rewound the tape and pressed 'play'. A low, scraping sound came out of the speakers that suggested metal under stress. There was something about it that augured catastrophic collapse, the imminence of a snapping wire or the buckling of a girder. He listened to himself dragging the coin along the strings at different rates, experimenting with various rhythms. Eventually, the tape reached the point where Faye's scream intruded. It was high pitched, urgent and quite chilling. Even though the scream had had to travel all the way from the bottom to the top of the house, the recording was remarkably clear. Christopher tilted his head to one side. The effect was quite interesting.

I could use it.

This thought, which felt slightly unnatural, almost like an insertion, was accompanied by a fleeting impression of wrongdoing, the sense that he shouldn't really be entertaining the idea of exploiting his daughter's accident. But it wasn't enough to stop him. A recording of a child in pain, a genuine recording, was hard to come by. Christopher was already considering how it might sound with reverb, or filtered, or played backwards.

Over the speakers he heard himself reacting, the dropped coin bouncing on the floor, his speedy transit; the door opening, the scream suddenly louder. Then somebody spoke: 'Turn the key gently. I shall have what is mine.' Faye howled, shocked by the sting of the glass, a world – previously safe – suddenly made cruel and dangerous. Then like an afterthought, reflective, spoken with tenderness and carried on a sigh, 'She is mine.' It was the unmistakable voice of Edward Stokes Maybury. 'She is mine.'

Christopher pressed 'stop'. The spools jerked to a halt and he looked around the studio. He did not expect to see anything, but an instinct, more animal than human, made him study his surroundings for some time.

That night, Christopher was lying in bed beneath a clammy cotton sheet. He pushed it down to his waist, exposing his chest, but this made little difference – he was still hot and uncomfortable. Even though the windows had been left open, the air in the room was motionless and tainted with the noxious reek of the Vale of Health pond. He was thinking about his travel arrangements, going over the details, ticking off items on a mental checklist: passport, tickets, francs. A cab was collecting Christopher early. His plane was scheduled to land at Charles de Gaulle airport at nine a.m. and he hoped to be in Paris by eleven. Henry had recommended a quiet hotel in St-Germain-des-Prés, not far from the Luxembourg Gardens.

Laura lifted the sheet and let it fall in order to cool herself. She had been restless too, unable to settle because of the humidity.

Since their earlier altercation they had managed to be perfectly civil to each other, but Christopher sensed that things weren't quite right yet; the subtle accords that make intimacy possible had not been fully restored, and he was uncomfortable going abroad without having first recalibrated their affections. He was superstitious in this respect, worried that if something horrible happened to him, if the plane crashed or he was run over, they would have parted for the last time without having resolved their differences.

Christopher slid across the mattress and pressed his body against Laura's. He kissed the nape of her neck and, reaching down, insinuated his hand between her thighs. Touch, closeness. He had faith in the healing properties of physical contact, the palliative effects of shared pleasure. Almost immediately, Laura rolled onto her back and let her knees fall apart. He was surprised by her acquiescence; he had expected her to need more coaxing, more encouragement. She pulled him between her legs and raised her hips. He felt a slight resistance, her flesh giving, and then immersion, engulfing warmth.

Their lovemaking was not particularly vigorous, but it wasn't long before Christopher began to experience fatigue. The muggy atmosphere made intercourse effortful. Christopher found that he was running out of breath and supporting the weight of his body was making his arms ache. The moon was casting just enough light to reveal Laura's expression. She did not look like a woman lost in a state of sensual abandon, but rather someone trying to solve a difficult mathematical problem. Her expression was determined, her lips pressed tightly together. Christopher still hadn't got used to her short hair.

It was evident that neither of them was very excited. They were both perspiring heavily. To avoid the embarrassment of having to give up, Christopher closed his eyes and thought of someone else to expedite his climax. The person he thought of was Amanda Ogilvy.

After their exertions, husband and wife lay next to

each other in silence, moisture evaporating off hot skin, arms extended, only their fingers touching. The taint of the stagnant pond water was now fortified by the pungency of their bodies. It had been a pointless exercise. The subtle estrangement that had existed between them was still there – only made more obvious by their perfunctory union. A mosquito or some other insect was producing an irritating whining sound, but it was not irritating enough to stop Christopher from falling asleep.

He was awake before the alarm clock sounded. He turned it off and crept to the bathroom where his clothes were hanging behind the door: a crumpled, pale linen suit and a cheesecloth shirt. After he had washed and dressed he went downstairs and picked up his travel bag in the hallway. He unlocked the door, being careful not to make any noise. As he did so, Maybury's last communication came back to him: *Turn the key gently. I shall have what is mine.* The reference to key-turning, which had up till then seemed obscure, now acquired uncanny resonances. It was as though Maybury had foreseen the moment of his departure and had judged it to be significant. Christopher closed the door, remembering the tender sighing that had followed. *She is mine. She is mine.* The sky was streaked with salmon-pink clouds and the birds were singing.

Emerging from the porch, Christopher walked to the

gate, where he paused and looked back at the house. He had been looking forward to getting away, but now something snagged. The sensation was almost physical, yet he immediately recognized that its nature was psychosomatic, that his discomfort was caused by a moral scruple – doubt, uncertainty. His leave-taking suddenly felt like an abrogation of responsibility, abandonment, neglect.

Laura and Faye weren't in any danger, surely? He had read too much into a chance observation, made false connections and ascribed meaning where there was none. There was nothing to fear. He took a deep breath and the fresh air of the new day cleared his head. The cab he had ordered seemed to glide smoothly into the Vale and he raised his hand to attract the driver's attention.

Second week in June

Laura wiped the surfaces in the kitchen with a damp cloth and then paced from room to room on the ground floor brandishing a duster. Everything was already spotless, but for some reason she couldn't settle and cleaning gave her something to do. She had tried to read a novel; however, after only ten minutes she had had to set it aside. She just couldn't concentrate. A new character had been introduced and she realized, belatedly, that she had no idea who he was supposed to be or how he was related to the other people in the story.

When she had finished dusting, Laura wandered around the house searching for other things to occupy her. She was looking for something undemanding, something that would keep her busy and provide her with a modest sense of accomplishment at its conclusion; something that would accelerate the passage of time and allow her to justify the reward of tea and biscuits that she was already planning.

'Come on, Faye,' she said to her daughter. 'Let's tidy the nursery.'

The child followed her mother up the stairs on all fours.

Laura encouraged Faye to pick up her soft toys and put them in a basket. The child copied her mother's actions with gleeful enthusiasm. While Faye was thus employed, Laura set about organizing the books in alphabetical order. On the lowest shelf she discovered the clockwork monkey. The last time she had seen it was in the empty room on the top floor. Chris must have brought it down. The thing was supposed to amuse, make children laugh, but the cast of its expression was not simply mischievous. The monkey's face had a sinister aspect and its grin was oddly twisted, almost a leer. Laura pushed the toy back on the shelf as far as it would go.

Faye was becoming fractious. She threw a miniature panda across the room and stamped her feet.

Laura asked, 'What's the matter, darling?'

The child looked annoyed and shouted the infantile equivalent of a profanity. Laura picked her up and held her close. 'Are you tired, honey?' She sat down on the window seat, stroked Faye's hair, and the child became less agitated. 'What a good girl, helping Mummy. Who's been a good girl?'

The garden was fabulously wild and colourful. Ivy had begun to climb up the sides of the gazebo and the gorse bushes seemed to have doubled in size. Long grasses and poppies surrounded the apple trees. The overall effect suggested reckless, paroxysmal growth. Many of the plants Laura couldn't name. Some were tall and strange, with massive petals and fleshy spikes. They were otherworldly and reminded Laura of the exotics that flourished in the steamy hothouses of Kew.

A thought came into her mind. *Sue's coming tomorrow.*

Laura was glad, not only because the garden was in dire need of attention, but also because she liked Sue and she was looking forward to seeing her again. That a professional visit from someone she hardly knew had become such an eagerly awaited occasion exposed the deadly monotony of Laura's day-to-day existence. She felt her throat tighten with emotion.

When Chris had announced that he was going to Paris she had reacted badly. The thought of being left in the house with only Faye for company – albeit for only a few days – had made her feel like she was teetering on the edge of an abyss. Chris's expression had been enquiring but she had managed to conceal her desperation. There was the old fear, of course, that familiar dread of loneliness, but in addition to this she was aware of something new, a fleeting apprehension of danger. She didn't know what it was but it made her feel weak and defenceless.

Faye was very still, nestled in the crook of Laura's arm. When Laura studied her daughter more closely she was surprised to discover that the child had fallen asleep. Laura stood up, drew the curtains, and walked over to the cot. With a single fluid movement she deposited Faye on the mattress.

'Sweet dreams,' she whispered.

Laura stepped out onto the landing and considered what she might do next. The need to remain fully occupied seemed even more pressing than before – a necessity rather than a choice. Directly ahead of her was a large cupboard that had clearly been designed for the purpose of storing linen. Ventilation lattices were positioned above both doors. This enormous space was where they – Laura and Christopher – had chosen to stash all of those things that weren't of any real value but which for various reasons (such as sentimental attachment) they had been reluctant to throw away. Laura grabbed the handles, pulled and found herself staring at a wall of junk. The interior was filled to capacity; chaotic and shabby, like a jumble sale. She saw a chipped Smith Corona typewriter, a teasmade, two tennis racquets (with broken strings), four lever-arch files, some glazed pottery figures, chocolate boxes, a Hornby steam locomotive, some model railway track and, stuffed into the gaps, several plastic carrier bags overflowing with bills, receipts and used-up chequebooks.

It needed a good clear-out.

Next to the typewriter was a pile of magazines. Most of them were editions that had been published between 1965 and 1967 and some had Laura's face on the front. After 1967 she had become quite blasé about her image appearing in magazines and thereafter was less inclined to save them.

She picked up a copy of *Harper's Bazaar,* flicked it open and saw a younger version of herself on the streets of New York. It had been a Richard Avedon shoot and the photographer had made her leap about on Broadway. The camera had caught her walking on air, legs straight, like an open pair of scissors, dressed in a short skirt, boots and a tight jumper that emphasized the pertness of her breasts. She dropped the magazine on the floor and examined the next one on the pile. It was *Cosmopolitan.* The scantily clad cover girl didn't really look like her at all. But it *was* her, at her thinnest, her ribcage visible through her pellucid skin. Then *Elle,* encased in a dark, figure-hugging suit – not a bad likeness; then *McCall's,* wearing a futuristic-looking gold dress and massive earrings, with pale, chalky lips and hair subjected to the harsh discipline of a severe geometric cut. One magazine followed another: some dropped, some tossed, some hurled across the landing in anger. There was another pile of magazines behind the first. Laura didn't look at any of them. She simply heaved the lot out and let them spill across the floor.

The shelf had been lined with thick wallpaper and this had been dragged forward with the magazines. Laura was about to slide the overhang back into position, when she noticed that something had been uncovered: a pattern of pale squares. She reached into the dark recess and tried to dislodge four pieces of stiff card that were stuck to the shelf. It was difficult and she had to use her fingernails. One of the pieces got torn in the process.

When she brought the cards out into the light, she discovered that they were old photographs. The edges were worn and the images were speckled with spots of mould. All of the photographs were of the same individual, a girl of about seven years of age. She was wearing what appeared to be a shapeless dress made from sacking and her face was smeared with dirt. Her expression was glum.

'Such a sad little face,' Laura murmured.

Only one of the photographs was taken without trickery. In all of the others the girl was, to a greater or lesser extent, transparent. They seemed to represent an early experiment involving double exposure. Laura looked at each photograph in turn and chanced upon a particular order that made the girl seem to vanish. Frame by frame, she faded almost to nothing, becoming, in the end, a featureless outline. The child's expression seemed to grow more fearful as the sequence progressed, but it was difficult to be certain because of the gradual loss of detail. Laura reversed the order so as to bring her back.

Chris would be extremely interested in these photographs. A week or so earlier he had been babbling excitedly about one of the voices he was now in the habit of recording: the voice of a Victorian stage magician who he believed had once lived in the house. Chris had said something else too, about Mr Ellis the builder and a camera in the attic, but she couldn't remember what exactly. She hadn't been listening. Chris had wanted her to go upstairs with him so that he could play her the voice he had recorded, but she had made some excuse or other. He had obviously been irritated by her indifference and he had left the room in a huff.

Laura wasn't impressed by his new musical project and she was finding his obsession with the dead rather unsettling. He sometimes chastised her for being unwilling to engage with the big questions, but why should she care about life after death? Life *before* death was challenging enough. She went down to the kitchen and returned with a dustbin bag. She filled it with the magazines she had removed from the cupboard and then, pausing for a moment, she considered the photographs. She didn't want to encourage Chris's morbidity. The mouth of the dustbin bag was wide open and inviting. For a moment she hesitated, but it was only for a fraction of a second. The photographs fell from her hand and slipped out of view. Laura knotted the plastic and closed the cupboard doors.

Didier Baumann, the producer of *Le Jardin des Reflets*, arrived at Christopher's hotel shortly after lunch. He was a middle-aged man with a weary, hangdog expression. Dark pouches of wrinkled flesh sagged beneath his rheumy brown eyes. Although he looked as if he hadn't slept for a week, he was smartly dressed in a white shirt and blue trousers. They made their way to the Rue de Rennes and then set off in the direction of the river. Heat rising from the asphalt made everything shimmer in the distance. Baumann talked about his production company and his association with several 'successful' projects, although Christopher had only heard of one of his films, a romantic comedy called *La Saison des Tempêtes*. The traffic had come to a halt and irate drivers were blasting their horns continuously. Baumann had to raise his voice to compete. 'There it is – where we are meeting.' He was pointing at Les Deux Magots, a cafe on the corner of Boulevard St-Germain and Rue Bonaparte. The interior was crowded and very noisy, but a quiet table was found for them on the pavement, in the shady corridor beneath a vast green awning. They sat drinking coffee. Time passed. Baumann consulted his wristwatch and looked around anxiously.

'Is there a problem?' Christopher asked.

'No,' Baumann replied. 'He will be here soon.'

Christopher wasn't convinced.

Half an hour later Fabrice Ancel arrived. Even though the sun was shining, he had chosen to don a black leather jacket over a polo-neck sweater. His hair was long, unwashed and tousled. He wore glasses with thick frames and his cleft chin was shadowed with stubble. Standing by his side was a blonde girl. Excessive quantities of mascara and lipstick could not hide the fact that she was still in her adolescence.

'Monsieur Norton.' Baumann gestured towards the young man. 'Fabrice Ancel.' The director gripped Christopher's hand firmly and said, '*Je suis honoré*,' before adding in heavily accented English, 'I have admired your work for many years.' Christopher thanked him and Baumann introduced the girl. 'Martine. A very talented dancer.'

Christopher bowed gallantly. '*Enchanté*.'

After a brief exchange of preliminary courtesies, Ancel launched into a detailed exposition of his objectives; occasionally he would say a phrase or two in English, but he appeared to be uncomfortable when he wasn't speaking his own language. He talked about illusion and reality, and made frequent references to the writings of a psychoanalyst called Jacques Lacan. It transpired that the central character of *Le Jardin des Reflets* was loosely based on one of Jacques Lacan's case studies, Aimée, a woman who had attempted to stab a famous Parisian actress. Ancel spoke at length about mirrors and identity, occasionally slowing his delivery to make some quasi-philosophical observation. 'A man sees himself in the mirror. But what does he see? In fact, he sees another man. We identify with an image outside of ourselves, something alien.' Christopher nodded, feigning interest, but actually he was finding Ancel's long-winded speech void of substance and rather tedious.

The girl was silent, but at regular intervals she threw a sideways glance at Christopher. When she crossed her skinny legs, he noticed that her tights were laddered. She had allowed one of her flat shoes to fall away from the heel of her foot and the ribbons holding up her vest had slipped from her shoulders. It was as though her clothes were causing her discomfort and she was eager to be free of any restraint. Christopher altered the angle at which he was sitting in order to remove her from his sight. The director was still grappling with the problems of identity. 'How do I know who I am? The ego functions to conceal inner fragmentation. It is an inauthentic agency. Thus, we can learn very little by asking ourselves this type of question.'

Christopher was becoming impatient. He wanted Ancel to stop talking about psychoanalysis and start talking about the film; he wanted to discuss the characters, their development, and the musical possibilities of the plot. Attempts to steer the conversation away from theoretical abstractions met with considerable resistance, and when Christopher became more insistent, Ancel simply talked over him. Then, quite suddenly, Ancel produced a notebook, scribbled something down and tore off the top sheet, which he held out for Christopher to take.

'What's this?' Christopher asked.

'My address,' Ancel replied in English. 'Could you come tomorrow afternoon?'

'What time?'

'Four o'clock?'

'I have a flight to catch.'

'Then one o'clock?'

Christopher looked at Baumann, who said, 'You will have enough time to get to the airport.'

'Very well,' Christopher replied, slightly confused. 'One o'clock.'

Ancel stood up. *'Au revoir, monsieur.'* He nodded curtly at Baumann and, without heeding a single social nicety, strode off down Rue Bonaparte. The girl picked up his cigarettes and followed, falling in behind him, keeping a distance of several paces. When Christopher turned to address Baumann, he was silenced by the producer's curious expression. The man was obviously in awe of Ancel and a faint smile of wonderment played around his lips. His eyes encouraged Christopher to speak, to acknowledge that they had just been in the presence of a higher being. When Christopher failed to deliver the desired response, Baumann was forced to supply it himself. 'Fabrice is very complex, a true artist. *Le Jardin des Reflets* will be a work of genius, I know it.'

*

As soon as the bell rang, Laura rushed down the hallway and opened the front door.

'Hi.'

The woman standing beneath the porch had struck a pose reminiscent of a pantomime 'boy' – legs set apart, hands on hips – and everything about her seemed to telegraph vigour and robust health. She was wearing denim dungarees over a khaki T-shirt and her complexion had been reddened by exposure to the sun. Her thick, streaked hair was pulled back into a single dense tuft.

'Sue.' Laura made a sweeping gesture. 'Please. Come in.'

'Another beautiful day.'

'Yes, isn't it?'

Laura showed Sue into the kitchen, where Faye was sitting in her highchair clutching a red crayon and scribbling on a sheet of paper. The child looked up and smiled. 'That's unusual,' said Laura. 'She's normally frightened of strangers.'

Sue went over to the highchair and examined Faye's drawing. 'What a lovely picture.' Then she brushed a knuckle against Faye's cheek. 'You don't need to worry about me, do you, darling?' Her voice carried a trace of cockney.

'Tea?' Laura asked.

'That'd be great,' Sue replied. 'Thanks.'

As the kettle was boiling they chatted about mutual acquaintances, all of whom were regulars at the bookshop in Islington, and when they sat down their conversation continued naturally, easily, broadening out, expanding to cover the novels they were reading and other topics of common interest. A second pot of tea was made and Laura, mildly curious, asked Sue how she'd become a gardener. Sue replied, 'I sort of fell into it,' and went on to explain how three years earlier her husband had been made redundant and she had started to do some odd jobs for her elderly neighbours: weeding, planting, mowing the lawn. They liked what she did and recommended her to others. She attended evening classes in order to study horticulture and subsequently sat an exam in garden design. During this period her husband became a heavy drinker and prone to angry outbursts, so she left him. 'Best thing I ever did,' she concluded with breezy indifference.

Laura reciprocated, telling Sue a little about her own past, about her childhood and her parents. 'They threw me out when I started modelling.'

'Why?' asked Sue.

'They thought it was undignified . . . wanton.'

'That must have been tough.'

'It was. I was still very young when I left home.'

'Were they religious, your parents?'

'Yes, and terribly pious – it was inevitable that I'd rebel. But, ironically, I've come to share their views. I don't think modelling is sinful – not like they did – but I think it's morally dubious. I wouldn't want Faye to become a model when she grows up.'

Laura discovered that her companion was refreshingly level-headed. Sue didn't become overly excited when Laura spoke about the glamorous world that she had formerly inhabited, nor did she ask any salacious questions about celebrities (which was what usually happened). When Sue learned that Christopher was a composer of film scores, her response was equally measured. Laura was impressed. She had enjoyed talking to Sue, and it was with some reluctance that she looked up at the kitchen clock and said, 'I suppose I'd better show you the garden.' Laura lifted Faye out of the highchair and led Sue down the hallway, into the drawing room and out through the open French windows. The air was buzzing, warm and fragrant. Two white butterflies took off and flew into the clear blue sky. Sue took some cigarette papers and a bag of tobacco from her pocket and with deft fingers made a thin roll-up, the end of which she glanced with a burning safety match. 'So what do you want?'

The bluntness of Sue's question took Laura by surprise.

'I don't know.'

Sue drew on her cigarette and surveyed the margins.

'There's a lot here that could be preserved. Well-established growth. I'd leave that well alone. I mean, look at those pyracanthas – beautiful – and that lovely purple berberis.' She took another drag. 'And what about the gazebo?'

'What about it?'

'Do you want to keep it?'

'I don't know. I'm sorry, I haven't thought . . .' Laura felt a little flustered. 'I asked you to come, but I haven't thought about what I want you to do at all. How stupid of me.'

'That's OK.'

'No. It isn't. Not really.'

'Look, I'll make a few suggestions and we can take it from there. All right?' Laura nodded. 'Do you mind if I take a look around?'

'How can you? It's like a jungle.'

'I'd like to see what's going on under those shrubs.' She pointed towards the far wall. 'See how high they are. I reckon there's an old rockery or something under there.'

'How will you get across?'

'I've got some tools in the van.'

'Do you want another tea?'

'No thanks. I'm fine.'

Laura carried Faye back inside and took her up to the nursery. She had meant to play a game with her daughter, but she found herself hovering behind the net curtains studying the woman at work below. Sue had put on a pair of canvas gloves and armed herself with a cutting instrument that she wielded with extraordinary efficiency. Within minutes, she had sliced a channel through the long grass and thorny bushes. For someone of slender build, she seemed to possess remarkable strength; she looked like an Amazon, a warrior princess, hacking and slashing, moving forward with merciless determination. Suddenly, Sue stopped working. She wiped the back of her gloved hand across her brow and turned round. Laura drew back so as not to be seen – as if she had been doing something wrong. She sat down on the floor next to Faye. 'OK. Let's play, shall we?'

Thirty minutes later, Sue called up the stairs, 'I've finished.'

Laura lifted Faye, balanced the child on her hip and descended the stairs. In the garden she discovered Sue standing by an upright shovel, the blade of which had been pushed into the earth. Sue's arm was outstretched and she was holding a cork in her hand. 'I just found this.' Laura took the cork and remembered Simon and Amanda's impromptu visit the day she and Christopher had moved into the house – champagne on the terrace. 'I think it must be one of ours,' said Laura, putting the cork in her pocket. 'This way,' Sue beckoned. Laura advanced along the freshly cut route through the grass and bushes. A fat, grumbling bumblebee bounced against her bare arm. On reaching the gazebo, Sue pulled the door open. 'Look inside. Someone must have been sleeping rough in here when the house was empty.' Laura saw a filthy tartan blanket, some pillows, a pile of empty cider bottles and some disintegrating newspapers. Grasping a mouldy plank, Sue pulled it away from the frame with ease. The wood cracked and splintered. 'Completely rotten. To be honest, I'm surprised it's still standing. You could get rid of it easily enough or, if you want to keep it, I could get a friend of mine to build you something similar . . . or make a copy . . . up to you.'

'I wouldn't mind something less fussy,' Laura replied, 'with more room inside, big enough for a table and chairs.'

Sue shaded her eyes. 'There's a rockery by the back wall, just as I'd suspected.' She chopped her visual field into sections with quick, downward hand movements.

'Rockery, orchard, lawn, flower beds. Not much work at all. Everything you need is already here. You just can't see it. Ah! Almost forgot.' She marched off in the direction of the apple trees, calling out, 'Mind the nettles,' and stopped next to a large bush. She pulled a branch back and said, 'Look in there.' Laura crouched down and peered into a shady hollow. Near the trunk was a statue – a cherub on a pedestal reading a large book.

Something seemed to pass in front of the sun. The light dimmed, but when Laura looked up there were no clouds in the sky.

'There could be more,' said Sue, 'The bushes are so thick round here, who knows what they're hiding. Do you want me to cut the branches away to expose it?'

Laura felt uneasy and in spite of the June heat a curious sensation made her shiver. 'No.' She shook her head.

'No?'

'It's probably best to just . . . leave things as they are.'

Sue's voice sounded distant. 'Are you all right?'

'Actually, I feel a bit . . .' Laura didn't know how to describe what she was experiencing. 'Odd.'

'Here. Give me Faye.' Laura expected her daughter to protest, but when Sue took her the child seemed perfectly happy. 'Must be the heat. Let's go back inside.'

Sitting in the kitchen, Laura began to feel better;

however, she noticed that Sue was looking at her differently. Her oblique regard suggested suspicion.

'What happened out there . . .' The sentence remained in limbo, neither a statement nor a question – an uncompleted thought expressed prematurely. Sue shifted uncomfortably before making a fresh start. 'You get feelings, don't you?'

'I'm sorry?'

'Strong feelings . . . intuitions?'

'Doesn't everybody?'

'Not everybody, no.'

Laura shrugged. 'I'm not sure what you mean.'

Sue nodded. 'Sure you're all right now?'

'Yes,' Laura replied. But she didn't feel all right. Something of the chill she had felt in the garden had insinuated itself into her bones.

Sue stood up and leaned against a wall. 'I could clear that rockery in an afternoon. It wouldn't take me very long, and then you'd have a nice place to sit.'

'I'd have to talk to my husband.'

'Don't worry about the money. I'd do it for you as a favour. It'd be no trouble at all.'

Laura protested. 'That wouldn't be right. I couldn't . . .'

Sue shrugged and glanced at her watch. 'I suppose I should be going.'

'No, don't go. Not just yet.' A note of desperation had entered Laura's voice. 'Please. Have another cup of tea.'

The hotel room was small but decorated ostentatiously: fake eighteenth-century furniture, heavy velvet curtains and antique prints of palaces and gardens in gilt frames. It was getting late, but Christopher wasn't tired. He had already bathed and put on a dressing gown, and he was sitting on the bed, legs outstretched, staring at his reflection in the cheval glass. *A man sees himself in the mirror. But what does he see?* Christopher remembered the young director's observations concerning the objectification of the self and found, to his surprise, that he was indeed experiencing his image as something extrinsic and foreign.

A trolley rattled down the corridor outside. There was a distant knock and muffled voices, then receding footsteps.

Christopher was disinclined to pick up the paperback he had bought at Heathrow airport. He felt uneasy and oddly despondent. This wasn't only because of his disappointing meeting with Ancel. Lately, it seemed to Christopher that the whole of his life had become unsatisfactory. He thought about Laura and their hopeless lovemaking the previous evening, and how afterwards they had stewed in the moist, rank heat, barely touching – or barely able to touch? And he remembered how, in order to bring their laborious union to a merciful end, he had had to think of Amanda Ogilvy.

About a year after meeting Laura, Christopher had rented a villa just west of Cannes for a month. It was a cool, spacious building, set on a headland with spectacular views over the sea. The outer walls were covered with red bougainvillea and a steep stairway led from the end of the garden down to a private beach and jetty. Two weeks after Christopher and Laura arrived they were joined by Simon and Amanda, who, at that time, had not been in a relationship for very long. Most evenings, the two couples would eat outside together, drink excessive quantities of red wine and watch the sun set. As darkness fell, the warm air would become fragrant with herbs and the scent of flowers. One night, Amanda produced a coal-black lump of cannabis. She rolled several joints which were passed around the table and the party talked and smoked and watched a crescent moon rise into a starry sky. Laura was the first to retire and shortly afterwards Simon said that he was feeling sick and that he would have to lie down.

Amanda continued rolling joints. When she spun the spark wheel of her cigarette lighter a tall, steady flame made her face vivid and vaguely infernal. She spoke about Marxism, poetry and Kandinsky, one word slurring into the next, until she was overcome by torpor. They sat in silence for what seemed like an eternity, pleasantly vacant, watching the moon scatter glittering streamers across the calm water. Amanda started to giggle and Christopher found that her amusement was infectious.

'Let's go down to the beach.' Her low, husky voice was bewitching.

'We're not capable,' Christopher replied. 'We'll fall down the stairs.'

'No we won't. Not if we're careful.' She started to laugh again. 'Not if we're very, *very* careful.'

She stood up and offered him her hand.

They made their way along the garden path, leaning against each other for support, and descended the stairs. Amanda dragged Christopher across the sand and they stopped when the surf cooled their feet. Across the cove on the next headland was another villa. None of its windows were illuminated.

'Isn't it beautiful?' said Amanda, throwing her head back and spinning like a child. She let her shawl drop from her shoulders and reached behind her back to undo the fastening that held her bikini top in place. Her breasts were suddenly exposed.

'What are you doing?' Christopher asked.

'I'm going for a swim. Are you coming?'

Everything became dream-like. Christopher felt light, airy and transparent. Amanda turned to face him. She took a deep breath and her breasts seemed to expand, becoming too magnificent to resist. Christopher pressed his palms against her blunt nipples and his fingers sank into her receptive flesh. A shudder of pleasure passed through Amanda's body. She fell to her knees and Christopher felt her exploring the contours of his rigidity through the cotton of his shorts. He heard the teeth of his zip separating, a soft tearing, and moaned as she discovered the secret of his release and took him into her mouth. He stood, gently swaying, listening to the waves until his eyes closed and his being dissolved and he became nothing but sensation.

The following day, no one got up until late afternoon.

Simon and Laura were sitting on the veranda and Christopher was squeezing oranges in the kitchen. Amanda entered and stood beside him. Her hair was wet and she was wearing a brightly coloured sarong.

Under his breath, Christopher said, 'It never happened.'

'That's right,' she replied, her voice full of gravel. 'There's nothing to discuss.'

And they never spoke about it again.

Christopher gazed at his reflection in the angled glass. The reality behind the mirror seemed to be disjointed with the reality in front, misaligned by several degrees.

For five years, Christopher had resisted the urge to exhume those memories or extract any pleasure from their content. Yet recently the recollection of his encounter with Amanda Ogilvy had become an increasingly necessary marital aid. Christopher released a long, melancholy sigh. Hotel rooms could be lonely places.

Laura was lying on the sofa in the drawing room flicking through a pile of magazines. When she had finished reading the articles that had interested her most, she sat up and gazed out into the garden. The light was failing and there was a curious absence of birdsong. Apart from the hiss of the baby monitor she could hear nothing. It was as if the house had been transported from the city to some remote location, a faraway place, beyond the reach of civilization. She began to feel a vague sense of disquiet; her chest tightened and she struggled to suppress a rising wave of panic. 'It's OK. Nothing's going to happen.' The words lacked conviction and Laura fled to the kitchen, where she opened a packet of biscuits and, one by one, ate them all. She made herself a cup of camomile tea and turned on the radio, hoping that the sound of human voices would stop her feeling quite so removed from the rest of humanity. The discussion programme she listened to was full of bleak predictions about the country's imminent demise, but she found the illusion of companionable, erudite conversation comforting.

When the programme was finished she was feeling calmer. She listened to the ten o'clock news, collected the baby monitor and then went to the bathroom where she washed and reluctantly swallowed a pill. Once again, she wondered about side effects. She remembered standing in the garden next to Sue and the way the light had changed; sudden chills, shivers, vivid nightmares – things seemed to be mounting up. For a brief instant she considered paying the doctor a visit, but she rejected the idea almost immediately, doubting her ability to remain civil while being subjected to more of his condescension and benign censure.

Laura crossed the landing to the bedroom, set up the monitor, climbed into bed and read a novel until she began to feel sleepy. She switched off the lamp, turned to lie on her side, and extended a hand over the mattress to the point where, ordinarily, her fingers would have made contact with her husband's body. To her surprise, she discovered that the coolness of the sheet made her sad. She missed him, although she wasn't quite sure what that meant anymore. Her thoughts became sluggish and incoherent and she gradually drifted into a state of semi-consciousness. She became dimly aware of something irregular, an unexpected sensory event, a perturbation, when really there should have been only blackness and the feeling of her mind slowly unravelling like a ball of wool. What was it? She didn't open her eyes, but forced herself to become more alert.

A knocking sound was coming from the baby monitor, distant but rhythmically distinct. Laura listened a little harder until Faye rolled over and there was a loud thud: the child's head colliding with the woodwork of the cot – unpleasant to hear but a common and largely inconsequential occurrence. The continuous hiss of the baby monitor returned. There was no more knocking, and Laura concluded that the noise had probably been caused by Faye's movements. Satisfied that there was no reason to ward off sleep any longer, she surrendered herself to a dark, rolling wave that folded her into its hollow and carried her away.

When Laura opened her eyes again she knew that she had not been asleep for very long. She raised her head and looked at the window for confirmation. There wasn't even a glimmer of sunlight in the strip of sky that separated the curtains. The reason why Laura's sleep had been disturbed soon became apparent. Faye was 'talking'. There were no gurgles or squeals, but a continuous stream of utterances that approximated adult speech. It was something Faye did occasionally, but only when playing a turn-taking game in which Laura would say a few phrases and Faye would try to copy them. Faye stopped chattering, paused, and then started again.

Laura was puzzled, because Faye usually slept until early morning, and if she did wake up in the night she nearly always became distressed.

As before, the utterances stopped briefly before their resumption. There was something about this repeated stop-start pattern that made Laura feel distinctly uneasy. She sat up in bed and switched on the lamp, feeling oddly vulnerable. When Faye ceased her babble, the silences that followed were absolute, suggesting that the child was listening intently, and when she started making noises again, it seemed to Laura that Faye was reacting to something. Each episode of speech seemed to contain slightly different registers of emotion: curiosity, wariness, surprise.

Laura got up and went out onto the landing. She turned the light on and hurried to the nursery; grasping the door handle, she pushed the door open and stepped inside. As Laura had expected, she found Faye standing in the cot, holding the wooden bars. The child was staring across the room at the bookshelves. She turned to look at her mother. There was no trace of a smile on her face, although her eyes widened slightly.

'Faye? What's the matter? What are you doing?'

The child's features softened and showed the first signs of recognition. Laura sighed, feeling oddly relieved. She picked up her daughter, who became limp in her arms, and tested the temperature of her forehead with the back of her hand. The child was hot, but that didn't mean much. It had been very hot all day and the house was like an oven.

'What is it, darling? You should be asleep.' Laura manoeuvred Faye's head so that it was resting on her shoulder and circled the nursery. She stroked the child's back and hummed a lullaby. Eventually, Faye fell asleep and Laura put her back in the cot.

On returning to bed, Laura found that she was feeling tense, so she retrieved her novel and started to read. The words on the page blurred as her eyes tired and in due course the book dropped from her hands and her chin fell against her chest.

Laura awoke feeling somewhat disorientated. She

examined her wristwatch, which she had laid on top of the bedside cabinet, and was amazed to see that the time was ten minutes past three. She had been asleep for over an hour. As she reached to switch off the lamp, Laura froze when the monitor crackled into life and emitted yet another stream of chatter. Like before, each of Faye's vocal experiments was followed by an interlude of silence, and Laura was reminded of her earlier, disconcerting impression that she was eavesdropping on one half of a conversation. She threw the bedcovers off and her book fell to the floor. Faye stopped talking, and it was then that Laura heard a man's voice. His speech was soft and obviously modulated to engage a child. It dropped from high to low registers and had a coaxing, encouraging quality. He may have laughed, but if he did, his laugh coincided with a burst of electrical interference and it was difficult to be sure.

For a few seconds, fear reduced Laura to imbecility. She sat on the edge of the bed, her limbs shaking violently, her bowels loosening with terror. It was only when she heard Faye's voice again that maternal instinct made her spring into action. She opened her bedside cabinet and took out a pair of scissors, which she gripped in her raised hand like a dagger. Then she crept out onto the landing and tiptoed to the nursery door, where she paused to listen. She could hear nothing except the pounding of her heart in her ears. Her fingers found the light switch and she kicked the nursery door open. It flew back and she leapt forward, ready to plunge the sharp point of the scissors into the intruder's chest. There was no one to attack. Confused, she jerked around and turned a full circle. Everything was just as it had been before. Faye was standing in her cot, grasping the bars, except this time she was staring not at the bookshelves but directly at Laura and her lower lip was trembling.

If there had been a man in the room, he couldn't have escaped without being seen. Laura walked over to the window, shaded the glass to block a reflection and looked down into the garden. It was too dark to see anything. Faye began to whimper, so Laura put the scissors on the windowsill and went to pick her up. 'There, there,' Laura said, 'There's nothing to be frightened of. Come with Mummy.' She was reluctant to leave the child on her own again, so she carried her back to the bedroom. Laura noticed that her novel was still lying on the floor, but she left it where it was and got into bed with Faye. She held her daughter close, kissing her soft hair and gently pinching her chubby cheeks. 'Go to sleep, honey. Go to sleep.'

Laura had definitely heard a voice, of that she was absolutely certain; a man's voice, coming through the monitor speaker. The device was still hissing, so she reached out and turned it off. She was about to switch the lamp off as well, but she hesitated and withdrew her hand. She did not want to spend the remaining hours of the night in darkness.

Ancel greeted Christopher and ushered him into a spacious room with tall windows and an intricately moulded ceiling. A pall of cigarette smoke made the interior look gloomy even though the light was strong. There wasn't much furniture: a low modern sofa, a matching armchair and a glass coffee table covered with well-thumbed scripts. Beneath a large abstract oil painting the separate units of a stereo system were arranged along the skirting board. A television, canting precariously on four spindly legs, was connected to a videocassette player by way of a twisted lead.

Christopher had been dreading his second meeting with Ancel all morning. He had had enough of the young director's haughty posturing and really didn't want to hear another word about Jacques Lacan, mirrors or psychoanalysis.

Ancel pointed at the sofa and said in English, 'Please sit.' As Christopher crossed the room, the sound of his steps on the bare floorboards was enriched by a slight echo. 'Can I get you something to drink?'

'No thanks,' Christopher replied.

Ancel lit a cigarette and sat beside his guest on the sofa. He reached for one of the scripts on the coffee table and turned a few pages. 'So,' he said in French, 'do you have any questions?'

'Yes,' Christopher replied, 'I do. Our conversation yesterday was very interesting; however, I wondered if – today – we might agree to focus on practicalities.'

Ancel drew on his cigarette. 'As you wish. What do you want to know?'

They started talking and, much to his surprise, Christopher discovered that Ancel was perfectly willing to discuss the structure of his plot, his characters, the style in which he intended to shoot the film, and, above all, the music he wanted Christopher to compose. 'I would like to play you something,' said the director, casting the script aside. He knelt and searched through his record collection, rapidly flipping one album cover against the next until he found what he was looking for. After sliding the vinyl disc out of its sleeve, he positioned it on the turntable and waited for the automatic arm to swing across and drop. A loud thud preceded the eerie opening of Stockhausen's 'Studie 1'. Ancel stood up and paced backwards and forwards, gesturing to indicate those effects that he hoped Christopher would be able to reproduce. When the piece came to its oblique conclusion, Christopher said, 'You know I worked with him – at NWDR in Cologne?'

Ancel made a minute adjustment to the position of his spectacles. 'Who? Stockhausen?'

'Yes, back in the fifties.'

The director was clearly impressed. He pushed out his lower jaw and nodded. 'Exciting times . . .'

'Yes. Exciting times,' Christopher repeated.

Christopher began to suspect that Ancel's appalling display of bad manners the day before had been an act put on for Baumann's benefit. The producer clearly considered rudeness to be a necessary condition of genius.

A door opened and Martine entered. Her hair was tousled and she looked as though she had just got out of bed. She was wearing one of Ancel's shirts and, Christopher guessed, little else. Ancel acknowledged her by raising his eyebrows and she responded with a shrug, before passing in front of the sofa like a lynx. She climbed onto the armchair, curled her legs beneath her buttocks and reached for the cigarettes and a lighter.

Christopher had been mesmerized by Martine's

progress, and when he turned to address Ancel he was relieved to find that the director had been occupying himself with the video player. The television screen began to glow and the opening credits of a film appeared. Christopher immediately recognized the music, because it was his own. Oscillators throbbed, a fairy gamelan suggested enchantment and limpid chords promised landscapes of ice. Ancel looked back over his shoulder at Christopher and spoke in English. 'This . . . this sound . . . for me, it describes perfectly the world of the unconscious.' The look on his face was almost pained. 'Your music expresses the inexpressible.'

'Thank you,' said Christopher. 'You're too kind.' He hadn't received a heartfelt compliment for so long he wasn't sure how to react.

'When Aimée looks in the mirror,' Ancel continued, 'this is what I want, this sound.' As the title of the film slipped from view a spaceship materialized in a field of drifting stars. The fairy gamelan and the chilling chords faded but the oscillators continued to throb like giant engines. Ancel pressed the 'pause' button on the video machine and reverted to his native tongue. '*Formidable*.'

Christopher was pathetically grateful.

Before getting the train to Charles de Gaulle airport, Christopher walked briskly through Beaubourg and Les

Halles to the Tuileries quarter, where he bought his wife a bottle of perfume. He was feeling penitent, having allowed himself the previous evening to dwell upon his illicit liaison with Amanda Ogilvy. As he waited to cross a busy road, he tilted his head back to catch the sun and felt, if not exonerated, then at least cleansed by its fierce heat.

Laura had pulled a chair out onto the terrace and as she sat, sipping beer from a can, she gazed steadily at the clump of bushes that had grown around the hidden statue. A smoky impression of the cherub's rounded features and its sly smile had persisted in Laura's memory. Faye was crawling around by the French windows, occasionally stopping to inspect one of the many stuffed toys and wooden bricks that were scattered on the flagstones.

Chris would be back soon, but this didn't make Laura feel any better. Her sense of being alone had become almost intolerable, a deep bedrock of pain over which alternate waves of boredom and anxiety endlessly rolled. Suddenly, she leapt up from her chair and lifted Faye off the ground. She marched into the house, picked up the telephone receiver and dialled Sue's number. The ringing tone sounded in the earpiece and she waited for a long time. She supposed that Sue was probably working, but she hung on regardless, hoping. Faye buried her hands in Laura's hair and emitted a pleasant, liquid gurgle.

'Come on,' Laura urged. 'Come on.'

The ringing continued, and then, after a beat of silence, Sue said, 'Hello.' She was a little out of breath. In the background there was a clattering noise, things falling onto a wooden floor. 'Shit. Sorry.'

'Sue? It's Laura.'

'Oh – hi – Laura.' Recognition raised the pitch of Sue's voice in three musical steps like the beginning of a major scale. 'I just got through the door and dropped everything. I've been to the garden centre.'

'Really? Which one?' It was a ridiculous question. Laura didn't know any garden centres.

'Pavilion. Enfield. What can I do for you?' Laura didn't reply. It was such a lengthy pause that Sue clearly thought the line had gone dead. 'Laura?'

'I was . . .' She hesitated before trying again. 'I hope you don't think I was rude yesterday.'

'Rude? What on earth are you talking about?'

'You offered to do me a favour and I think I may have appeared unappreciative.'

'Oh, forget it. You weren't feeling well.'

'And I was wondering . . .' Again she faltered. 'I've been sitting with Faye on the terrace today, and . . . well, it isn't ideal. It would be much nicer to sit by the rockery.'

'You've changed your mind? Not a problem. As soon as I'm free I'll pop over. I'll get rid of the overgrowth and clear a space by the wall.'

'Would you?'

'Sure.'

'Coloured stones or a gravel surround.' Sue shared her thoughts. 'I can see how it would work; something simple but effective.'

'Great. That's really great.'

They spoke for a few more minutes and when Laura put the phone down she was feeling a lot calmer.

Last week in June

'With respect,' said the politician, 'since the beginning of March the value of sterling has dropped by over ten per cent and the Bank of England is almost without reserves. We borrowed two billion dollars from the IMF in January which has already been squandered propping up the pound. The situation is very serious indeed and it is essential that the British public accepts that cuts are absolutely necessary.'

Laura switched the radio off. When would there be some good news? She remembered what Simon had said the last time he'd come to dinner: *Shanty towns on the heath, no food in the shops*. It was all so very frightening. There had been so much optimism, creativity and hope in the sixties, how was it possible that the country could be so utterly transformed in less than a decade? *The real issue, of course, is whether democracy can survive if things get any worse.* Laura didn't want to think about what might happen if the pessimists turned out to be right – it was just too awful. She gazed at her daughter, who was sitting in the highchair scribbling on a piece of paper. *What a world to bring a child into.* She had had the same thought the morning after the Birmingham bombs, the morning she'd come to see the house for the first time with Christopher. The words vibrated in Laura's mind like the refrain of a Greek chorus; however, they were no longer a lament but an accusation. Something made her turn, a liminal event that demanded her attention, an impression of movement in the margins.

'Oh, how disgusting,' she said out loud.

A column of ants was crawling up the wall and into a kitchen cupboard. She opened the door and saw that the tiny creatures were flowing over everything: jars, tins, bags of sugar and flour. Laura traced the column backwards to establish where the ants were coming from, but when it reached the floor the ants thinned out and the line became almost impossible to follow. She emptied the cupboard and threw away those items that had been contaminated. A transparent bag of brown sugar hadn't been sealed properly and was seething with activity. After soaking a sponge in disinfectant, she wiped the ants off the empty shelf and brushed the broken corpses into the waste bin. She mopped the floor, put the tins and unopened bags back in the cupboard and made a list of items that needed to be replaced. When she had finished her skin was flushed. Perspiration had soaked through the material of her T-shirt, producing unsightly dark patches. She leaned against the fridge for support and fanned her neck with her hand.

While Laura had been rushing around the kitchen, Faye had been hunched over her drawing; she hadn't raised her head once or produced a single exclamation. Laura noticed that Faye was no longer scribbling. The movement of the crayon over the surface of the paper was slow and appeared to be more controlled than usual. There were no furious strokes that typically left marks on the white Formica. Faye's expression was serious and Laura detected a presentiment of adulthood in her daughter's knitted brow. She thought about the cruel certainties that lay ahead for her – disappointments, heartbreak, loss – and was surprised by a stab of pity that made her eyes prickle. The unexpected arrival of such an intense emotion made her acutely aware of her own fragility. She pressed the moistness out of her eyes and went over to the highchair.

'What's keeping you so busy?'

Laura looked down at Faye's drawing and found that there was something about it that held her attention. She saw the usual mass of scribble but it was contained in a crude box divided by straight lines of varying length. The background had been coloured red. Laura bit her lower lip and noticed that if she focused on certain areas the drawing acquired a hint of perspective. Was it supposed to be a room? The image was resonating with something in her memory; however, it took a few more seconds before she made the connection, and when she did, Laura shook her head in disbelief. The vertical lines reminded her of hanging chains and the red background suggested stains on a wall. Faye had drawn Laura's nightmare.

'No,' Laura whispered. 'It can't be.' She was being suggestible and here was yet another example of how her volatile state could make her credulous and irrational. Clearly, her memory of the nightmare was influencing her perception of the drawing; she was resolving ambiguities prejudicially.

Faye had stopped moving.

'Baby?'

The child loosened her grip on the crayon and it fell out of her hand. A moment later she slumped forward.

Laura resisted the urge to scream. She sank down to Faye's level and saw that her daughter's eyes were closed. The child was still breathing and her inhalations were accompanied by a mucilaginous snore. It appeared that Faye had simply fallen asleep, which, on reflection, wasn't so remarkable given how hard she had been concentrating. Laura sighed and was grateful that, on this occasion, she hadn't let panic get the better of her. She pulled Faye's drawing out from under the crayons and studied the image. It was just a box, some vertical lines and scribble; yet a small doubt persisted, a dimly insistent feeling of disquiet. Laura scrunched the paper up, squeezed it into a tight ball and threw it into the bin along with the dead ants and spoiled food. She had hoped that a decisive, symbolic gesture of this kind would rid her of any residual anxieties, but she was quite mistaken. Somewhere in the depths of her unconscious was a windowless chamber in which hanging chains had been stirred into collision: *clink-clink-clink*.

Laura lifted Faye out of the highchair, carried her up the stairs and entered the nursery. She put her daughter down in the cot and covered her with a thin cotton sheet. The child rolled over onto her stomach and settled with her face squashed against the mattress. Laura opened the window a fraction, drew the curtains and went downstairs to make some tea – camomile for herself and English breakfast for Christopher.

She did not enter the studio immediately. Instead, she waited outside for a few moments and listened to the muffled sound of voices coming through the door. It was like listening to a party, but a party in which the background music was supplied by a kind of industrial orchestra. Production-line hammering was punctuated by blast-furnace roars. Laura didn't knock. She opened the door and saw Chris seated in the middle of his equipment, his hands operating slide controls and his eyes fixed on a row of jittery VU meters. He looked more like an astronaut than a composer. When the voices faded he reached up and switched off two tape machines.

'I've made you some tea.'

Christopher's office chair rotated through one hundred and eighty degrees. 'Thanks. How long have you been standing there?'

'Not long.' Laura advanced and handed her husband the mug. 'You're working on it again – the piece?'

'Yes.'

'What about the android film? I thought that had to be finished soon.'

'It's almost done – plenty of time – there's no rush.'

'I'm going to the shops later. There were ants in the kitchen and some of the food got spoiled. Do you want anything?'

'No. No thanks.'

She wanted him to stop; she wanted him to erase those voices. She could feel something like pressure building up in her chest, a pressure that promised, on release, to provide the means of voicing her objections. But at the very last moment, her courage deserted her and she experienced a sudden deflation that made her think of air escaping from a balloon.

'OK,' she said.

The office chair turned and she found herself facing the back of Chris's head. He rewound the tapes and a moment later the babbling voices and the factory rhythms returned. Clutching her tea with both hands, she left the studio and kicked the door shut behind her.

The rest of the day was dull and tiring. Laura walked to the shops, did the laundry, then the ironing, and prepared the evening meal. When Christopher came downstairs to eat, the radio was left on and they barely spoke to each other. Laura retired early and Christopher returned to his studio. He did not stay there long. Thirty minutes later she heard him coming down again, and, after he had attended to his ablutions, he got into bed, naked. Laura supposed that this meant that he would want to have sex with her, but he made no approaches and they sat, side by side, propped up by pillows, reading – she a novel, and he the book he had bought about the recording of spirit voices.

Laura did not find it easy to concentrate. She kept on thinking about Faye's drawing, the man's voice coming through the baby monitor and the chill she had experienced in the garden; nightmares, hallucinations and sudden changes of body temperature. The idea that all of these might be side effects of her medication was appealing, but she didn't believe it. She was simply trying to prove to herself that she was still capable of being rational. What she really thought was that these disturbing phenomena were all connected with Christopher's recordings. She was concerned that he might be opening a door, extending an invitation, or, even worse, letting something in. Laura put her novel down and said, 'Chris? Can we talk?'

He turned a page and said, 'What about?'

'Something happened when you were away. I didn't mention it before, I don't know why.'

Christopher used the inside flap of the book jacket to mark his place. 'Oh?'

'I heard a voice coming through the baby monitor – a man's voice. It was in the middle of the night and I was really frightened. I thought there was someone in Faye's room, but when I looked, there was no one there.' She continued, giving more detail and explaining how it had seemed to her as if the voice had been addressing Faye directly, and how Faye had listened and responded. 'It was really strange – unnerving.' Christopher remained silent, the slow nod of his head betraying a thought process that he did not feel obliged to share. Laura took a deep breath. 'I wonder if . . .' She hesitated before clumsily completing her sentence. 'I wonder if it's got anything to do with what you've been doing.' Christopher frowned. 'The voices. The recordings . . .'

'It's possible, I suppose.'

'I was worried about Faye.'

'Why? She wasn't in any danger, was she? Not really.'

'I don't know.'

'Darling, it was only a voice.'

'But it was talking to her.'

'You don't know that.'

'No, I can't say for sure. But that's what it sounded like.' Laura fiddled nervously with the ribbon on her negligee. 'You're dabbling with the supernatural and—'

'I wouldn't call it dabbling,' Christopher said, quite plainly piqued.

'Sorry, wrong word.'

'Look, I can see how it must have been frightening. But what actually happened? Faye got woken up a few times and you had to take her out of the nursery.'

'*Come to me, Faye*? Remember that?'

'Of course I do.'

'Well then.'

'I don't understand. What are you suggesting?'

The bluntness of the question made her stop and reflect for a few moments. Chris wasn't party to her inner world; he didn't know about the nightmare, Faye's drawing or the coldness that had seeped into her bones. She *could* tell him everything – that was an option – but it would be difficult to express the subtle registers of feeling that had accompanied her experiences and she might end up sounding like a hysteric. The prospect of explaining herself suddenly seemed too problematic and arduous. She waved her hand. 'It doesn't matter. You're right, I'm overreacting.'

'Darling, I didn't say *that*.'

'I know, I know. But you're right. Nothing happened – not really.'

'It's a big house. You were on your own . . .'

'Yes.' Laura rotated a finger close to her temple. 'I let my imagination run wild.' She picked up her novel again and attempted to sound breezy. 'I'm going to see Sue next week. What shall I say about the garden? Her quote was very reasonable, I thought.'

'I'll check how much we've got in the savings account. Then we'll make a decision.'

'She said she'd do the rockery for free.'

'Why would she do that?'

'We're friends.'

'As long as she doesn't expect anything.'

Laura put her novel on the bedside cabinet and turned off the lamp. Christopher read for a few more minutes and then turned his lamp off too. The mattress tilted as he edged over to her side of the bed. She had her back to him and he moulded his body against hers. He flung an arm over her waist and pulled her close.

'Is the French film going to happen?' Laura asked.

'Yes. I'm seeing Henry tomorrow. There won't be much money.'

'How much money do we need?'

'Always more than we've got.'

As Christopher descended the stairs he could see a letter on the doormat. He walked down the hallway and squatted to pick it up. His knee joints clicked and a sharp pain at the base of his spine reminded him that he was no longer young. Until recently he had found such daily reminders of his own mortality depressing, but since embarking on his electronic voices project, he was more inclined to be philosophical. The prospect of decline and his ultimate physical demise was less daunting given that he now believed that something very clearly followed, although he was still agnostic concerning its exact nature. The voices he had recorded had not been very instructive and Christopher had had difficulty reconciling their brief, sometimes incoherent declarations with notions of a Christian afterlife. Indeed, he tended to think of the spirits existing in some vast, unknowable expanse. Supposing that a familial bond might facilitate communication, he had considered trying to contact his parents, but he had found the idea vaguely repellent, in the same way that he had found their bedroom vaguely repellent when he was an adolescent. Something dark and Freudian prevented him from disturbing their eternal slumber.

Christopher opened the envelope and registered his solicitor's letterhead at the top of the page. A single paragraph explained that when Christopher had purchased the house, a comprehensive search for title had been undertaken and that the office copy entries confirmed Mr Edward Stokes Maybury to be one of several former owners. An invoice was stapled to the letter and Christopher tutted when he noted the exorbitant fee.

Here then was final proof that the spirit voices he had recorded were authentic. He really was doing something completely new. A ripple of excitement produced a private, self-satisfied smile. He put the letter and invoice back in the envelope, folded it to reduce its size, and tapped it into the breast pocket of his shirt.

On entering the kitchen, he saw Laura standing on a chair looking into an open cupboard.

'They've come back again.'

'What?'

'The ants.'

'Must be something to do with the heat. It's more like Athens than London.'

'I don't know where they're coming from.'

'You'll have to get some poison . . . bait – that's what they call it, I think.'

'Is it safe?'

'I suppose so. Actually, I can get some. After I've had lunch with Henry I'll buy some in Hampstead village.'

'OK.'

He paused before leaving. 'What you were saying last night . . .'

Laura stepped off the chair and flicked an ant from her finger. 'Yes.'

'The voice that you heard . . . was it the same voice that said *Come to me, Faye* on the recording I played you?'

'I don't know. He was speaking too softly.'

'OK.'

As Christopher was about to leave, Laura asked, 'Why?'

Christopher responded with artful nonchalance. 'Just a thought.'

At twelve thirty he was sitting opposite Henry Baylis in Le Cellier du Midi. Baylis had brought three contracts for Christopher to sign and, as usual, Christopher didn't bother to read them. He turned the pages until he found his name typed beneath a dotted line.

'All pretty standard,' said Baylis before biting into an oval of sliced French bread. Christopher grimaced when he saw the trifling sum he was going to be paid. 'Yes, I know,' Baylis continued. 'Pitiful, but there it is.' He handed Christopher a pen. 'I'm so glad you and Ancel hit it off. And what's this Baumann character like? I've only had the pleasure of talking to him on the phone.' Christopher finished signing the contracts and handed them back to Baylis, who checked the signatures and said '*Splendide!*' At that moment, a waitress appeared with their entrées – *crêpe aux épinards et saumon* for Baylis and *escargots de Bourgogne* for Christopher. Baylis topped up their glasses from a bottle of Merlot.

'Henry.' Christopher leaned forward. 'Do you know anything about Victorian stage magic?'

Baylis assumed an exaggerated expression of bemusement. 'I can't say that I do.' He raised his glass. 'To *Le Jardin des Reflets* and the Palme d'Or.'

Christopher humoured his agent. The touch of their glasses produced a pure, delicate chime, and Christopher repeated the toast. 'You see,' he continued, 'I want to find out about a Victorian magician called Edward Stokes Maybury.'

'Why do you want to do that?'

'He used to live in my house. I found some of his things in the attic when we moved in. Props . . . I think.'

'And you want to know where you can get a good price for them?'

'No, not at all. What I found was broken, worthless. I just want to find out more about Maybury.'

Baylis sampled his crêpe. 'Delicious. Well, you could try the British Library of course . . .' His face was suddenly illuminated by inspiration. 'No. Not the British Library, the Magic Circle. If they can't tell you anything about him, then no one will. That said, the Magic Circle is a private members' club and they don't extend a warm welcome to strangers. They can be very cagey.'

'Oh,' said Christopher, disappointed.

'Even so,' Baylis continued, his eyes twinkling mischievously, 'that might not prove to be an insurmountable problem.'

'Don't tell me that you're a member!' Christopher exclaimed.

'No, no, no. Don't be ridiculous. But I know someone who is. Bill Loxley. He's actually a criminal barrister – that is to say, a barrister specializing in criminal law rather than a barrister with a penchant for crime. We were in the same set together back in the Dark Ages. He's a real character. When he isn't defending rogues he does magic shows as Balthazar, Master of Miracles. He also writes very scholarly articles on the history of magic. It's one of those peculiar passions, like early music or exotic pets – unaccountable and all consuming. Bill might know something about your Maybury chap. He might even be able to use his advocacy skills to get you into the Magic Circle library. You'll have to buy him lunch, of course.'

'Naturally.'

'So, this Baumann fellow?'

'You won't forget, will you?'

'What?'

'Loxley.'

'No, I'll give him a call tonight. Well?'

'There's not much to say about Baumann.'

Henry rolled his eyes at the ceiling. 'God give me strength!'

'Well, there isn't.'

'And Ancel?'

'I thought he was a bit arrogant at first, but I warmed to him in the end.'

Henry dabbed his forehead with a handkerchief and refilled his glass. 'Come along now, catch up. I've got a good feeling about this film, you know.'

'You always do, Henry.'

Halfway through their telephone conversation, Christopher had realized that Loxley would have agreed to meet him even without Baylis's intercession. 'That's fascinating, quite fascinating.' The man had clearly been eager to learn more about what Christopher had discovered. Loxley had arrived early and was waiting for Christopher outside Goodge Street Underground station. Identifying him wasn't a problem. He was tall, big-boned, and the high dome of his head was completely hairless; a Van Dyck beard and tapering ears suggested a certain diabolical but hammy glamour. They greeted each other, shook hands and walked to the headquarters of the Magic Circle in Chenies Mews while exchanging polite generalities. On entering the building, Christopher remarked on the absence of members. 'Magicians,' Loxley confided, 'have a tendency to rise late. Let me show you around.'

Christopher, who had expected his companion to be more secretive, was guided to a small theatre – 'one hundred seats' – and an extraordinary club room, the floor of which was decorated with all of the signs of the zodiac arranged between concentric circles. Above the zodiac was a canopy surmounted by an enormous witch's hat. There were also display cases in which the paraphernalia of several famous magicians were displayed.

'Take a seat,' said Loxley.

Christopher lowered himself between the arms of a rather grand wooden chair while Loxley dragged another away from the wall and turned it so that he could sit facing Christopher.

'So,' said Loxley, 'Edward Maybury.' He crossed his legs and removed a notebook and silver pen from his jacket. 'Would you mind? I'd like to go over a few details.'

'Not at all.'

'When we spoke on the telephone you mentioned finding a theatre bill.'

'Yes. There was a framed theatre bill promoting a Maybury show.'

'Do you recall the venue?'

'I'm afraid not. And there was a traveller's trunk with the letters E.S.M. engraved on the nameplate.'

Loxley raised his hand, indicating that he wished

Christopher to slow down. 'Please . . . The theatre bill – can you recall anything about the show?'

'The audience were promised secrets of the ancient world . . . vanishings . . . automatons.'

'Automatons?'

'Yes.'

'You're quite sure?'

'Yes.'

'That's interesting. I didn't know Maybury used automatons. What else did you find?'

'There were some large mirrors and some wire.'

'How thick was it?'

'Not very. And some lacquered boards decorated with Chinese dragons. They looked like the sections of a folding screen.'

'Were they large?'

'Yes.'

'How many of them?'

'Four, I think.' Christopher paused.

'Please . . .' Loxley gestured for Christopher to continue.

'There was a broken camera and some old 78 records. I suppose the camera might have belonged to Maybury, but not the records.'

'He didn't die until 1914. It's possible they were his.'

'And some toys. I kept one of them for my daughter – a clockwork monkey.' Christopher tried to remember what else he had seen but nothing came to mind. 'That's all there was, I think.'

'And everything you found was thrown away?'

'Yes. Everything except the monkey. The mirrors were broken, the boards were split. None of it looked valuable. I'm sorry.'

Loxley shook his head. 'It's unfortunate, but how were you to know?' He smiled, plainly attempting to compensate for the regretful tone of his voice. After making a few more notes he raised his head and continued in a lighter register: 'Let me tell you what I know about Edward Maybury. It isn't very much and I trust you won't be too disappointed, but his career was relatively brief and I don't suppose he was ever, even at the height of his fame, regarded as a very considerable magician. We know about his act from reviews and he's mentioned – in passing – by some of his contemporaries. Our most important source is a memoir by George Briscoe, not a performer himself, but a talented engineer who created illusions for others. Now, this Briscoe was an associate of John Nevil Maskelyne, who was, at that time, the most important magician in London. He used to put shows on in the Egyptian Hall in Piccadilly . . . Just wait here a moment, we have a rare photograph of the Egyptian Hall stage in the library. I won't be a minute.' Loxley got up, walked across the room, and ascended a curious staircase made of alternating half-steps. When he returned he was carrying two old volumes. He opened one of them and showed Christopher a grainy view of a proscenium arch, beneath which a distant figure in a suit was holding up a large square of silk. 'You can't really tell from this bookplate, but it was a splendid venue – the walls were decorated with hieroglyphs, and papyrus leaf columns supported the balcony. They called it England's home of mystery.' Loxley turned a few pages and showed Christopher a line drawing of the auditorium as seen from the stage. A cupola was clearly visible in the centre of the ceiling. 'Maskelyne hired Maybury to perform at the Egyptian Hall in 1874. Briscoe tells us that Maybury had perfected a vanishing illusion that neither he nor his associates could fathom. It was called the Siamese cabinet.'

'The boards in my attic?' Christopher asked.

'If so,' Loxley continued, 'one wonders whether Maybury had succeeded in fooling Briscoe into believing his methods were more ingenious than they in fact were.'

'Why do you say that?'

'You found mirrors.'

'Is that how it's done then?'

Loxley feigned horror. 'I couldn't possibly say.' He took the book back from Christopher. 'Maybury travelled to America shortly after his Egyptian Hall performances and eight years later he returned to England a wealthy man. He must have made some shrewd investments. As far as I know, he never worked in magical theatre again. Although I suspect there was no love lost.'

'Why do you say that?'

'Harry Vignoles and Arthur Pratt – one a journalist and the other a composer of music-hall songs – mention Maybury in their diaries. They both describe a bitter, rather conceited man, who believed that he had never been given the recognition he deserved. To make his point, Maybury performed a card trick that left Vignoles and his companions utterly astonished, but sadly the reporter didn't trouble to record the details of the illusion, so it's difficult to assess whether their astonishment was merited.' Loxley opened the second book and offered it to Christopher. 'This, as far as I know, is the only surviving photograph of Edward Maybury.'

Christopher took the book reverentially and inspected a plate that was discoloured with age. It showed a man in a frock coat and top hat, surrounded by children. They were dressed in rags and looked like street urchins. The photograph was of such poor quality it was impossible to get a very clear idea of what Maybury looked like.

'Who are the children?' Christopher asked.

'They were part of his act.'

'What did he do with them?'

'He made them disappear.'

First week in July

Amanda Ogilvy was sitting up in bed writing a poem. She had thrown a silk scarf over the lamp stand and the walls were patterned with crimson shadows. Two joss sticks burned and crumbled as the album on her Wildcat portable record player revolved and filled the air with sitar music. A mournful melody was augmented by the shimmer of sympathetic strings.

The feeling of the pencil in her hand and the slight traction of the graphite on the thick, textured paper was gratifying. As the pencil traversed the page, it left a trail of looping, childish script: *What was it that she fell for? His beak, plumage, webbed feet . . . or was it the prospect of convenience, a daughter hatched from an egg?*

She was working on one of her satires inspired by Greek mythology – Zeus's shape-shifting seduction of Leda, for which purpose the god had assumed the form of a swan. Amanda had given it the capricious title 'Bird Watching'. The theme of the poem was gender differences, a topic she frequently explored in her writing.

Amanda was a complex person. A pleasure-seeker, a voluptuary, but at the same time, ever since the early years of her adolescence, she had been strongly attracted to anything that betokened intellectualism: the romance of the coffee house, intense conversation, art, revolutionary politics. In her youth, she had yearned for the company of men with vision and purpose (none of whom, she soon discovered, lived anywhere near her parents' house in Pinner). She would return from juvenile parties drunk, aroused from being kissed – and touched – fall into bed and still feel the need to read before sleep – Kafka, Orwell, Camus. Her mother and father, neither of whom read for pleasure, were vaguely suspicious of her expanding library of second-hand paperbacks. She was attracted to dissident cliques and hung out with like-minded students in smoky bedsits, listening to impassioned conversations about modernism that lasted all night and didn't end until daybreak.

All of her lovers at university were would-be novelists, but none of them ever succeeded in getting anything published. Simon was the first 'real' artist that she had ever met and this made him irresistible. She would sit for hours watching him improvise at the piano, entranced by the glamour of his authenticity; however, she had had to make concessions. He could be cold and distant, cerebral to the point of frigidity. It had become increasingly difficult to accept the conditions of their compact of late, particularly so since she was now an artist in her own right and generally less impressed by Simon's accomplishments. From the very beginning the match had been imperfect. Amanda, the pleasure-seeker, the voluptuary, had made significant sacrifices over the years.

The record came to an end and Amanda got out of bed in order to put it back in its sleeve. She heard the front door opening and Simon's inept attempt to close it quietly. He crept up the stairs, tripping where the carpet was loose, and entered the bathroom. Amanda slid back between the sheets and waited. She listened to him showering and eventually the door handle turned and he appeared, his hair still dripping. He was fragrant with excessive cologne.

'Still awake?'

She glanced at the alarm clock. It was one o'clock in the morning. 'Yes, I've been writing. I hadn't noticed the time. You're late.'

'Douglas wanted to go out for a drink after the rehearsal.'

'Where did you go?'

'We went to a pub first and then on to his club.' Simon walked over to the lamp stand and pulled the scarf off. The light in the room changed colour from red to yellow.

'You know, you really shouldn't do that. You'll start a fire.'

'It's only a thirty-watt bulb. It doesn't get very hot.'

He squeezed the scarf. 'You say that, but . . .' Suddenly, he lost the urge to argue the point. Instead, he folded the material into a neat triangle and placed it on the dressing table.

'How was the rehearsal?' Amanda asked.

'Excellent,' he replied. 'The cello solo was sublime. Shall I turn this off?' He tapped the lampshade.

'All right.'

The room was plunged into darkness.

Amanda's body bounced as Simon got into bed. They lay apart for a few moments before she rolled onto her side. She slipped her hand beneath his pyjamas and trifled with his chest hair. 'I'm so tired,' Simon yawned. 'It really was a very exhausting evening.'

'I'm sure it was.' A little too much emphasis on the word 'sure' introduced scepticism into an otherwise supportive response.

Simon either didn't notice or wilfully ignored the hint of bad feeling. 'Another long day tomorrow,' he said, adding a laboured sigh for effect.

'Yes,' Amanda repeated, 'another long day.'

She closed her eyes and thought once again about Leda surrendering herself to the amorous swan. The emotion that accompanied images of this bizarre union was dangerously close to envy. A half-dream of brightly illuminated down, like falling snow, ensured a smooth transition from wakefulness to sleep.

When Amanda opened her eyes again it was morning. She could hear Simon's regular exhalations and felt discomfited by a full bladder. Pulling the covers aside, she got out of bed and went to the bathroom. While seated on the toilet, her gazed wandered. Simon's clothes were hanging on the back of a chair and he had pushed his shoes between its legs. She noticed that the shoes were dirty. After wiping herself and pulling the chain she went to take a closer look. They were covered in dust, and when she turned them over she saw that mud had collected in the corrugated rubber soles.

The rehearsal had taken place in a West End church. That's what Simon had told her. In which case, why were his shoes so filthy?

Christopher switched off the radio and listened to the new recording. After his introductory remarks an old woman's voice floated out of the continuous static. 'God have mercy.' There was a short pause and the quivering contralto continued: 'I dare not approach while he reposes near thy heart.' Somewhere deep in the radio noise, he thought he could hear a distant cry, a dreadful keening. He stopped the tape, rewound it for a few seconds and pressed 'play'. There was nothing but static. He checked the rev counter but the cry seemed to have disappeared. Christopher's perplexity was mild. He had become accustomed to the occasional experience of auditory hallucination. Listening to static for long periods of time seemed to encourage the brain to overinterpret the slightest perturbation. He let the tape run on. A young man, desperate, almost hysterical: *'Ich stehe allein! So ganz allein!'* The voice was unusually clear. *I stand alone! So utterly alone!* There was a sob, followed by the words: *'In meinem kleinen Zimmer.' In my little room. 'Mir wird so eng!' I feel trapped.* This was followed by two minutes of empty whooshing, after which the static began to ripple with faint, incomprehensible whispers. A burst of flutter preceded the old woman, who returned to issue a warning: 'Do not heed the speech of shadows.' The remaining ten minutes of the recording were void. Christopher pressed 'stop' and removed his headphones. 'Not bad,' he said out loud. It had been a productive night.

The studio was unbearably hot and when he changed position, he found that his shirt was damp and sticking to his skin. He could smell his own perspiration, his lips were dry and he was thirsty.

In the kitchen, he poured an inch of concentrated orange juice into a tumbler, filled it with tap water, and stirred the mixture with a fork. He gulped the sweet liquid down his parched throat and put the bottle back in a cupboard. There were some dead ants next to the ant bait. Although tired, he didn't want to go to bed, so he went to the drawing room and lay down on the sofa. 'The speech of shadows,' he said, savouring the alliteration. It would make a good title. Up until that point he had only thought of his composition as 'the piece', but giving it a name seemed to advance the project a stage further and he felt a sudden rush of excitement. He imagined seeing those same words printed in the *Radio Times* or on the front of a concert programme. The prospect of his critical rehabilitation made him feel slightly agitated so he got up and began pacing around the room.

He had completed several circuits of the sofa before he was halted by his own reflection in the French windows. His hair was sticking up, his shirt was hanging out and he needed a shave. There was something about his self-neglect that made him look older. Through his reflection,

Christopher thought he could see a glimmer of light. He walked to the window and peered out into the garden. There was indeed a faint luminescence and he judged that its source was in the vicinity of the gazebo.

'What the . . .' A slight increase in brightness confirmed his thinking. The gazebo materialized momentarily like a lantern, a skeletal structure of posts and struts. The light was clearly coming from inside. Was it a fire?

Christopher rushed to the kitchen and found a torch in one of the cupboards. Then he returned to the drawing room, unlocked the French windows and stepped out onto the terrace. The light had vanished. He made his way to the gazebo and flashed the torch around the interior. He saw a blanket, bottles and some newspapers. Nothing was smouldering or scorched; however, he detected a trace of tobacco smoke in the air, which troubled him a little, but not for long. He noticed that the neighbours, who smoked excessively, had left one of their windows open. Christopher scratched his head. He was sure he had seen a flickering light.

There was a sudden noise – the swish of long grass – and an impression of movement. He swept the torch beam around the garden. An animal, a cat – or was it a fox? – appeared in the circle of illumination and then leapt out of view. There was more sound, scrabbling, a thud, and then silence. His heart, which was hammering in his chest, began to slow down again.

Christopher walked back to the house and checked the side entrance. The beam of his torch penetrated the darkness, revealing a dustbin and a ladder lying on its side. Mr Ellis – the builder – had neglected to collect the ladder after his departure and Christopher had failed to arrange for its disposal. Beside the dustbin was a cardboard box that had been stuffed to capacity. Its sides bulged and some of the contents had spilled onto the ground. Christopher crouched down to pick up one of several magazines. He was surprised to see that the cover girl was a younger incarnation of Laura. It was a 1960s edition of *Glamour.* She was pouting at the camera and looking very sexy. The torch beam travelled across the ground and came to rest on another image of his wife. There she was, sitting on a chair, the shortness of her miniskirt revealing the full extent of her slender legs. Her hair was a glorious fountain that fell to her shoulders and curled upwards. She looked like the quintessential sixties 'dolly bird'. Christopher shone his torch into the box and discovered more magazines of a similar vintage, all of them graced with images of Laura in her elegant prime.

The following morning Christopher entered the kitchen and found that Laura and Faye had already finished their breakfast. Faye was playing with some plastic farm animals and Laura was inspecting the cupboards to see if any more ants had appeared.

'The bait worked,' said Laura.

'Good,' Christopher responded, before inserting a spoonful of cornflakes into his mouth. They managed to sustain a superficial conversation, but Christopher wasn't really listening. He was rehearsing the confrontation that he was about to instigate. He knew that what he intended to do was unnecessarily theatrical, a provocation, but he couldn't desist. It was as though he had become detached from his own mental processes. He got up, left the kitchen, and returned carrying the box of magazines he had discovered the night before. Like a robot, he held the box over the kitchen table and let it go. The crockery jumped and the spoons rattled. Faye looked at him quizzically then went back to playing with her animals.

'What do you think you're doing?' Laura asked.

He removed a magazine from the box and tossed it in Laura's direction. She looked down at her own image.

'I found them last night. Why on earth did you throw them away?'

'I've been having a clear-out.'

Her face was blank, her lips pressed together. Christopher noticed a burgeoning surplus of flesh beneath her chin.

'I don't understand,' he said, throwing his hands up and letting them fall again. 'I just don't understand.'

'What don't you understand?'

'Why you'd throw these away?'

She shrugged. 'I don't want them anymore.'

'But it's your life. It's what you did.'

Laura sighed. 'I modelled clothes, Chris. That's all.'

He pulled another magazine out of the box and held it up. '*Vogue.* They put you on the front cover of *Vogue*.'

'So what?'

'Doesn't it mean *anything* to you?'

'Not now. No. It's the past.'

'What about Faye?'

'What about her?'

'Don't you think she'd like to see these magazines when she gets older?'

'I hope not. I hope she'll be interested in a lot more than clothes and make-up.'

'She's a girl! Of course she'll be interested in clothes and make-up. And there's nothing wrong with that, is there?' Laura's expression encouraged Christopher to reflect on his rhetoric. He responded defensively. 'Being feminine won't stop her from becoming a doctor or a lawyer.'

'But being *feminine*,' Laura said, inscribing the air with quotations marks, 'as you put it, makes it hard for a young woman to get taken seriously, especially if being *feminine* means showing your legs and painting your face. I don't want Faye to grow up thinking that her mother was particularly proud of being a professional clothes horse.'

'Don't be so ridiculous. The kind of work you did had genuine artistic value. Some of those shoots really captured the spirit of the time. Children are naturally curious about what their parents got up to when they were young. It'd be nice for Faye to see some of these.'

'Please. Take the box outside and leave it by the dust-bin. Those magazines are mine, not yours, and I want to throw them away.'

'I don't know . . .' He was too exasperated to continue speaking. He took a deep breath and tried again. 'I don't understand. What's the matter with you?'

'Ah.' It was only a single syllable, but it communicated sudden, grave insight – resentment and anger. Christopher was too het up to detect such nuances. He did not register the portent in her eyes. He only saw the severe, masculine cut of her hair and the pendant bulge beneath her chin. 'I don't know what you're becoming – what you're turning into.'

Laura stared at the magazine in front of her. A red rash had suddenly appeared on her neck.

'You want me to be like this again, don't you?'

The truth of the accusation had the effect of leaving Christopher speechless. Eventually, he replied, rather weakly, 'No.'

'Well, it's not going to happen. OK?' She picked up the magazine and placed it on top of the others in the box. 'Now, please. Take it outside.'

Christopher conceded defeat and silently did as he was told.

Before going up to his studio he went into the bedroom to find a thinner T-shirt. Although it was still early in the day the temperature had started to climb. On Laura's dressing table he saw the bottle of perfume he had bought for her in Paris. It was unopened.

For the rest of the morning Christopher couldn't concentrate. He tried to focus on his music but he kept on thinking about Laura, and when he listened back to what he had recorded he was disappointed. It didn't compliment the scene he had been watching on the TV screen:

androids converging on a moon base surrounded by parabolic dishes. The soundtrack lacked urgency and the textures were too thin. He was tempted to erase the tape and start again, but he resisted the urge. What he needed was a break, some fresh air to clear his head. In the hallway, he shouted out, 'I'm going for a walk, OK?' Laura didn't respond. He shrugged, slammed the door and walked down to the gate.

As he crossed the road he noticed that the tarmac was tacky. The soles of his shoes stuck to the ground and when he lifted his feet he heard a tearing noise. He had to curl his toes otherwise his shoes would have come off. The sun was so strong the tarry surface had begun to melt. He had never seen anything like it before. Apart from a little thundery rain on the first Sunday of the month, the sun had been a permanent fixture and temperatures had soared into the eighties every day. The sky had become a glaring dome of blue-yellow haze. London was burning up. He remembered a headline he had read in the *Express* a week earlier: 'Sweat It Out For Fifty Years'. Scientists had just discovered an atmospheric phenomenon called the 'greenhouse effect' and experts were predicting longer and fiercer heatwaves to come. In a final twist of fate, the weather had joined forces with the inept politicians, striking unions and terrorists to hasten the end of Britain. The whole nation was about to spontaneously combust.

Christopher hurried onto the shaded path beneath the trees on the opposite side of the road and began to penetrate the wooded margin of Hampstead Heath. Once again, he began to think about Laura. What was happening to her? She had been changing for some time now, but the process of transformation had accelerated over the last few months. Throwing away her magazines was a symbolic act, a disavowal of her past. In effect, she was declaring that she was no longer the person who he had fallen in love with. And if that was true, didn't it follow that their relationship would suffer or, even worse, become unworkable? Yet neither he nor she could just walk away from their shared commitments. There was Faye to consider. Christopher suddenly felt tension arising as two contradictory impulses pulled in opposite directions. On the one hand, he accepted the responsibilities of marriage and family, but on the other hand, the artist in him balked at the prospect of confinement in an unhappy domestic situation. A photographic image of Ancel's apartment clarified in his mind: the tall windows, the oil painting, the scantily clad young lover. Christopher felt envy curdling in the pit of his stomach. Like many men of his generation, he had heard Cyril Connolly's assertion that *There is no more sombre enemy of good art than the pram in the hall* repeated more times than he cared to remember. Perhaps there was some truth in it after all.

Once out of the woods, Christopher ascended a path which took him up to the Bronze-Age burial mound known locally as Boadicea's Grave. He noticed that the surrounding fields were mottled with brown patches. The absence of rain was causing the grass to shrivel and die. After crossing the south meadow and the duelling ground, he negotiated the hump of a quaint stone bridge and made his way up towards the eighteenth-century stucco facade of Kenwood House.

The heat had made him thirsty so he bought himself a cup of tea in the cafe and searched for a table outside. He stopped dead when he saw Amanda Ogilvy sitting beneath a sun umbrella reading a book. She was wearing a lacy white summer dress that emphasized the darkness of her Mediterranean complexion, and her black hair was tied back. Loose coils framed her face and when she moved they bounced like springs.

'Amanda?'

She looked up. 'Christopher? What are you doing here?'

'I've been walking. Mind if I join you?'

'Of course not.'

He pulled a chair out from under the table and sat down.

'What are you reading?'

'Stevie Smith – *Collected Poems*.' She held up the cover so that he could see for himself.

'Stevie Smith . . .' He repeated the name in a slightly distracted way.

'You *do* know her work.'

'Do I?'

'Those lines about being further out than you thought and not waving but drowning?'

'Ah, yes. Fancy that. I'd completely forgotten the name.'

'But not the poem – you only need to hear those lines once and you never forget them.'

'Are you having a day off?'

'No, it's summer. Or hadn't you noticed?' Amanda gestured at the blazing sun.

'So it is.'

Their conversation flowed easily and required no effort. Amanda talked about films, television and the recent announcement that Benjamin Britten had accepted a life peerage. 'Have you ever met him?' she asked.

'No.'

'Simon has. One of Simon's chamber pieces – the movement for flute, harp and cello – was performed at Aldeburgh.'

'I remember.'

'He had dinner with Britten after the concert. I wasn't invited.'

A sparrow landed on the edge of the table, hopped once and then flew off again. Christopher drained his cup. 'Would you like some more tea?'

'Yes please. Thank you.'

Christopher went inside the cafe and returned with a tray loaded with metal teapots, milk and fresh crockery. As he poured and stirred he became conscious of Amanda watching his movements. Their eyes locked. She was frowning slightly. 'Are you all right, Chris?'

'Yes. Why do you ask?'

'You seem a bit subdued.'

The argument with Laura had put him in a bad mood; however, he hadn't given Amanda any reason to suspect something was amiss – or so he'd thought. As far as he was concerned, he had been behaving normally, yet he felt obliged to acknowledge her observation and he responded accordingly. 'I've got a lot on my mind at the moment. There's this score I'm writing and I can't seem to get the bloody thing finished, probably because I've been spending too much time working on something else: a serious piece – my first in years.'

'The one with the voices – the spirit voices.'

Christopher started. 'You know about it?'

'Yes, Simon told me.' She appeared flustered and a little anxious. 'That was OK, wasn't it? For him to say, I mean.'

Christopher waved his hand in the air. 'Of course, it's not a secret.'

'I thought the concept sounded very interesting. But *that* isn't it.' Her eyes widened. 'No, there's something else troubling you, isn't there?' She leaned forward, as if she were trying to get a better view of his soul.

'Well, I suppose you're right,' Christopher replied. 'There is something else . . .' He wondered whether it would be wise to continue. But suddenly the weight of his dissatisfaction pressed down on him, and he felt an overwhelming need to unburden himself. Amanda was an old friend and someone who he could trust with confidences. And who else did he have to talk to? There was no one better qualified to hear his confession. 'I'm not sure that things are as they should be with me and Laura.'

'Oh?' said Amanda, leaning even closer. 'What do you mean?' She had tried to sound casual but her eagerness was transparent.

Christopher made some abortive attempts at translating his feelings into words, and discovered that the task was more challenging than he had expected. His sentences gradually became less fragmented and his speech gathered momentum. He found himself saying that Laura had become distant, cold, almost a stranger, and that she was even looking different these days. 'It's as though she's rejecting everything she once was.' An account of the argument in the kitchen followed. 'She insisted that I take the magazines back outside. She's thrown them all away. I can appreciate that she wants to move on – doesn't everybody? – but why does she have to deny her past?' Christopher was aware that his voice had acquired an unattractive whining tone, and he made an effort to pitch his subsequent complaints in a lower register. Amanda nodded, her sympathetic expression rigidly set, unconditionally accepting his grievances. He found the ventilation of his feelings curiously satisfying.

'Look,' said Amanda, 'this might not be an appropriate question for me to ask, so just tell me to stop being nosey, if that's how you feel – I won't be offended – but are you still . . .' She halted before whispering, 'Intimate?'

Christopher looked down, embarrassed. He studied Amanda's feet. She was wearing sandals and she had painted her toenails the colour of maraschino cherries. 'Well, yes. But it isn't what it used to be. It's all become rather . . .' He searched his memory for the right word. 'Indifferent.'

Amanda tried to comfort Christopher. She urged him to be patient and suggested that Laura might be going through a 'phase'; she reminded him that it wasn't unusual for women to experience an 'identity crisis' after having a baby and she added that she was sure that they – Laura and he – being mature adults, could 'work it out'. But there was something missing from Amanda's counsel. Her jargon sounded trite. She seemed to be quoting from an article or a work of popular psychology rather than speaking from the heart. Perhaps she was aware of this deficiency, because soon after she abandoned language altogether and rested her palm on the back of Christopher's hand. For a few minutes, physical contact relieved them of any need to talk, but in due course Amanda said, 'Relationships. Appearances can be so deceptive. You know, me and Simon . . .' Her lips puckered to form an odd smile. 'It's never been perfect, particularly in *that* department.' The cast of her face changed. 'But you must have guessed.'

'No,' Christopher replied, puzzled. 'I had no idea.'

'Well, if things had been better, between me and Simon, then our . . .' Her forefinger oscillated between them. 'Our . . . I don't know what to call it.' She sighed and concluded, 'It probably wouldn't have happened.'

Christopher was shocked. The subject of their illicit

liaison had always been strictly taboo. 'I had no such excuse. Not at that time. Laura and I were very happy.'

'You say that . . .' Amanda let her incomplete sentence fill the ensuing hiatus with implications.

'What?'

'We were stoned. We were very stoned. But isn't it the case that we do what we really want to do when we're out of our heads?'

'Should we be having this conversation?'

'Probably not, but life's complicated, isn't it?' She lifted her hand off Christopher's and bent down to rummage in her macramé bag. The front of her dress became slack, exposing the pale floral border of a bra. While she was searching for her cigarettes, she noticed Christopher's shoes. They were covered in brown dust. It reminded her of the dust she had seen on Simon's shoes the morning after he had returned late from rehearsals. She realized that she was seeing something significant, but now wasn't the time to think about it. Sitting up, she offered Christopher a cigarette.

'No thanks. I've given up.'

'Be a devil.' The huskiness of her voice made this modest incitement persuasive. She held the box out in front of her.

Christopher's resolve crumbled. 'Oh, all right. Bugger it.'

When they started talking again, their conversation was more philosophical. Instead of discussing personal unhappiness, they took up more general themes – the knotty problems of the human condition, the best way to live. It felt like a retreat from a precipice, a withdrawal to safer ground. They had both taken a step back.

Amanda stubbed out her cigarette and looked at her wristwatch. 'Oh shit, I was supposed to be meeting a friend in the village. I'm going to be really late.' They both stood and made some final remarks preliminary to parting, and Amanda offered Christopher her cheek. He bent to aim a chaste kiss on her smooth, olive skin, but she was not quite still enough to ensure perfect accuracy, and instead their lips made partial contact. Christopher detected a fractional lingering, and when they separated, he thought that he saw something new in her eyes – a fleeting presentiment of intent. Or was he just imagining it? 'Goodbye,' said Amanda. 'It's been nice – talking like this.' She hung her bag over her shoulder, turned and rushed off, her stride widening until she achieved a rather lazy half-trot. Her jet-black hair was suddenly lustrous in the sunlight, paradoxically gleaming. Christopher watched her until she disappeared. He sat down and looked at the crushed filters in the ashtray. One of them was stained with lipstick. It was then that he noticed Stevie Smith's *Collected Poems*. For a moment, he considered chasing after Amanda, but he realized she might have gone left or right beyond the terrace, and he had no way of knowing which. Both directions would get her to Hampstead village, depending on how she intended to get there – by car or bus. He pressed his hands together as if in prayer and fell into a deep, contemplative state.

That evening, Christopher telephoned Amanda.

'It's Christopher.'

'You've got my Stevie Smith?'

'Yes. Shall I drop it over?'

'Look, we're going to be away for a few weeks. Could you give me a call at the end of the month?'

'Sure.'

Had she planned it? He had read a little Freud, and, as far as he could tell, the great psychoanalyst did not believe in accidents. Ultimately, forgetting was always motivated. The famous Stevie Smith couplet that Amanda had paraphrased came back to him. It was easy to drift out further than you thought and to find yourself not waving but drowning. Inevitably, he wondered how far out he had travelled during the course of that afternoon.

Last week in July

She was searching for Faye. Once more the house had become a magic box of secret compartments that seemed to unfold and multiply. It was the same nightmare, although not identical in every respect. Previously, she had arrived on the top floor without using the stairs. On this occasion, however, she found herself labouring up a structure reminiscent of an Escher lithograph. Flights and stages defied the logic of conventional geometry. She climbed and climbed, her legs becoming heavier, and almost collapsed when she finally reached the uppermost landing and staggered into the unused room.

Mummy. Mummy, help me.

Faye's impossibly articulate voice drew Laura towards the alcove. She passed through the wall and emerged in the windowless chamber, where she came to a halt and looked around, registering the paraffin lamp, the ochre-stained bricks and the swaying curtain of chains. Instruments of butchery and torture were laid out on the table, but among the meat cleavers and surgical implements she now noticed a Rolleiflex camera, a piece of equipment she associated with her early modelling career. She glanced down at the champagne bucket. It was no longer empty. This time, a bottle of Dom Pérignon was half buried in the slushy ice and a hotel keyring had been hooked over the cork. A metal tag attached to the keyring was engraved with a room number – 18. Laura sensed that these two digits were connected with some event of personal significance to her, but when she tried to remember what it was her memory supplied no clues.

Somewhere behind her a door opened and closed, and, as before, she heard footsteps approaching but she could not turn. The tip of a cane made contact with the floor. Chains were brushed aside and subsequently produced a metallic clatter. *Clink-clink-clink*. The skin at the nape of her neck began to prickle. *Clink-clink-clink*. It was just behind her, less a person, more a presence – a twisted appetite; merciless, repulsive; eager for depravities, for peeled flesh, exposed inner parts and savage, irregular pleasures. She tried to call for help, but all that she was able to produce was a pathetic whimper.

Laura opened her eyes and stared into the darkness. Her husband made a grumbling noise and coughed. She clutched the under sheet as though clinging onto something material would prevent her from tumbling back into that terrible place. Her quick, loud respiration subsided, but the world was not quite right; the dream had not been properly sealed off from reality and she was aware of a stray thread of terror, something odd that had carried over, something that persisted.

Clink-clink-clink.

Laura sat up, held her breath, and listened. It was the sound of chains colliding; faint and swathed in a continuous hiss. The source was close to her right ear – the baby monitor. For a few seconds, Laura was made immobile by the same paralysis she had experienced in the dream. Then a siren seemed to sound in her head and she leapt out of bed. On the landing, she flicked a light switch and ran into the nursery. Faye was fast asleep. Laura studied her daughter then glanced about the room. Her rapid survey required quick jerky movements and she suddenly felt dizzy. She reached out and grasped the rail of the cot so as to steady herself. Her mind seemed to make a late calibration and the room acquired a more solid aspect. Had she been fully awake when she had heard the *clink-clink-clink* of the chains? She wasn't sure.

'What are you doing?' Christopher's voice startled her. She turned and saw him in the doorway, yawning and raking his hand over his scalp. 'Is something wrong?'

Laura wasn't sure how to proceed. 'I thought I heard

something again. You know, something strange – coming from the monitor.'

'A voice?'

'No, something else. I'm not sure.'

'You woke me up,' said Christopher. He sounded a little irritated.

Laura nodded. 'Yes, I'm sorry.'

Christopher shrugged and returned to the bedroom. When she was sure that the dizziness had passed, she joined him.

'What did you hear?' Christopher asked. 'If you didn't hear a voice, what was it?'

'A noise – clicking. I may have been dreaming. I really don't know.'

She heard her husband tut. What did he mean to communicate? Rebuke? Mild disapprobation? Impatience?

He rolled away, taking most of the bed sheet with him. Laura made no attempt to retrieve her share. The night was hot and she doubted that she would fall asleep again.

Christopher found Laura sitting on the terrace. She was lying back in a garden chair with a bottle of suntan lotion within easy reach. Her skin glistened and exuded a sharp, lemony scent. She was wearing a long skirt, but she had hitched most of the material above her knees, exposing long, shapely legs, blemished only by a small number of mosquito bites. A pair of sandals had been kicked off and had come to rest some distance from her feet. Christopher's shadow fell across her face. She stirred, and behind the tinted lenses of her enormous Yves Saint Laurent sunglasses, her eyes opened.

'Faye's waking up,' said Christopher.

'OK.' Laura straightened her back. 'Sue's coming this afternoon.'

'Is she?'

'Yes. I told you yesterday.'

'Did you?'

'Yes.'

'What's she coming for?'

'To do the rockery, remember?'

'Oh, yes.'

'Did you check the savings account?'

'I thought you said Sue wasn't going to charge?'

'I did.'

'No, I didn't check the savings account.'

'Then what shall I say to her about the rest of the work?'

'Tell her that we definitely want it done. It's just a

question of when.' He inspected his shirt cuffs. Before Laura could respond, Christopher reminded her that their daughter was awake and he hurried back into the house. On returning to his studio, he watched more scenes from *Android Insurrection* and felt somewhat disheartened. There was still a great deal of music to compose and the prospect didn't excite him.

While he was cutting and splicing tapes, he heard the doorbell ring downstairs, then faint voices and a peal of laughter. He didn't let the gardener's arrival distract him. After an hour or so, Laura knocked and entered. 'Sue's here.'

Christopher looked up. 'Yes, I heard.'

'I'm driving into the village to get some things,' Laura continued. 'We're running out of milk. Sue said she won't be leaving until about five.'

'OK.'

The studio was beginning to feel like a greenhouse. Two bluebottles were orbiting Christopher's head and no amount of swatting could persuade them to alter their trajectories. The buzzing that they produced was like a chainsaw and a heavy sensation, situated somewhere behind Christopher's brow, was threatening to become more readily identifiable as pain. It was time to take a break. He spliced a final length of tape, hung the loop on a hook, and descended through the house to the kitchen.

While waiting for the kettle to boil he walked idly to the table and his gaze fell on two paperback books that he hadn't seen before. The first was titled *House Arrest* and was written by a sociologist who lectured at the University of Essex. Several paragraphs of text had been underlined. On the inside cover, he found the name Susan Kent scrawled in biro. The second book was titled *Against Our Will: Men, Women and Rape*. Beneath the title it said: '. . . a conscious process of intimidation by which all men keep all women in a state of fear.' Such casual use of the word 'all' annoyed Christopher intensely. He scowled, picked up the book, and flicked through the pages. Again, he observed that certain passages had been underlined.

He was disturbed by the sound of footsteps and when he looked up he discovered a woman was standing by the door. She was wearing a vest-like T-shirt, denim shorts and a pair of large black boots. Her thick, sun-bleached hair was tied back with a scarf.

'Hi,' she said, stepping forward and making an arc with her right hand as if she were cleaning an invisible window. 'I'm Sue. You must be Christopher.'

He nodded and held up the book. 'You're lending this to my wife?' His use of the possessive pronoun was emphatic.

The woman looked puzzled. 'What?'

'*All* men,' said Christopher, tapping the offending word. '*All* men keep *all* women in a state of fear. That's a bit sweeping, isn't it?'

'Perhaps you should read it first. I mean, before you . . .'

'I'm not sure I need to.'

Attempting to lighten the atmosphere, Sue smiled and knowingly recited a cliché: 'You should never judge a book by its cover.' She crossed to the sink, filled a glass with water, and raised it to her lips. Her thirsty gulping was clearly audible. When she had finished drinking she turned to face Christopher and wiped her chin with a polka-dot handkerchief. Her skin had been burned by the sun and was peeling.

'It's divisive,' said Christopher bluntly.

Her expression, which for a moment had been illuminated by hope, was immediately eclipsed by disappointment. 'Look,' said Sue, 'I think we've got off on the wrong foot here.' Christopher's tightly compressed lips offered her little encouragement. 'A book like *Against Our Will*,' she continued, 'is a bit extreme, I'll grant you that. But sometimes you have to shout loudly to be heard . . . you know?'

'It doesn't help . . .' Christopher muttered, vaguely. He wasn't really addressing the gardener. A half-formed thought had simply slipped out.

'I'm sorry?'

'Men, women . . .' Christopher's irritability had made him inarticulate. 'How we get along together . . . it's all so inflammatory.'

'Well, so is rape.'

His instinct was to rip the book apart and scatter the shreds like confetti, but instead he laid the dog-eared paperback down on the table next to the spider plant. A cloud of steam was escaping from the kettle.

'I'm making a cup of coffee,' said Christopher, trying to keep his voice steady and level. 'Would you like one?' He wasn't going to give this woman the satisfaction of seeing him lose his temper. He wasn't going to confirm her prejudices.

'No thanks,' she said. 'I need to crack on.'

After her wary departure, Christopher could still smell her: earth, freshly mowed grass and a hint of tobacco. It was as though her physical departure was incomplete. An olfactory ghost remained. Christopher made his cup of coffee and returned to the studio; however, it was some time before he could concentrate on his work. He kept on thinking about his brief but intense encounter with Sue.

Much later, Christopher returned to the kitchen. Laura was cooking and Faye was seated in her highchair. The gardener had evidently gone.

'Have you seen the rockery?' Laura asked. She was unusually animated; even her voice sounded different, brighter and purer in tone.

'No, I haven't,' Christopher replied.

'Take a look.'

'OK.'

From the terrace, Christopher could see a stone cascade where previously only shrubs had obscured the rear wall. It was an attractive feature. Getting closer, he saw that the downward flow of the rockery was interrupted by horizontal flower beds of different shapes and sizes. A crescent of coloured stones had been spread around its base and an adjacent area of ground had been cleared. From this vantage point it was now possible to enjoy an unrestricted view of the house in all its Gothic Revival splendour. Christopher felt a pang of guilt. It hadn't even occurred to him to thank Sue.

'It's great,' said Christopher, as he stepped back into the kitchen. 'I can't believe she did it all for free.'

'Yes,' Laura replied. 'It was kind of her, wasn't it?'

'We must get her something – for her trouble. A small gift.'

Laura indicated the books on the table.

'What did you say to Sue about these?'

'Why do you ask?'

'She said that you'd had a chat about them and she'd got the impression that you disapproved.'

The gardener had obviously chosen to be diplomatic. Christopher experienced a second pang of guilt. 'Well, look what it says on the cover. All men are rapists! You can't possibly believe that!'

Laura tensed and responded firmly, 'I'll read the book.'

Simon Ogilvy was sitting in a nondescript office in the bowels of Broadcasting House with Hugo Hasting-Bass, a senior producer for BBC Radio 3. Hasting-Bass was a shabby individual whose mode of dress did little to betray his privileged background. His hair was a frizzy, undisciplined grey mop, and his glasses listed precariously on the bridge of his retroussé nose. He wore baggy cord trousers, a checked shirt with a crumpled collar and a V-neck sweater with well-worn, threadbare elbows.

Hasting-Bass had been enthusing about a new programme idea when his assistant arrived with three mugs of coffee. 'Ah, thank you, Roderick.' The young man sat beside his superior. Hasting-Bass was middle-aged and plump, whereas Roderick was a vision of lithe, golden youth – blond curls, Russian cheekbones, full, sensual lips and eyelashes that actually glinted when they caught the light.

'You know,' said Hasting-Bass, tilting his palms at the ceiling, 'I think a little humility is in order. We can learn a great deal from today's pop musicians. I'm not talking about groups who achieve success in the hit parade, of course, but rather those who attempt to construct intricate works on a larger scale, those who make – for want of a better term – concept albums. These chaps are able to challenge their audience, make them concentrate for longer periods of time, because they provide an overarching theme. Have you listened to any . . .' Hasting-Bass hesitated, as if what he intended to say next was collecting in his mouth like an excess of saliva, 'progressive rock?' Coming from Hasting-Bass, the words sounded forced and absurd.

'A little,' Simon replied. 'My wife occasionally plays records that her students give her. To be honest, I'm not overly impressed. I find it all rather crude and episodic.'

'Indeed,' said Hasting-Bass. 'But that's rather beside

the point.' He bristled for a moment before smiling benevolently at his assistant. 'Roderick has been introducing me to some of these artists and I must say I'm intrigued. The more experimental passages are almost atonal. Yet these groups reach an audience of millions, an audience who, until recently, were only prepared to listen to three-chord love songs lasting for less than three minutes. My feeling is that these more sophisticated pop musicians are able to push their audiences beyond their habitual listening habits because of the conceptual element. A narrative – a theme, a concept – makes their music far more accessible. Now, my thinking is this: if it works for them, there's a good chance it'll work for us too. I'm keen to broaden our appeal and I'm convinced that conceptual pieces will be the key to our future success.'

'That's very interesting,' said Ogilvy, although his voice sounded moribund.

Hasting-Bass transferred four heaped teaspoons of sugar from a plastic bowl to his coffee mug with reckless haste, producing a trail of white granules on his desk. 'Needless to say, something of yours will almost certainly be broadcast in our new programme – *The Pit and the Pendulum*, perhaps, or *Epitaphs*. However, I'm still looking for more pieces, particularly works that haven't been performed before, but they *must* be conceptual.' Hasting-Bass brushed some sugar from his trousers. 'Do you have any recommendations? Are any of your colleagues, perchance, working on something that might be suitable?'

Roderick smiled encouragingly. His teeth were alarmingly white and there was something about his physical perfection that saddened Simon, although he couldn't specify what it was exactly. 'No,' said Simon. 'I'm afraid not.'

After the meeting with Hasting-Bass, Simon walked to his car and found that he could barely touch the steering wheel it was so hot. He had to conduct some of the heat into his own hands before it was possible to begin the journey home. About halfway, he pulled over in order to use a telephone box. He called Amanda and said that he had been delayed and wouldn't be back until late. 'Hasting-Bass wants to discuss a new programme he's producing. There might be a commission in it, one never knows.'

Amanda responded with her usual guarded neutrality. 'OK,' she replied, 'I hadn't cooked anything.' An odd thing to say, Simon thought, because she rarely prepared his supper.

He drove up to Jack Straw's Castle, where he sat at a table nursing a beer and waiting for the sky to darken. He would need several drinks before venturing outside, beyond the car park and down the dusty track that led to the woods of West Heath, where his shame and confusion could be concealed, not only beneath the cover of night, but behind a final bastion of thorny bushes. Looking through the amber lens of his glass, he thought once again of Roderick. The boy (he could only think of him as a boy) had looked like Dorian Gray.

Laura was tired because she hadn't slept properly for two nights. Throughout the hours of darkness, she had been tense and excessively sensitive to the slightest sound. Every knock and creak had lifted her heart into her throat and when the baby monitor crackled or buzzed she had strained to hear more – a distant voice or the dreadful *clink-clink-clink* of swaying chains. After rising, she had examined her face in the bathroom mirror and had been depressed by the appearance of two dark crescents beneath her eyes. She had decided, about a month earlier, to relinquish petty vanities, but she was feeling fragile. Consequently, she had scooped dollops of moisturizing cream from a tub and rubbed the cool white paste into her skin. This ritual, which she used to perform several times a day, had felt comforting.

Now, lying on the sofa, absorbed by the intricate curlicues of the ceiling rose, she felt guilty. She had been weak. What did it matter if she had bags under her eyes? And what was the point of trying to preserve her looks? Beauty – or at least her kind of beauty – was unsustainable. She did not want to be defined by appearances anymore. It was so shallow. She thought about her husband, how Chris had been angry because of her insistence on throwing away her collection of magazines. He just didn't understand. Nor could he understand, ever, because in all probability he would never know what the real cost of her success had been.

The door was ajar and Faye crawled out of the room.

'Faye?' That's all she ever seemed to do, call out her daughter's name, not only in reality but also in her dreams. 'Faye? Come back, darling.' Sometimes the child responded, but not very often. 'Come on, honey. Please.' Laura sat up, finding that repositioning her body was far more effortful than it should have been. 'Do I really have to come and get you? Faye? Please, honey.' Laura sighed and, feeling annoyed (as much with herself for not bothering to shut the door as with her daughter), she stood and stomped across the floor.

Laura found Faye standing at the bottom of the stairs, her head tilted backwards.

'Faye?'

The child didn't move. She seemed to have entered a trance-like state, just as she had before, when Laura had discovered Faye staring at the wall in the empty bedroom on the top floor. Her little body was so still that she looked like a doll, the limbs of which had been manipulated to achieve an even distribution of weight. Laura began to tremble, but she did not lose control. She wanted to study her daughter more closely, to make observations that might inform a diagnosis. The doctor had said that there was nothing wrong with Faye, but he was clearly mistaken. This wasn't normal.

Laura sat down on the bottom step and passed a hand in front of Faye's face. The child didn't flinch. Leaning forward, Laura examined Faye's eyes, which were very much like her own. The light was providently striking her daughter's irises at the precise angle required to turn them gold. Faye's stare was so fixed, so rapt, that it made Laura uneasy. Against her better judgement, she found herself glancing over her shoulder to make sure that there really was nothing remarkable to look at on the stairs or first-floor landing. Laura clicked her fingers next to Faye's ear and brushed a knuckle against her cheek. 'Faye, darling, what's wrong?' The child's eyelids began to droop and the upper half of her body rocked backwards and forwards. When she fell, Laura caught her and clutched her close, kissing her soft blonde curls. Faye began to cry. 'It's all right, honey,' Laura murmured. 'Don't cry – everything's fine.' She stroked Faye's spine and kissed her again. 'Everything's fine.'

When Christopher came down from the studio to have his lunch, Laura told him what had happened.

'It was the same thing. Identical.'

'Yes, but the doctor said she was OK.'

'I think he's wrong. I'm going to take her to see him again.'

'OK.'

'Can you come with me?'

'I'm working. Why do you need me to go?'

'I don't think the doctor listens to me.' Christopher's expression was so disdainful that Laura quickly added, 'All right. There's no need. I'll deal with it.'

Christopher expressed his frustration by making juggling movements with his hands. 'Of course the doctor will listen to you.'

She shut down the conversation with a curt repetition. 'I'll deal with it.'

Three hours later she was sitting in the doctor's waiting room dandling Faye on her knee. There were six other patients, one of whom had a bad, rattling cough. A spritely old woman made polite conversation, remarking on Faye's beauty and disclosing with pride that she was the mother of four 'strapping' sons. 'A daughter . . .' she said with some regret. 'I've always wondered what it must be like to have a daughter.'

In due course the doctor appeared and invited Laura to enter his surgery. Over the flat expanse of his desk, she addressed a bald patch that had started to show on the doctor's crown. He remained hunched over his notes, occasionally emitting a protracted humming noise, while she described Faye's trance. When she had finished the doctor still didn't look up. 'You were here in May,' he said.

She wasn't sure whether this was a statement or a question. Judging that it would be rude to remain silent, she replied, 'Yes. I was.'

Finally, the doctor looked up and made eye contact. 'You know, children are not so very different from us adults. They get tired, their minds go blank, they nod off to sleep. It's been two months since you were here last. I suspect that if these absences were indicative of a significant underlying problem, then they would have become more frequent in the intervening weeks. And look at your daughter, Mrs Norton. Really.' It was remarkable how this one small word – *really* – pronounced with particular emphasis – questioning, sceptical, accusatory – completely undermined Laura's sense of being an intelligent adult. 'Isn't Faye a picture of health?' His forced smile begged Laura to reflect on her folly.

'I've never seen children do this before,' she responded.

'Do you have a great deal of experience with children?' It was a question with one purpose only – to expose her lack of authority, to embarrass and belittle her.

'No,' she mumbled. 'No. Not really, but . . .'

The doctor talked over her unfinished sentence. 'As I said to you before, I could refer your daughter to a neurologist . . .'

'But you're not going to.'

The doctor raised one of his eyebrows before adopting a tone of casual familiarity. 'My son used to go to sleep while he was eating. And – if I'm not mistaken – it started happening when he was about Faye's age now.'

'She wasn't asleep. Her eyes were open.'

The doctor ignored this objection and leaned forward. His gaze became penetrating. So much so that Laura detected a hint of stagecraft in his melodramatic attitude. 'And *you*, Mrs Norton. Tell me, how have *you* been recently?'

'All . . . all right, I suppose.' Dishonesty made her stumble over her words.

'You see,' the doctor intoned gravely, 'I can't help wondering whether the problem – as you describe it – is only a problem in so far as it reflects your own anxieties.'

She surprised herself by snapping. 'No! That's not it. That's not it at all.' The doctor withdrew. 'I'm worried about my daughter!'

'Are you taking your medication?'

'Oh, Jesus Christ . . .' Laura shook her head. She wanted to scream. She had feared this would happen.

The doctor spoke firmly. 'Mrs Norton, I can't help you if—'

'Forget it. Just forget it.'

She got up and placed Faye in the pushchair.

'Perhaps you should come back tomorrow. You're obviously quite distraught today.' He pushed his chair back and stood, demonstrating that he had not forgotten his manners. When Laura reached the door she turned and sighed. She considered apologizing, but then dismissed the thought. 'I can fit you in first thing tomorrow morning,' the doctor persevered.

'I don't think so,' she said, opening the door and manoeuvring the pushchair through the gap and out into the waiting room. The man with the cough was wheezing into a handkerchief held over his mouth. A few ominous red stains were visible on the white material.

As she rushed away from the practice she began to cry. She was furious and her head filled with the militant language that she often heard at the bookshop in Islington. *Chauvinist! Male chauvinist pig!* He had no right to treat her like that – no right at all. She carried on walking for some time, not paying very much attention to where she was going. Eventually, her pace slowed and she became more aware of her surroundings. She was walking down a wide, leafy road with large red-brick houses on either side. Her temper cooled and she sat down on a bench. Faye had gone to sleep.

She remembered the argument with her husband over the magazines. He had stood beside her, bemused, perhaps even horrified, and said, 'What's the matter with you?' It was obvious that he didn't like what she was becoming. The memory came to her in a peculiar form, like a black-and-white photograph taken from a third perspective. She saw herself sitting at the kitchen table and Christopher, his expressive hands arrested in the air like a shop-window dummy. It was a desperately sad image.

'What's the matter with you?' She repeated his words

out loud and suddenly she was besieged by doubt. 'I don't know,' she whispered. 'I really don't know.'

Christopher waited until he was alone in the house before he telephoned Amanda Ogilvy. There was always a chance that Simon would answer, but there was nothing he could do about that. As he listened to the ringing tone, he was conscious of a fluttering sensation in his stomach. He was relieved when Amanda's voice sounded in the receiver. Their conversation was light in tone and he fancied that her frequent laughter was uncharacteristically girlish and, perhaps, somewhat nervous. 'Your book,' he said. 'When shall I bring it over?'

'Just a minute.' She put the phone down and went to consult her diary. Christopher could hear an aggressively discordant toccata being played on a piano. He thought of his friend seated at the keyboard, engrossed in his music, oblivious. Amanda returned and said, 'How about tomorrow morning?'

'Yes,' Christopher replied. 'That would be fine.'

'Ten thirty?'

'Yes. Ten thirty.'

The following day he scraped the bristles off his chin with a razor and applied a little too much aftershave.

Subsequently, he drove to Muswell Hill, where he parked his car – not outside the Ogilvy residence, but in an adjacent side street. Fortunately, there were no twitching curtains.

Christopher pressed the doorbell and some chimes sounded inside the house. He listened for a piano, but couldn't hear anything apart from the birds and the constant low rumble of London traffic. Amanda had decorated the bay window with coloured transfers, just like those he had seen at The Earth Exchange – two mandalas and a CND peace symbol. She opened the door and invited him in, but it was only when the door was closed that she offered him her cheek to kiss. He handed her the book. She took it, thanked him for taking the trouble, and put it on a shelf.

'Do you fancy a coffee?' Amanda chirped.

'Yes, thanks,' he replied.

On entering the kitchen, she said, 'Simon's got a rehearsal today. He won't be back until this evening.'

'Right,' said Christopher.

An hour later they were in bed together.

When they had finished making love they rolled apart, hot and needing to cool down. A fan, placed on a chair by the window, was rattling loudly but having no effect on the temperature. Christopher turned to look at Amanda.

She was lying on her back with her eyes closed, her arms thrown above her head and her legs spread. Her dusky skin was coated in a film of perspiration that gave it an appealing, smooth sheen. He found the ampleness of her body satisfying. He liked the slight bulge above her waist, the generous girth of her upper thighs, and her breasts which, even when deflated by the redistributive force of gravity, still retained a residual curvature. Her pubic hair was thick, fleecy and remarkably black – a black so intense that it fascinated him.

The room was hazy and humid.

Amanda lit a cigarette and let clouds of smoke rise up from her mouth in silky, braided columns. Even though the curtains were drawn, the light was strong enough to penetrate the material. Everything was bathed in a decadent, reddish luminosity.

A conversation of sorts began: a rather superficial conversation about what they were both going to do later that afternoon. They were not ready to discuss implications, consequences. It was far too early. Christopher asked for a cigarette and when he drew on the filter the nicotine rush made him shiver with pleasure.

After a lengthy silence Amanda said, 'I suppose that counts as unfinished business.'

'What?'

'You know – the beach.'

'How do you mean, unfinished?'

'Well, we didn't get very far last time, did we?'

'What?'

She repositioned herself so she could see him more clearly. 'We didn't get very far,' she repeated.

'Far enough. Isn't *all the way* far enough?'

She smiled. 'God, you must have been stoned.' She rolled off the bed and stood up; the sight of her hair tumbling down her back and the loveliness of her buttocks stopped him from responding. Amanda slipped her arms through the sleeves of a kimono and left the room.

Later, in the car driving home, Christopher wondered what she had meant. They *had* gone all the way. He could remember, albeit dimly now, the warmth of her moist interior, made inordinately exciting because the sea that they had been standing in was cold. The contrast had produced an extraordinary amplification of sensitivity. He could remember the moonlight on her wet shoulders, her husky groans close to his ear. Amanda was flattering herself. Perhaps she wasn't as robust as she thought. It wasn't he who had been heinously stoned, but her. Yes, that was the explanation. It must be. Nevertheless, as Christopher pressed his foot to the floor and accelerated down Hampstead Lane, the idea that they both possessed conflicting memories of the same event made him feel strangely uncomfortable.

Christopher felt nervous in the presence of his wife. Her powers of intuition worried him. When, all those years ago, they had driven down to the villa near Cannes, Christopher had been amazed by Laura's map-reading skills. Her directions were faultless. In due course he had noticed that she wasn't really looking at the map at all, but making consistently correct guesses nevertheless. It had amused him at the time, although now, he supposed, he would find such behaviour rather irritating – in the same way that he now found her ability to guess what he was searching for rather irritating. He avoided Laura for the rest of the day and informed her over a hurried supper that he intended to work late. In fact, he spent the remainder of the evening listening to French piano music and thinking about Amanda.

It was past midnight before his mawkish reverie came to an end. Still disinclined to go anywhere near Laura, Christopher considered how he might busy himself, and, judging the pin-drop hush of the house to be propitious, he decided to record more spirit voices. Making the usual appeal to 'unseen friends', he let a tape run for ten minutes before playing it back. There was nothing, not even a distant whisper. A second attempt was equally disappointing; yet he persevered, doggedly inviting the 'unseen friends' to communicate. On the third attempt he allowed the tape to run for twenty minutes before pressing 'rewind' and 'play'.

The voice that he subsequently heard was perfectly clear; so clear, in fact, that he started and looked over his shoulder. It seemed inconceivable that such clarity could be achieved in the absence of a living body, vibrating vocal cords, a tongue and teeth. Moreover, his bewilderment was compounded by the tonal quality of a voice that was entirely different to anything he had heard before. The treble register was so unexpected that several seconds had elapsed before Christopher realized he was listening to a child, a girl of about seven years of age – or so he estimated. 'Now I lay me down to sleep, I pray the Lord my soul to keep.' The recording was also unusually long. 'If I shall die before I wake, I pray the Lord my soul to take.' A pause was followed by a solemn 'Amen.' Christopher continued listening, alert, until the rev counter showed that the tape had been running for twenty minutes. The prayer was the only communication.

He played it back several times, noticing additional

details with each repetition. The child spoke in a pronounced cockney accent and had difficulty articulating the letter R. Between the first and second couplets she inhaled, causing some phlegm to rattle in her lungs. Her final 'Amen' was oddly despairing. It wouldn't be necessary to clean up the recording as every syllable was distinct. Even something of a background acoustic had survived transmission from the spirit realm – a slight echo.

As Christopher listened to the prayer he became increasingly excited. He had been struggling with the problem of how 'The Speech of Shadows' was going to reach its climax, but now he could see what needed to be done. All of the other voices would fall away, leaving only one voice. The girl's delivery was so affecting and the words of the prayer so apt, he couldn't help thinking that the spirits approved of his project and were helping him to realize his creative vision. Heady with inspiration, Christopher imagined that he might have been, in a sense, chosen, and that his art might ultimately fulfil some higher purpose. His skull became crowded with possibilities: vast soundscapes, rolling waves of harmony, fundamentals produced by the motion of stars; expanding nebulae, nurseries of light, cosmic orchestration. He couldn't operate the controls fast enough. He introduced the voice of the girl into the mix and the effect was thrilling.

The sky was beginning to brighten but he wasn't tired. Indeed, he hadn't felt quite so good since the early days of his career when he often worked through the night. He felt invigorated, confident, invincible. Even when the sky had turned fully blue he was still refining harmonies and repositioning the faders. It wasn't until he heard Laura getting up that he looked at his watch and conceded that the heaviness in his limbs must be fatigue. He closed his eyes and when he looked at his watch again two hours had passed.

After breakfast he tried to resume where he had left off, but something had changed. Fleeting images of Amanda's body kept distracting him. They flashed into his mind like a pornographic slideshow. Arousal made him restless, agitated, and he couldn't settle. Every time he tried to develop a new idea, he was distracted by ghostly recollections of caresses and kisses, and he was returned to the ruby half-light of Amanda's bedroom. He wanted her to hear his new composition.

Abandoning the pretence of industry, he left his studio and descended the stairs.

'I'm going for a walk,' he shouted.

From somewhere in the house – he wasn't quite sure where – Laura called back, 'What about lunch?'

'I'm not hungry.'

Outside, the warm air smelt faintly of burning wood – the subtle fragrance of a log placed on dying embers. He crossed the soft, yielding tarmac and followed a winding pathway through the trees. A carpet of dry leaves crunched underfoot. Even the leaves on the bushes crumbled like wafers as he brushed past. Christopher pressed on until he joined a wider path that led to a Victorian viaduct. Tiny flying creatures clouded the air and it became necessary to bat them away with his hands. When he leaned over the iron railing to look down, he saw that the water level of the lake below had dropped, exposing steep banks of cracked mud. The still surface was covered with algae and resembled a sheet of emerald.

He thought about the music he had composed in the night and felt a frisson of pleasure. Once again, he began to fantasize about concerts and interviews and appearances on radio arts programmes. He remembered Loxley talking about Maybury – *a bitter, rather conceited man, who believed that he had never been given the recognition he deserved.* It was a terrible thing, to be overlooked.

Christopher entered another area of woodland and continued until he emerged at the foot of Parliament Hill.

His climb to the top was arduous and on the way he noticed something very unusual. The English were keen sun worshippers and rarely missed an opportunity to soak up its rays. Yet the slopes of the hill were empty, a wasteland of bleached dead grass. The sun was so strong it felt sickening, like an aggressive medical treatment that would make one's hair fall out.

When Christopher reached the summit he stopped to catch his breath. He was panting and his shirt was sticky with sweat. Beyond the heath and its hinterland of high-rise housing, the whole of central London was submerged beneath a layer of pollution, a horizontal brown strip that shadowed the horizon. St Paul's Cathedral was the only significant landmark distinguishable in the haze. He couldn't find the slim cylinder of the Post Office Tower because it was hidden behind a bush. A low-flying passenger jet flew overhead, the roar of its engines creating an awful din. It banked and glinted before veering off to the west.

Looking south once again, he saw a figure ascending the hill. Even at two hundred yards the mop of bright orange hair was conspicuous and vivid. An irregular, limping gait was also apparent. Christopher watched and felt an increasing sense of unease as the figure got closer. It was a man, a young man, whose limbs were extremely thin and wiry. There was something about his step suggestive of a manikin made from pipe cleaners and animated by stop-motion photography. His labouring ascent continued and the gap between them diminished. The youth was dressed so bizarrely, Christopher assumed that he must be a psychiatric patient: a ripped T-shirt held together with safety pins, long chains hanging down from beneath the hem, tight, tapered jeans and big military boots. A razor dangled from his left ear in lieu of an earring and around his wrist he wore a thick leather band festooned with sharp metal studs. The youth paused a few feet in front of Christopher and took a swig from a can. His mean, slit eyes were full of menace.

It seemed fitting that this young man had dragged himself up the hill from the direction of the city, the great, murky sprawl sweltering beneath its blanket of bad chemicals. He was like a new life form, an urban monster that had spontaneously arisen out of the primordial soup of London's broiling atmosphere. Christopher realized it was extremely unwise to stare, but he was fascinated. How old was this juvenile horror? Seventeen, possibly sixteen; certainly still young enough to be plagued by a disfiguring outbreak of suppurating acne. His ugly expression promised violence and Christopher tensed up. The backdrop of high-rise housing in the middle distance reminded Christopher that this part of the heath abutted several districts where squalor and casual aggression were commonplace.

The boy sneered, tossed the beer can aside and lunged forward. Christopher raised his arms, a clumsy warding off; however, his spastic gesticulations proved entirely redundant when his presumptive adversary swerved away. 'Wanker,' the boy growled before hawking with bitter vehemence. A moment later the lame adolescent was dragging his leg down the scorched incline on the other side of the hill in the direction of Highgate.

Christopher let out a sigh of relief, but when he bowed his head he saw a thick string of mucus attached to his linen trousers. 'Little shit!' He picked up an empty crisp bag and used it to remove the sputum, a task that proved remarkably difficult. For the next twenty minutes he sat on a bench, recovering from his unfortunate encounter and gazing out over a landscape of post-apocalyptic emptiness.

On his way home he discovered a dead dog. It was an elderly, overweight mongrel that must have dehydrated. Flies were crawling in and out of its mouth and buzzing around its head. 'Jesus,' said Christopher, almost reverentially. The freakish weather was making London unrecognizable. The last time he'd seen a dead animal in a public place was during a holiday in Sicily.

The house was silent when he stepped into the hallway. He wondered whether Laura had gone out for a walk too, but then he spied the pushchair parked beneath the stairs. He went to the kitchen and drank water directly from the tap. It was difficult to stop once he'd started, and he carried on gulping until his stomach felt uncomfortably distended. He re-entered the hallway and craned around the drawing room door. Laura was standing by the French windows and she turned to look at him. He hadn't made any noise and it was odd how she seemed to have sensed him there. She then provided him with the answer to the question he was about to ask: 'Faye's upstairs, asleep. The heat is exhausting her.'

'It's exhausting all of us,' he replied.

As he was about to withdraw, Laura protested: 'No, don't go. We need to talk.'

Surely he hadn't been found out already? How could that have happened? He thought of Amanda. How well did he know her, really? Doubts began to multiply. Had Amanda spoken to Laura? Or had she confessed to Simon and was it Simon who had called? His mind became a chaotic hubbub. Laura saw that something was wrong and asked, 'What is it?'

'Nothing,' he replied, stepping into the room. 'I think I overdid it on the heath, that's all. I shouldn't have gone out when it's like this.' He fanned his face to emphasize the point.

'Can we sit?'

'Sure.'

Laura looked anxious. She placed her hands in her lap and they moved against each other as if she was washing them very slowly. Christopher noticed that her eyelids were rimmed with pink and her cheeks were puffy. It was obvious that she had been crying.

'Well?' His voice was a dry croak.

'Chris . . .' She offered him a faint, tormented smile, but seemed unable to find the language to express her thoughts.

'Yes?'

'I'm not happy here.'

'What do you mean?'

'I'm not happy here . . . in this house. I want to move.'

For a few seconds he experienced an airy lightness that threatened to become laughter; however, this euphoria soon melted away when the meaning of his wife's words finally sunk in. 'I'm sorry?'

'I want to move.'

'We can't. We don't have enough money. It cost us a fortune getting this place sorted out; we can't move again, just like that!' He snapped his fingers in such a way as to suggest that the satisfaction of her wish would require an expedient as outlandish as stage magic. 'Why on earth do you want to move?'

'I told you. I'm not happy here.'

He knew that she took pills. Didn't everybody these days? Especially women. Pills to lift you up, pills to let you down. He had tried to talk to her about her 'moods' but on every occasion she had underplayed their significance. 'Hormones,' she had replied dismissively. As a result, Christopher had consigned her 'hormonal problem' to a category of female biological mysteries traditionally ignored by men.

'Moving house won't make you happy.' He paused to select his words with greater care. 'What I mean is . . . if you're unhappy, then maybe that's because of other things. You can't blame it on the house. Maybe you should see the doctor.'

'He doesn't listen. I told you.'

'All right, see another doctor – someone private, someone in Harley Street.'

'I thought you said we didn't have any money.'

'Harley Street doctors are expensive, sure. But not as expensive as moving home.'

'Chris, I know what I'm asking is a lot—'

'No. No.' He couldn't allow her to continue. She was

being ridiculous. 'It's just not possible, OK?' Laura removed a piece of dark fluff from her smock and stared blankly at her feet. 'You need to find the right specialist,' Christopher added.

Laura looked up again and Christopher watched sunlight collecting in her eyes until they turned gold. 'You want me to see a psychiatrist. That's what you want, isn't it?'

'No, I said you need to find the right *specialist*. If you think that your hormones have got something to do with it, then go and see an endocrinologist. But if you did need to see a psychiatrist . . . if that's appropriate, why not? As long as you get the right treatment and get better.' She had been such a striking woman. She had looked like a goddess. Now only her eyes attested to her former divinity. Christopher took one of her hands and squeezed it. He noticed that several of her fingernails were torn and ragged. She would never have been so remiss in the past; her nails were always filed to perfection and expertly painted with varnish. 'You haven't been yourself, have you? Not for a long time, probably not since Faye was born.'

She responded as if she hadn't really been listening to him. 'I want to move. And please don't pretend you don't know what I'm talking about.'

'Well, I don't know what you're talking about,' said Christopher.

'I'm worried about Faye.'

'The doctor said she was fine.'

'I've got a bad feeling.'

'That's because you're not well, not because of the house.'

She wanted to tell him more: she wanted to tell him about her recurring nightmare and Faye's drawing, and how she had seen correspondences between them. She wanted to tell him about how she had felt something terrible, something cold and unspeakable, when she had stood by the stone cherub that Sue had discovered in the garden. She wanted to tell him about the strong intuitions she had had throughout her life, and how she had always ignored them or suppressed them because they had frightened her. But she couldn't say any of these things, because the thoughts were coming into her head too fast and if she opened her mouth the words would come tumbling out and she knew that she would sound hysterical. So instead she said a single sentence as calmly as she could. 'Please stop recording those voices.'

Christopher shook his head. 'No. You can't expect me to do that. I haven't felt so excited about a piece in years.'

The previous exceptionally productive night was still fresh in his memory.

'Please, Chris. You're out of your depth. It's making me very uneasy . . . and I'm worried about Faye.'

Christopher withdrew his hand. Laura could feel his anger building and saw his expression turning ugly as he struggled to control himself. His efforts failed. 'Just when I find a really worthwhile project, a project guaranteed to make people take me seriously again, you want me to drop it. Well, isn't that just typical!'

Laura turned away as though he had slapped her across the face. How was it *typical*? she wondered. There were no precedents for the conversation they were having. Christopher was snorting like an enraged bull. 'Listen to yourself. Just consider for a moment what you're demanding. You want to move. You want me to stop working on my new piece. Anything else I can do for you? Any other *reasonable* requests?' He paused before continuing even more emphatically. 'We don't have the money to move and I don't see why I should stop working on my piece. I know you're worried about Faye, but that's another issue. You're imagining things!'

Ordinarily, Christopher wasn't a man prone to outbursts. Consequently, it wasn't long before he was feeling slightly ashamed. 'Look,' he started up again, his voice softer. 'I'm sorry, I shouldn't have shouted. But what you're suggesting . . . it doesn't make sense. It's all too drastic. Why don't you see someone and maybe all this,' he continued, making a sweeping gesture that invited Laura to consider the ornate fireplace and the plush furnishings, 'won't seem *so* bad. Please?'

Laura was still looking away from him. 'Just leave me alone for a minute, will you?' This was not said as a rebuke. There was no hostility in her voice. She was simply expressing a genuine need for solitude.

'OK,' he whispered. 'I'll be upstairs.' And with that, he stood up and walked to the door, pausing before his departure to look back at his wife as she curled into a compact ball and rested her head on a cushion. The tableau was so pitiful he was overcome with regret.

Surprisingly, Christopher found that he was able to compose. Sometimes emotional upheaval made concentration impossible, but at other times it seemed to facilitate an escape from reality. The creative process became a refuge, a place of safety or healing. He worked for almost an hour before the telephone rang. Laura didn't answer it so he went down to the bedroom and picked up the extension.

'Christopher. It's Henry. How are you?' They made a little inconsequential conversation before Henry said, 'I spoke to Mike Judd today, and he'd like to hear something soon. What shall I tell him?'

'The deadline isn't up yet.'

'True. But it isn't terribly distant either.'

'There are a few more scenes that I need to work on.'

'Yes, but if Judd wanted to pop over and listen to what you've done so far, that wouldn't be a problem, would it?'

'It isn't convenient, Henry.'

'There isn't anything wrong, is there?'

'No. Nothing's wrong.'

'You see, Judd's getting a bit jittery.'

'I'll be finished on time.'

'Will you? Because if you're in any doubt—'

'I'm not.'

'Any doubt at all, it would be advisable to give me advance warning so I can launch a precautionary charm offensive.'

'You won't have to do that.'

'Good. How did you get on with Bill Loxley, by the way?'

'We got on very well indeed. He was extremely knowledgeable.'

'Knew about your man then, did he?'

'Yes.'

'Extraordinary.'

'Thanks for putting me in touch with him, Henry. I appreciate it.'

'Where did you take him to lunch?'

'A little Italian place near Russell Square – a bit dilapidated but the food is always very good.'

'Perfect. Listen, there's a chap pressing his face against the window so I think I'd better see what he wants before he gives my new secretary a fright. She's a bit neurotic and I haven't got a clue what to do if she faints.'

'OK.'

'I'll tell Judd that everything's under control.'

'Yes, you do that, Henry.'

'Bye, Chris.'

'Bye, Henry.'

Later, the door of the studio opened and Laura appeared holding Faye. 'OK,' she said, as if she were continuing the conversation that they had had earlier and there had been no interval. 'I'll talk to Martha.'

'Martha?'

'The psychotherapist I met at the bookshop in Islington. I'll ask her for some names. I'll try to get some help, but if I'm still unhappy at the end of the year, I want to move.'

Christopher got up and walked over to his wife. He put his arms around her and his daughter and hugged them both before kissing Laura on the lips and rubbing his nose into Faye's curls. 'OK,' he said. Christopher observed their reflection in the window and it struck him that they looked like an ideal family in a TV commercial. But at the same time, he understood that although all three of them were touching, their points of contact were few.

'I love you,' he said to Laura. It was the first time he had said those words in over a month and they made his betrayal complete.

Even with the curtains drawn the bedroom was already full of light by five o'clock in the morning. Simon Ogilvy was able to study the network of fine red lines on his wife's back at leisure. She was still fast asleep. It was not the first time he had seen such marks and he knew what they represented. Over the years he had learned how to read his wife's body like a book. He could even tell her lovers' particular preferences by the location of the bruises. The symmetrical patterns of discolouration positioned above the kidneys showed clearly where she had been grabbed from behind. How ironic. And then there were the more obvious tokens of her infidelity: the excessive use of perfume, coinciding with the appearance of her most expensive underwear in the laundry basket.

Who was it this time? he wondered. A colleague, perhaps, or one of her students? He could see the attraction of the latter. Students were never around long enough to cause problems. After completing their A levels, they obligingly left the capital for university towns and were generally never heard of again. All very convenient.

Did he care? Yes, he did. Was he jealous? Yes, in a way. But how could he object to her adultery? He had deceived her as much as she had deceived him. More so, in fact.

Could their marriage last for much longer? It seemed improbable. It was coming apart just like everything else was in the intolerable heat. Surfaces were slipping, edges curling. Whatever had been stuck together was loosening and separating, falling open to reveal stringy cobwebs of goo.

And what would happen when Amanda finally lost patience with his sterile affections? He had imagined and reimagined the scenario time and time again. Amanda packing her bags, the front door slamming shut, the sound of the car engine fading into the night. What then? Would he have the courage to be himself? Or would he continue to inhabit a world of lies.

Ogilvy got out of bed and walked to the window. He tugged the curtain aside and blinked at the harsh brilliance of a vindictive sun.

August 1976

Christopher stared up at the screen and watched the silent, steady progress of the android. It stopped and the camera zoomed in for a close-up of the machine's eyes. The glowing red irises swivelled to the left and then to the right, suggesting suspicion.

Why had he lied to Henry? He had been working intermittently on the score of *Android Insurrection* but not enough to ensure its completion before the deadline. As a rule, Christopher was a consummate professional, but on this occasion he had allowed himself to become completely preoccupied by 'The Speech of Shadows'. He had spent far too much time recording the voices of the dead, clarifying their messages, and devising new effects to give their communications a fitting context. If he made a concerted effort, there was a slim chance that he would be able to finish the score of *Android Insurrection* by the end of the month; however, he resented having to work on anything other than his 'serious' piece.

Christopher forced himself to concentrate on the action.

The android was firing a laser gun and pursuing a child through a warren of metal corridors. Christopher had patched the routing matrix and adjusted the control-panel settings of the VCS3 synthesizer in order to produce a repetitive beat that resembled the noise of helicopter rotors. He moved the small joystick and altered the quality of the sound, removing some of its harsher registers. It was an acceptable effect, one that created a sense of urgency, but an element was missing: an ingredient that would express the child's terror.

Christopher got up from his chair and walked over to a shelf on which a number of slim boxes had been placed in a neat row. Each one had a handwritten label on the side and he ran his finger along the containers until he found the word 'scream'. He opened the box, took out the spool, and wound it onto the Akai 4000DS, after which he pressed 'play' and listened. A child's scream filled the studio. It was Faye's scream, the scream that he had inadvertently taped in June when his daughter had stepped on broken glass in the kitchen. He recorded his improvisations on the synthesizer and then introduced Faye's scream into the mix – a lazy way to heighten emotion, but effective nevertheless.

When Christopher played the soundtrack and the video clip simultaneously he was surprised by the result. Even though he had felt uninspired, he had managed to create an accompaniment that was genuinely disturbing. He congratulated himself, decided that a reward was in order, and went downstairs to the kitchen where he took a beer from the fridge. He held the cold can against his forehead for a few moments before tugging the ring pull. The noise it made was like a human exhalation.

Laura had left the radio on. For as long as Christopher could remember, the ten o'clock news had been heralded by the portentous chimes of Big Ben, but it was now introduced by the less dramatic expedient of the Greenwich Time Signal. This was because Big Ben, the clock that once regulated a prosperous global empire, had broken down. Christopher took a swig of beer and laughed; it was such an apposite symbol for the demise of Great Britain, almost too just, almost too contrived to be accepted as an example of mere happenstance. Its precise irony suggested divine intervention, the existence of a frivolous God prone to displays of sharp, merciless wit.

The newsreader began his dismal litany. And *how* dismal! It was difficult to believe what was being said. The country was bankrupt and the government had had to go cap in hand to the IMF to beg for a £2.3 billion rescue package. A commentator pointed out that such a large sum of money would not be given unconditionally and that demands for drastic cuts in public expenditure were inevitable. 'It will be the IMF, not the government, who will determine domestic policy from now on.' And there was even more bad news to follow: a report on the British army's attempt to regain control of no-go areas in Belfast, Derry and Newry. Christopher considered the term 'no-go areas'. When the drastic financial cuts imposed by the IMF began to take effect, would there be 'no-go areas' in London too? He gulped the remainder of his beer and crushed the can in his hand. It was oddly satisfying, the illusion of superhuman strength. His mind wandered but he was still dimly aware of a continuous stream of grim announcements. A change in the newsreader's tone signalled a final, lighter item, which concerned the imminent West End opening of the controversial musical *Jesus Christ Superstar*. Again, Christopher laughed. If ever the country needed a saviour it was now.

Christopher switched the radio off and dropped his empty can into the bin. Flies were hovering above the fruit bowl and the sink smelt of drains. He heard footsteps and when he turned, he saw Laura standing in the doorway. She was wearing one of her baggy smocks, cotton trousers and a pair of clogs. 'I'm going to bed.'

'OK,' Christopher replied. 'I'll be up in a minute.'

'OK.' The heat was so enervating that Laura was obliged to push against the architrave in order to gain the necessary impetus for movement. She floated out of view like a tropical fish in an aquarium – languid, spiritless. As soon as Laura had gone Christopher went to the drawing room and collected a packet of cigarettes that he had hidden in the bureau. He let himself out into the garden and walked around to the side entrance. His eyes had not adapted to the dark and he tripped over Ellis's old ladder. He grazed his hand on the wall and cursed under his breath. It felt faintly absurd, at his age, to be sneaking around like a naughty schoolboy behind a bicycle shed, but he was sure that, when embarking on an affair, it was prudent to conceal *any* changes of behaviour, however minor. Anything might arouse suspicions.

Christopher lit a cigarette and the act of smoking had the effect of making him feel in some curious, abstract way closer to Amanda. He wanted to be with her again, he wanted to observe her mannerisms and listen to her pleasing, husky voice. Already, lust was becoming complicated by deeper feelings. Where would it end? An important question, but he had no appetite for dissection and analysis at that moment. He drew on his cigarette and his shoulders relaxed. Amanda had said that Simon was going to be away the following Tuesday. 'Do you want to come again?' she had said, straight-faced, but perfectly aware that her words possessed two meanings. 'Yes,' he had replied. 'I'd love to come again.' He counted the days that remained before he would see her and found the exercise consoling.

There was a rustling sound in the air, the whispering of desiccated long grass swayed by a gentle breeze. At first, Christopher thought nothing of it, but its persistence made him feel vaguely uneasy. He wasn't able to identify the cause of his disquiet, until it occurred to him that the night was hot and exceptionally still. There *was* no breeze, yet the long grass continued to whisper. He emerged from his place of concealment and, as he did so, the rustling suddenly stopped. Christopher froze and stared into the darkness. The light from the drawing room allowed him to see as far as the orchard, but beyond that he could discern nothing. He stepped off the terrace and waded out into the garden, his trousers catching on the prickly shrubs. It wasn't possible to go very far and he came to a halt in the middle of the lawn. He felt sure that he wasn't alone, that something was out there with him. Common sense dictated that it was an animal of some kind – perhaps the elusive fox that he had encountered before – and he was tempted to clap his hands loudly to make it startle and run, though he didn't want to attract Laura's attention. Christopher made his way back to the side entrance and disposed of his cigarette.

Again, a swishing sound suggested movement in the grass, but it was short-lived and by the time Christopher had returned to the garden, the silence was dense and fathomless. He crossed the terrace, looked out into the darkness one last time, then stepped back into the drawing room. Reaching out, he grasped the door handle and pulled hard. Displaced air made the curtains billow. The bolts were old-fashioned and he was reassured by their size and weight. As he fixed the upper bolt, he was troubled by a thought. *What if I've locked something inside, instead of outside?* He shook his head. Infidelity was a hard game to play. It had put his nerves on edge.

Laura opened her eyes and a few seconds passed before she achieved self-awareness. She seemed to coalesce out of nothingness, the parts of her personality gradually collecting around an indefinable core. When the process was complete, she guessed that she had been roused from sleep. Something was detectable at the boundary of sensation, something faint and vestigial, like the final iteration of an echo. Allowing her gaze to drop from the ceiling, she observed the orange-grey strip of luminescence that separated the curtains and guessed that it was still very early – one o'clock, perhaps? Her whole body was tense with expectation and she held her breath in order to listen.

When the voice came through the baby monitor, it was surprisingly loud and clear. 'Toys, toys, penny toys!' The speaker began his rhyme with incongruous gravity. 'Toys for girls and toys for boys. Toys for tots who scarce can crawl, toys for youngsters stout and tall.' Laura stretched her arm across the bed and rocked her husband's body. He responded with a grumble and an unconscious, inarticulate protest. 'That is how the toyman talks, as through London Town he walks.' The speaker paused before adding with decisive emphasis, 'Come, child. It is time.' Laura heard Faye make a pathetic mewling noise and then there was silence, a silence so absolute that it seemed as if the whole world had been swallowed up.

'Chris!' Laura gripped her husband's shoulder and gave it a violent shake.

His grumbling stopped and he said, 'What? What is it?'

'I heard a voice again.'

'OK.' He was still half asleep so she prodded him with a rigid finger.

Christopher grunted and anger made his speech more intelligible: 'Christ. That hurt.'

'Then wake up!' She switched the lamp on and got out of bed.

Christopher shielded his eyes from the light and asked, 'Where are you going?'

'To check on Faye – to see if she's all right.'

Come, child. It is time.

Laura removed the scissors from her bedside cabinet. Even though she accepted that whoever it was that had spoken those words was dead, she did not have the courage to enter the nursery without arming herself. The clarity of the voice suggested embodiment, the possibility of physical threat.

'What are you doing with those?' Christopher asked.

'I'm scared.'

She watched her husband's expression change. Exasperation and irritation were replaced by anxiety and then something close to alarm. It was obvious what he was thinking. He was thinking that she was mad.

'Look,' Christopher said, making downward movements with his hands. 'Let's try to keep calm.' Even though she was in a distressed state, Laura still registered the condescending inclusivity of his language. 'You don't need those scissors,' he added, venturing a false, mollifying smile.

'I'm going to check on Faye.'

'Put the scissors away. You heard a voice, that's all. A voice.' She shook her head and turned to leave. Christopher called after her – 'Laura?'– and when she didn't stop he vented his frustration by striking the mattress with a clenched fist.

The distance from the bedroom to the nursery was relatively short, but to Laura it seemed to stretch out before her, its elasticity negating her forward momentum. She was seized by a visceral sense of foreboding that located itself in her gut; her legs became weak and she struggled to make progress. She groped awkwardly at the landing light switch and thrust the door open. Instinctively, she scanned the corners and recesses to see if there was anyone – or anything – lurking in the shadows. Then, when she was satisfied that she was alone, she wheeled around to face the cot.

At first, her mind failed to accommodate the evidence. What she saw was so wrong, so impossible, that it was immediately rejected and reclassified as an optical illusion. She flicked the wall switch and even when the nursery flooded with light and her initial impression was confirmed, she still couldn't absorb the truth. She leaned over the cot rail and ripped the sheet aside, as if Faye's concealment beneath its awful flatness was an actual possibility. A few moments of puzzled silence followed, before Laura's mouth opened wide and she produced a sustained wail.

An instant later, Christopher stumbled into the room shouting, 'What is it?' Laura pointed at the empty cot. 'Where's Faye?' He had asked the question so many times it sounded much the same as usual, confined by habit within narrow emotional limits. Nevertheless, when he repeated the question, his voice quivered with desperate urgency. 'Where's Faye?' Laura was mute and shaking, her face contorted to such an extent she was barely recognizable. Christopher dashed past his wife and leaned out of the open window.

'Is she . . .' Laura choked on a sob.

'I don't know. It's too dark to see anything.'

'She's never climbed out before,' Laura cried. 'Never. She's too small.'

Christopher moved away from the window. He pushed past his wife and leapt down the stairs, taking them two at a time. In the drawing room, he snapped the bolts back and opened the French windows. Suddenly, he balked at the prospect of what he might discover. He paused, fought to control the revulsion that made his mouth taste of bile, and forced himself to proceed. The light from the drawing room was sufficient to illuminate the terrace and he sighed with relief when he saw that nothing was crumpled on the flagstones – no broken body, no shiny black lake of blood. But his relief was swiftly succeeded by bewilderment. Christopher looked up and saw Laura craning out of the nursery. 'She's not here,' he said. Laura shook her head and drew back into the house. The night was humid and Christopher used the sleeve of his pyjama jacket to wipe the sweat from his brow. 'Where is she?' he said out loud. 'Where the fuck has she gone?' His mind was clouded by shapeless apprehension.

Laura heard Christopher's voice floating up from below. She dropped the scissors, charged out of the nursery and began opening doors and looking into cupboards. 'Faye, for God's sake,' she called. 'Where are you?' In her distraught state, the house seemed infinite and she found herself reliving her nightmare. Spaces multiplied and receded as in a hall of mirrors. The house seemed to expand in every direction and she ran and ran until she became confused and disorientated.

Christopher found his wife pacing around the empty room on the top floor.

'Laura?' She seemed unaware of his presence and he

had to stand in front of her to make her stop. He grabbed her arms, pinned them to her sides and forced her to remain still. 'Laura?'

'What are we going to do?' she moaned.

'I don't know.'

'What are we going to do?' she screamed, demanding an answer.

The ferocity of her gaze became intolerable and he looked away. She shook herself free of his grip and stepped backwards. Running her hands through her disordered hair, she grimaced and made helpless gestures. Then she began to wail once again; however, this second outburst of anguish was very different from the first. This time, the wail was pitched low and suggested a painful drawing out. She doubled over, clutched her stomach and bellowed like a dying animal.

Detective Inspector Barnes was a thick-set man with swollen features, which appeared unfinished, hastily shaped, like a sculptor's preliminary experiment with clay. His hair was closely cropped and when he spoke the stresses in his sentences were subtly displaced, suggesting a childhood spent in the North East. He was accompanied by a skeletal but excessively polite assistant, who said very little and scribbled continuously in a notebook. The sound of heavy footsteps could be heard crossing the ceiling. On the first floor, a team of officers were taking photographs and attempting to obtain fingerprints. Christopher held his wife's hand but it was limp and lifeless.

'You woke up,' said the inspector, 'and you heard a voice coming through the baby monitor.' Laura nodded. 'Did you recognize it?'

She hesitated before answering. A fleeting change in her expression convinced the inspector that she was about to reply in the affirmative and he leaned forward, his posture betraying his presumption, but the light in her eyes dimmed and she replied, 'No.'

'Are you sure?'

'Yes.' Laura's assertion was not delivered with confidence.

The inspector glanced at his assistant before saying, 'A man, was it?'

'Yes, it was a man's voice.'

'What kind of voice?' Laura seemed confused by the question and the inspector qualified his enquiry. 'Young, old . . . any trace of an accent?'

'Not a young voice. Middle-aged, perhaps. And there wasn't any accent, no. He sounded quite . . . refined.'

'Refined?' the inspector repeated, surprised.

'Well . . . perhaps not refined . . . educated.'

'What did he say?'

'He recited a poem about a man . . . a man who sells toys. And then he said, "Come, child. It is time."' Laura shuddered and closed her eyes. A tear seeped out and ran down her face. When she opened her eyes again the inspector was observing her with a calm, steady gaze.

'What happened then?'

'I heard Faye – my daughter . . . she made a sort of whimper and I woke my husband.'

The inspector addressed Christopher: 'You didn't hear this voice?'

'No,' Christopher replied. 'How could I? I was asleep.'

The inspector spoke to Laura again: 'How much of the poem did you hear?'

'A few lines,' Laura replied.

'Can you remember any of them?'

'Toys, toys, penny toys, some for girls and some for boys.' Her brow wrinkled as she tried to recollect more. 'Some for tots that scarce can talk . . . this is what the toy man says . . . as through London Town he walks.' She shook her head. 'I'm sorry. I can't get it exactly.'

'Had you ever heard the poem before?'

'No. Never.'

'So what happened next?'

'I got out of bed and found a pair of scissors.'

'Scissors?' His head tilted to the side.

'So I could defend myself.'

'I see. And what were *you* doing, sir?'

Christopher sighed. 'Actually, I wasn't sure it was the right thing to do. I might have suggested to Laura that she put the scissors down.'

'But she didn't.'

'No. She ran out of the room and the next thing I knew she was screaming.'

'There was nobody in the nursery,' Laura interjected. 'And when I looked in the cot . . .' Her chest heaved. 'When I looked in the cot Faye was gone.' Again, she closed her eyes.

'We'd left the window open,' Christopher continued, 'because of the heat. My first thought was that Faye had managed to get herself out of the cot and there'd been a dreadful accident. She's too small to do that really, but that's what I was thinking. I couldn't see the terrace – it was too dark – so I went downstairs to take a look.'

'And did you notice anything unusual?'

'No.'

'Or hear anything?'

'No.'

The inspector paused, squeezed his lower lip, and then asked, 'What was your daughter wearing?'

'I don't know. I can't remember.'

Laura opened her eyes and said, 'Cotton pyjamas.'

'Were they distinctive in any way – patterned?'

'Yes. They were white with little pink flowers.'

The inspector wanted to go over Laura's account several times. She repeated her answers, occasionally recalling some new, insignificant detail, but more often than not she simply duplicated what she had already said in a manner that became increasingly mechanical. Throughout the interview, she had felt the strain of maintaining a semblance of normality. She wanted to abandon all pretences and shout, 'No, no. This is wrong.' She wanted to tell the inspector about the voices; she wanted him to understand that there was more to Faye's abduction than he realized. Yet even though she was exhausted and numb with shock, she was still conscious of social pressures corralling her speech down acceptable channels of expression and she withheld her objections. Besides, what good would it do? Transparency would serve no purpose. Chris had said nothing about the voices. Even prior to the police's arrival, when there had been no necessity for them to collude in order to create an impression of soundness, he had been behaving as if their daughter's disappearance was completely unrelated to his activities. To Laura, this constituted the ultimate proof of her marginalization. Chris had demonstrated a growing tendency to dismiss her concerns and underplay the potential risks of dabbling with spirit communication. Perhaps he was in denial now, completely unable to accept that it would have been wise to heed her warnings.

Dawn was breaking and policemen with torches appeared in the garden. 'Excuse me,' said the detective. He got up from his chair and went to the French windows. After sliding the bolts aside he exited onto the terrace and was followed by his assistant.

The couple remained seated on the sofa, watching the inspector direct his team. They saw him pointing at the back wall and then at the gazebo. Some of the men were carrying shovels.

Christopher tried to get Laura to rest her head on his shoulder, but she resisted.

The house had gone very quiet and although they could see what was going on outside, they couldn't hear a thing. It was as if they had slipped out of time and were now isolated from the rest of humanity, trapped in a hellish moment from which there was no escape. They were touching, but the distance between them was immeasurable. The inspector disappeared from view for a few minutes and when he returned he called into the drawing room, 'Mr Norton?' His voice was a welcome reminder of reality. 'There's a ladder in the side entrance. Is that where you usually keep it?'

'Yes,' Christopher replied. 'Although it's not *my* ladder – it belongs to a builder. He left it here last year and never came back to pick it up.'

'Would you mind joining me, please? Your wife can stay where she is.'

Christopher followed the inspector round to the side entrance. The inspector pointed at the ladder.

'Has it been moved?'

'I don't think so.'

The inspector rubbed his chin. 'The side door was unlocked – did you know that?'

'We often leave it open. The Vale's usually very safe. It's like a village here.'

'If the abductor did use this ladder, it's odd that he should have troubled to put it back where he found it.' The inspector shook his head. 'Although that's not half as odd as reciting a poem.'

Christopher cleared his throat. 'I'm not sure that my wife did hear an intruder.'

The inspector turned sharply. 'Oh? Why do you say that?'

'I think she may have heard some sort of interference, a radio broadcast that was picked up by the monitor.'

'Is that possible?'

'I believe so.'

'How does it happen?'

'I'm not sure about the technical details. But a baby monitor is basically a receiver, isn't it?'

'Yes, I suppose . . . that makes sense. There wasn't enough time for an intruder to make an escape. Your wife heard a voice, woke you up, and a few seconds later you were both in the nursery. How could an intruder climb out of the window with a child and remove a ladder so quickly?'

'But my wife said she heard my daughter.'

'She heard *something*, I'm sure – more interference, perhaps?' The inspector offered Christopher a cigarette. Christopher took one and the inspector lit it for him before lighting his own. 'No,' he continued. 'By the time your wife woke up they were long gone.'

The two men stared down at the ladder as if prolonged scrutiny of its rotting rungs and rusted brackets might eventually yield some precious insight. Birds were singing, a frenzied chorus of tweets and chirps that suddenly became very loud. Shovels made contact with the earth.

'Why are you digging?' Christopher asked.

The inspector's face was blank. It was as though Christopher hadn't spoken. 'If you don't mind,' said the inspector, 'I'd like to ask you a personal question.'

'Go ahead.'

'Are you a wealthy man?'

'No. Far from it.'

'But you write music for films.'

'I did very well in the sixties, but recently things haven't been great. I don't get much work these days.'

'Your wife is a famous model.'

'She *was* a famous model, but not anymore. She gave it all up.'

'Even so,' the inspector grimaced, 'some might think a film composer and a retired fashion model were very well off.'

'There are richer people than us living in Hampstead.'

'I'm sure. But it's more a question of perception.'

Christopher blew out a cloud of cigarette smoke. All he could say was, 'Jesus Christ.'

'Perhaps you'd better get back inside,' said the inspector. 'Your wife . . .'

'Yes,' said Christopher, 'Of course.'

*

Inspector Barnes made off in the direction of an officer who had started digging by a row of bushes. He was a young man and stood to attention as his superior approached. The inspector nodded and the officer relaxed.

'Look at this, sir.' The young man pulled a branch aside, revealing a statue of a cherub.

'Is that all you've found?'

'Yes.'

'Nothing else?'

'No, sir. Well, you can't get very far – inside there, I mean. You'd get torn to pieces.' He let go of the branch.

The inspector looked at the ground and kicked it with the toe of his shoe. 'So what are you doing now?'

'Digging, sir.'

'Does the ground here look as though it's been recently disturbed?'

'The bushes have been cut back.'

'Indeed,' said Barnes. 'But the ground?' He stamped his foot on the baked earth.

The young man winced. 'No, sir. The soil isn't very loose.'

'Not very loose? I'd say it was like fucking concrete.' The inspector's regional accent became more pronounced when he swore. 'Now stop pissing about here and go and join Collins and Crane by the rockery.'

'Yes, sir,' said the young man, balancing his shovel on his shoulder like a rifle. 'I'll do that right away, sir.'

The inspector lit another cigarette and followed his subordinate.

Amanda and Simon were sitting in their customary positions at the kitchen table. Between them lay an open newspaper. They were both staring at a particular column of print with frozen, horrified expressions. The radio, sounding softly in the background, dignified their distress with a Chopin prelude of sublime majesty. When the final chord was struck Simon touched the newspaper and withdrew his hand quickly as if his fingers had been burnt. 'It's unbelievable,' he said. Then, after a lengthy pause, he repeated the same sentence an octave higher.

'What shall we do?' asked Amanda.

'I'm sorry?'

'What shall we do?'

'We can't do anything.' Simon threw his arms wide open. 'Can we?'

'Shouldn't we call them?'

'Call them? What would one say? I wouldn't know where to begin.' The radio announcer introduced another piece by Chopin – the Waltz in A minor. 'And would it be the right thing to do? Now, I mean.'

'I don't know.'

'I doubt it.'

'But we're their friends.'

'Do *you* want to call them?'

'No, I didn't say that.'

Neither felt equal to the challenge. They talked for some time, exchanging brief, nervous sentences that gave shape and substance to their inadequacy. Together they demarcated their disappointingly small emotional boundaries and furnished themselves with the perfect justification for leaving the telephone in its cradle: 'We could so easily do more harm than good.'

Simon shut the newspaper, made sure that the individual sheets were properly aligned, then folded it into a neat rectangle. It was like an act of containment.

'God,' said Amanda. 'It must be so terrible for them.'

'Unimaginable,' Simon agreed.

'And that poor child . . .'

'Don't.'

'I wonder where she is.'

'Don't. It's too awful to contemplate.'

Amanda found her cigarette lighter and waved the flame under a lump of cannabis. She broke a piece off and crumbled the scorched resin into a pile of tobacco. After constructing a makeshift filter out of a flap torn from a box of cornflakes, she rolled a joint, lit it, and inhaled deeply. Two jets of aromatic smoke poured from her nostrils and drifted across the tabletop. Simon, who only rarely indulged, held out his hand. He needed something. The first drag made him feel slightly sick, but the second began to unravel a knot of tension between his shoulder blades. He closed his eyes for a few moments and the Chopin seemed to become more prominent. The music invited him to enter its shady arbours and ornamented interior, to leave the world and its troubles behind. When he opened his eyes again he noticed that Amanda's shoulders were shaking.

Crying did not come easily to Amanda. The effort required to conceal her distress made her face unusually volatile. She seemed to explore the entire spectrum of feelings before her features hardened into an ugly grimace and tears coated her cheeks with greenish mascara.

Simon balanced the smouldering joint on the outer rim of an ashtray, rose from his seat, and walked around to Amanda's side of the table. In a hapless attempt to dispense comfort, he pulled her head against his crotch. Amanda remained there for a few seconds, more out of politeness than anything else, before pulling away. 'God,' she sniffed. 'I can't imagine what they must be going through.' Those were her words. But the causes of her distress were far more complex and confused.

Days passed, one blurring into another. Christopher and Laura waited for a ransom note to arrive in the post, but it never came. Inspector Barnes returned and his questions became increasingly oblique. He wanted to know more about Laura's estrangement from her parents; he wanted to know more about their friends and associates; he wanted to see passports, bank statements and other private documents. Moreover, he seemed to take an almost prurient interest in their domestic arrangements, the minutiae of their marriage. Who did the shopping? Who did the cleaning? Did they have a babysitter? How often did they go out together as a couple? He asked to see their bedroom once more, and stood by the window staring at the disordered sheets and eiderdown. Christopher found his presence discomfiting and invasive. The harsh sunlight threw the inspector's lumpy features into sharp relief, such that he looked (when viewed from the side) as if he were afflicted with a disfiguring disease. He carried too much of the world's violence with him. His black shoes seemed indecently large and offensive on the delicate weave of the Persian rug. Why so many questions? And to what end? Christopher felt increasingly uneasy in the inspector's presence and it took him a while to determine the cause. It seemed outrageous and ludicrously unfair, but, if he was not mistaken, the inspector had started to treat them as suspects. His eyes narrowed too easily and the frequency with which he exchanged complicit glances with his assistant had increased. He was more content to let unnerving silences extend indefinitely while he studied husband and wife with clinical detachment.

Laura retreated into herself and became incapable of speech. She lay on the bed from morning till night, crying softly, incapacitated by grief. A combination of heat and self-neglect caused her lips to crack and her skin to flake. She forgot to wash and began to exude a feral odour. Christopher thought that her decline was so pitiful it would be enough to persuade the inspector of their innocence. But the policeman still asked to see Laura and seemed unmoved when she hobbled into the drawing room, confused and blinking, the glimmer of fresh tears on her lashes. He still pressed her for more detail.

When Christopher tried to comfort his wife, she simply pushed the air and turned her back on him. She refused to eat and her excess pounds melted away. The process was more like decomposition than weight loss. Soon, she looked like a corpse – supine, hands by her sides, sunken cheeks, shadows collecting in the hollows of her eyes. Christopher wondered how long she could go on like this. If she didn't get better, he would have to get her admitted to a hospital.

Historically, work had always been Christopher's refuge. Early on in his life, he had discovered that personal suffering could be mitigated by industry. Total immersion in the task of composition was his panacea, a constant and reliable comfort in troubled times. Yet when he entered the studio and let his gaze travel across the banks of equipment – oscillators, tape machines, speakers and the mixing desk – he felt oddly repelled. A flicker of remorse made him turn on his heels.

After Faye's disappearance had been reported in the press the telephone had started ringing. One of the callers was Sue, the gardener. Christopher explained that Laura wasn't well enough to talk. The woman was quite persistent, so much so that Christopher had had to be firm: 'No, I'm sorry. It *really* isn't possible.' She had responded, 'But I think I might be able to help.' He wasn't sure what she had in mind. 'It's kind of you to offer, but my wife wants to be alone right now.' He cut her off before she had an opportunity to say anything else. When Henry called, he struggled manfully to find the right words to express his condolences. In the end he was defeated by the magnitude of the tragedy. Accustomed only to superficialities, he accepted his shortcomings and brought their conversation to an abrupt close. 'You know I'm here if you want me.' It was the best he could do.

Laura was getting worse. On one occasion, Christopher found her sleeping in Faye's cot. She was curled into a foetal ball, her bony knees tucked under her chin, her thumb in her mouth – a bizarre substitution for the absent child. She was asleep, but the repetitive contractions of her pouting lips were accompanied by an urgent sucking noise. It was as though she was trying to get Faye back by sympathetic magic. On another occasion, she shut herself in the nursery and surrounded herself with Faye's dolls for an entire afternoon.

'Where's the monkey?' Christopher had asked.

'I don't know,' she had replied while adjusting a red bow in a mane of artificial tresses.

She had never liked the Victorian toy that he had rescued from the attic and he suspected that she had thrown it away, although he wasn't sure whether she had done so before or after Faye's disappearance. The possibility that his wife might be telling the truth was one that he dared not countenance.

One night, they were lying in bed together when the baby monitor began to crackle. Christopher switched on his lamp and got out of bed. He walked round to Laura's side and removed the monitor plug from the wall socket.

'No,' said Laura, 'don't do that.'

'It's keeping me awake.'

'Please. Plug it in again.'

'Why?'

'It was how I heard her . . . the last time.'

'You heard *something*, Laura . . .'

'I heard *her*.'

'You know that can't be right.'

'What if—'

'No. Don't even think about it.'

'*Come, child. It is time* – that's what I heard him say.'

'There was no one there.'

'Exactly.'

'People see things – hear things – when they wake up. Things that aren't really there.'

'Who says?'

'Inspector Barnes.'

'What does he know? He thinks we killed our own child.' Her voice had become bellicose.

'Laura—'

'There's no ransom note, Chris. Think about it.'

Christopher sat down on the edge of the bed. 'Laura, this isn't helping. You're thinking crazy thoughts. I know how upset you are about my tapes. I know you thought Faye was in danger, but—'

She had stopped listening to him. 'Why us? It doesn't make any sense.'

Christopher carried on talking, regardless of her inattention, more for his own benefit than for his wife's. 'And maybe you did have some kind of premonition. But ghosts don't kidnap children. OK? It just doesn't happen. It can't happen. My tapes have got nothing to do with Faye's abduction. OK? Nothing.'

Laura reached down and forced the plug back into the wall. Her eyes were wide and aglow with fiery defiance.

The telephone stopped ringing and the house became silent. Even Inspector Barnes failed to return.

Christopher detected a slight improvement in his wife's condition. She no longer lay on the bed all day and very occasionally she picked up a book. At mealtimes she toyed with her food but usually managed to eat a little before rising from the table. Her hours became more regular. Sometimes, she would surprise Christopher by responding to a question and a short, stumbling conversation might follow. They were like actors reading lines at a rehearsal, familiarizing themselves with an obscure, intractable script. She remained, however, indifferent to her appearance. Her hair was uncombed and she dressed in the same grubby outfit every day until he confiscated her dirty clothes and put them in the laundry basket. Vitamin deficiency had caused the corners of her mouth to rupture and these lesions had developed into unsightly sores.

Laura was never entirely mute. Her silences always hummed with the potential for accusation. He lived in fear of a sudden discharge of words that would connect him directly with her anger. Consequently, in order to evade that possibility, he spent an increasing number of hours walking on the heath. Away from the house, he found himself able to lower his defences and consider Laura's position. Had anything happened that might support her belief in supernatural abduction? Anything at all that a rational individual would accept?

There had been the *Come to me, Faye* message, but he had originally interpreted it as *Come Tommy. Fate!* Then there had been the *She is mine* message. He had recorded many similar phrases and this one only became sinister (rather than, say, romantic) with hindsight. And as for Edward Stokes Maybury, Christopher supposed that many Victorian entertainers must have used children in their acts. The fact that Maybury made children disappear was actually quite predictable: children have flexible joints and are small enough to squeeze behind mirrors. Furthermore, the slum areas of London would have afforded Maybury a constant supply of cheap labour. All of these elements could be linked together in order to produce a narrative consistent with Laura's standpoint, but the fact remained that what she believed was fundamentally impossible.

Christopher was glad that he had told her nothing about the *She is mine* message and hardly anything about Maybury. Such information would have produced even deeper entrenchment in the quagmire of her madness (although it was also true that Laura had been largely indifferent when he had first spoken to her about Maybury). Christopher didn't doubt that she had heard voices coming through the baby monitor – genuine communications, radio interference or auditory hallucinations, it didn't really matter which. Shock had amplified her pre-existing anxieties and the conclusion she had reached was absurd.

Christopher sat on a tree stump in a former grassy

hollow that was now a dustbowl. The sun punished the back of his neck and the air was fragrant with hot sap. He recognized that he had been engaging in a form of self-deception. His willingness to consider Laura's point of view wasn't really an example of open-minded fairness, but rather a means of reassuring himself that he wasn't to blame for his daughter's disappearance.

'Impossible,' he said out loud, while gripping the tree stump to remind himself of the material world and its certainties. Believing in spirit communication through electronic devices was, for him, the acceptable limit of credulity, but anything beyond that was clearly insane.

Faye had been abducted by a person or persons unknown. He remembered those occasions when he had heard noises in the garden and how he had assumed that they were produced by an animal. And then there had been the light in the gazebo and the signs of vagrancy. Perhaps someone had been planning to abduct Faye for months, patiently observing, biding their time, hidden behind the gorse bushes or lying in the long grass. Another memory: Laura, eight and a half months pregnant and looking out of the French windows. She had seen a man wearing what she thought was a frock coat . . .

The ransom note had not materialized, which meant that they – whoever *they* were – didn't want money. No, they wanted Faye for some other purpose. The thought made him feel sick and he leaned over the grass and started to retch.

What would they do to his sweet little girl?

It wasn't the dead that should be feared, but the living.

There was an alternative scenario. He had read about childless women who kidnapped babies and infants because they had a pathological need to find an outlet for their pent-up maternal urges. Their compulsion to love was overwhelming. Christopher hoped that Faye had been abducted by such a person, but it was a frail hope, a brittle confection of spun sugar that soon snapped and disintegrated. All too easily his thoughts returned to vile sexual perversions, torture and, ultimately, murder. One day, the telephone would ring and he would be summoned to a morgue to identify her abused and discarded body. The thought was so terrible it made him feel faint with grief.

He didn't know how long he could tolerate the uncertainty. In a way, not knowing what had happened to Faye was worse than receiving news of her death. His life would be held in abeyance, he would not be able to move forward, and he would be forever tormented by futile hopes. As the years passed, he would study every child in the street, and then every adolescent, and then every young woman, looking for the daughter he had lost. The strain would be too much to bear. He would lose his mind.

An instant later he had an idea that made him sit bolt upright. It seemed to electrify him into a state of rigid alertness. He didn't have to accept a life of uncertainty because he had the means – equipment, tools – to find the answers. For months he had been communicating with the dead. He could try asking them for some help, and if Faye had already passed over to the other side, they might be able to tell him.

Late August 1976

Christopher spent days in his studio whispering different variants of the same question into a microphone while the tapes rolled. 'Is my daughter with you? Do you know where she is?' When he played the recordings back they contained nothing. He listened to the empty hissing that issued from the speakers and felt deeply troubled. Where had they gone, his 'unseen friends'? Raudive's procedure didn't always work – far from it – but Christopher had never experienced such a protracted period of silence. He had become accustomed to capturing at least something on tape, albeit an incomprehensible crackle that only approximated human speech. Continued failure produced an uneasy feeling that intensified and mounted.

He gazed into the implacable blackness beyond the windowpane and fancied that only a void existed beyond the glass. This impression of a vast emptiness found a disturbing internal resonance and he suddenly felt his grip on reality slip. Had it all been an illusion? Had he really been recording the voices of the dead, or had he simply imagined it all? He felt untethered, adrift and panicky. Christopher stood up too quickly and his office chair spun away and crashed into the VCS3 stand. He grabbed a cassette labelled 'Speech of Shadows: third movement' and hit an 'eject' button. A vertical door sprung open in readiness to receive the cartridge. He slotted the cassette into place, slammed the door closed and pressed 'play'. A chord gradually assembled itself, one note at a time, and when it was complete an attenuated female voice declared, 'The ocean has no end.' Christopher sighed and pressed the 'stop' button. 'Jesus,' he said, brushing a fallen lock of hair from his forehead. 'What's happening to me?'

The next day he received a telephone call from Henry. His agent was clearly uncomfortable.

'Chris, I really didn't want to make this call, but I'm obliged to let you know what's happening, I hope you understand. The *Android Insurrection* people are beginning to get very impatient. I've informed them about the . . .' He hesitated before changing his choice of words. 'Your situation, and sadly, they aren't being terribly sympathetic. In fact, they're *demanding* to hear what you've got.'

'It isn't convenient,' said Christopher. 'I told you.'

'Yes, of course . . . but really, Chris, can't we sort something out? I could send a cab over. How about that? You wouldn't have to speak to anyone. Just hand over the tapes and leave the rest to me. I'm sure I can handle Mike Judd.'

'No, I don't think so, Henry.'

'But what's your objection?'

'I'm not . . . ready.'

'No one will ask you to do any more work, I'll see to that. Not now at any rate.'

'Give me another couple of weeks.'

The conversation continued unproductively for several minutes, until Christopher, exhausted by its pointless circularity, brought it to an end. 'I can't talk anymore, Henry. I'll call you back.' Nothing had been decided. Immediately afterwards, Christopher fixed himself a large, medicinal gin and tonic.

He trudged upstairs to the studio, sat next to a tape machine, pressed 'record' and spoke softly into a microphone. 'Faye, darling? If you're there, let me know that you're OK. It's Daddy. Please, darling. I love you.' Tears collected on his chin and finally fell in quick succession, spotting the material of his trousers.

*

Christopher had spent the whole day recording and replaying silence. He turned the volume up high and listened intently for perturbations in the continuous hiss. Outside, the light was ebbing away and the cloudless sky was becoming textured with shades of pink and violet. The heat was intolerable. He had finished the bottle of gin he had started drinking in the morning and a dull ache was spreading behind his eyes. Was there any point in continuing? He was about to switch the tape machine off when he heard something – a kind of soft juddering embedded in the noise. It subsided and then started up again, increasing in volume and acquiring a halting rhythm. When he grasped what he was listening to, he felt as if a cold hand had reached into his chest. There could be no mistake – it was the sound of a child crying. Each sob resonated in a cavernous acoustic that recollected the interior of a church. Echoes proliferated. The child was becoming more desperate, its breathing more ragged, until it wailed, the tonal arc rising and falling through a spectrum of emotions – rage, fear, anguish, abandonment – before dying away until all that remained was a pitiful whimpering. The introduction of pitch brought with it intimations of character. 'Oh Christ!' Christopher groaned. 'No, no, no.' He had no doubt he was listening to his daughter. The crying started up again and she suddenly shrieked. Pain made her squeal and an uncharacteristically low moan preceded more helpless sobbing. What did it mean? Where was she? He wanted to clap his hands over his ears, but he forced himself to carry on listening.

'What are you doing? What's that?' The voice was harsh and urgent. Christopher thought that it was on the tape but the sound of Laura's clogs on the floor alerted him to her presence. He rotated the chair to face her. 'Chris? What is it?'

'I don't know.'

'Tell me. What is it?'

'Nothing.' He tried to sound nonchalant. 'Go downstairs, Laura.'

Christopher leaned back to press the 'stop' button.

'No, leave it alone,' Laura barked. She walked up to one of the speakers and tilted her head, listening. Her face slowly filled with horror; her mouth opened, her cheeks collapsed, and her eyes seemed to swell out of their sockets. There was something almost operatic about the scale of her emotion. She was like a diva striking a pose, inhabiting her role before the challenge of a demanding 'mad scene'. Turning to look at Christopher, she said, 'It's Faye.' Her voice quivered. 'When did you record this?' He couldn't bring himself to say. Christopher reached for the 'stop' button again and was surprised when Laura grabbed his wrist. Her grip was like a manacle. She glared at him, but as she did so, the twilight infiltrated her eyes, turning them gold, and he was reminded of the woman he had once loved and lost. Something on the tape reclaimed her attention. She released his wrist, the blood drained from her face, and she stared at the speaker as if it were an apparition. 'No,' she whispered.

'What?' Christopher asked.

'Can't you hear it?'

'What?'

Her reply was almost whispered: 'Chains.'

'What do you mean, chains?'

The sobbing subsided for a moment, and he thought that he might be able to discern a faint clicking noise in the background, perhaps, but nothing that would explain Laura's obvious terror. She stumbled, as if her legs had given way beneath her, and she thrust both hands onto the mixing desk. Christopher got up from his chair to offer her support, but she shouted, 'Don't touch me!'

'Laura,' he pleaded, 'I don't understand.'

She was breathing heavily. Hunched over the faders, she did not make eye contact and when she spoke her voice contained a note of wonder. 'You recorded this *after* she was taken.'

He turned the tape off and summoned the strength to say, 'Yes.'

There was a beat of silence before she yelled, 'You stupid bastard, you *fucking* stupid bastard!' She picked up a handful of his cassettes and threw them at the wall. They shattered and the parts skittered across the floor. Rounding on him, she screamed, 'You stupid, stupid bastard!' He felt the force of her anger like a punch in the stomach. 'Oh my God,' she growled, throwing her head back. 'What have you done? What *have* you done?' She kicked the VCS3 stand and it toppled over. Then, ripping a curtain of tape loops off their hooks, she cast them into the air like party streamers. 'What did I tell you?' she demanded.

'Laura, please . . .'

'What did I tell you?' She jabbed a finger at him.

The force of her verbal assault rendered him speechless.

Laura dashed out of the room and slammed the door. He listened to her running down the stairs and for a few moments he could not move. His mind became blank. Gradually, his senses reconnected with the world and he snapped out of his malaise; he pushed his palms down on the arms of the chair and launched himself at the door.

He found Laura on the first-floor landing. She was

leaning over the banisters, not crying, but making odd moaning noises. Approaching her warily, he said, 'Laura, listen. Please.' She turned to look at him. 'You were right,' he nodded, encouraging her to acknowledge his admission. 'I shouldn't have made those recordings. I didn't know what I was doing . . . and I don't know what any of it means.'

Laura's grief was so intense it manifested as a kind of rapture. A peculiar half-smile flickered into being. 'You invited something unspeakable into this house and—'

'No, Laura,' he interrupted, 'we don't know that. Not for sure.'

'It was Faye.'

'It sounded like Faye.'

The back of Laura's hand hit the side of his face hard. He took a step backwards.

'You *selfish* bastard!'

She raised her hand again, and, anticipating the next slap, he twisted awkwardly. He was standing at the top of the stairs and he tried to grab the banister rail to prevent himself from falling, but he missed, and the world began to revolve rapidly.

Laura watched him bounce down the steps and she was reminded of a marionette being jerked this way and that by an incompetent puppeteer. His arms wheeled around and his legs were suddenly up in the air. He tumbled, head over heels, and when he reached the bottom, at the point where he might reasonably have been expected to come to rest, he seemed to gain extra momentum. Like a gymnast ending an acrobatic display with a final flourish, he somersaulted and travelled an extra yard. Even though she was delirious with rage, Laura registered the oddity.

The house was still and very silent.

Laura used the banister rail to aid her cautious descent. She staggered forward and came to a halt beside her husband. His head and neck were askew, projecting from his torso at an acute angle. She didn't need to check his pulse. He was clearly dead.

The interview room had bare grey walls and contained only essential furniture: a laminated table and three plastic chairs. A fluorescent strip on the ceiling emitted a flickering light. Inspector Barnes and his assistant sat on one side of the table, Laura on the other. Damp patches had begun to appear on the inspector's blue nylon shirt and the smell of his body odour was overpowering. The air was hazy with smoke. Barnes lit another cigarette and leaned back in his chair. 'So you were arguing . . .'

'Yes,' Laura replied.

The unsteady illumination made the inspector and his pale, bony companion look sinister. It made their movements appear discontinuous.

'What about?'

'It's difficult to say exactly.'

'Try.'

She wanted to tell him the truth, but how could she? 'Chris could be very selfish. I suppose that's always the case with creative people. They get so caught up in their work . . . you know?'

'I can't say that I do, to be honest.'

'He locked himself away in his studio and never came out.'

'Were you angry with him?'

'Yes, I suppose so. He'd been in the studio all day. We started talking, and – I don't know – things escalated, I got upset.'

'But what were you arguing about, specifically?'

'He'd stopped listening to me. It was like talking to a brick wall.'

'Oh?'

'I wanted to move house, but he didn't take any notice. He didn't take what I said seriously.'

'Why did you want to move house?'

'Isn't that obvious?'

It was past midnight and Laura was exhausted. The strain of thinking up plausible answers to Inspector Barnes's questions was beginning to show. She clasped her hands together in order to conceal a tremble and attempted to remain focused; however, she was only partially present. A part of her had been unable to escape from the studio; a lesser self, like a photographic negative, was trapped in the past, listening, in perpetuity, to Faye's cries and the *clink-clink-clink* of swaying chains.

Inspector Barnes tapped his cigarette over a cheap metal ashtray and said, 'I thought you were happily married. You didn't say any of this before.'

'Well, no,' Laura replied. 'I didn't think it was relevant to your investigation.'

A wry smile invited her to reconsider what she'd just said. Inspector Barnes took another drag from his cigarette. 'What happened next?'

'I lost my temper. I broke some of my husband's tapes, pushed an instrument over, then I ran downstairs and he followed me. Things got a bit . . . physical.'

'What? He hit you?'

'No, no. I'm afraid I hit him.'

'Why?'

'I was just . . .' She shook her head. 'Really upset.'

'How did your husband react?'

'He turned away . . .' She found it difficult to speak coherently. 'It was an accident. I suppose he tripped. I don't know . . . it all happened so fast. And then he fell.'

'Down the stairs,' Barnes added, as if her final words required clarification. Then he surprised her by being even more precise: 'The *first* flight of stairs, the stairs that you see when you enter through the front door.'

'Yes,' she said, confused by his pedantry.

The big man glanced at his assistant and then returned his attention to Laura. 'Did you move your husband after his fall?'

'He wasn't breathing. There was no point. I dialled 999 right away.'

'You're quite sure?'

'Yes.'

The detective lifted the cigarette to his mouth and the tip became bright as he inhaled. His lips parted and he allowed the smoke to float out slowly. 'That's odd.'

'What's odd?'

Barnes took his time answering. 'Where we found your husband's body would suggest that he fell from the landing.'

Laura shook her head. 'Well, he didn't. He fell down the stairs.'

'Then why wasn't he at the bottom of the stairs? Why was he off to the side?'

'He fell in a peculiar way. I saw it happen. You're quite wrong – he didn't fall from the landing. He couldn't have fallen from the landing, not by accident, because he'd have had to go over the banisters.' She said this confidently. Nevertheless, the detective's response was unexpected. He appeared to be quietly amused.

'No,' he said, 'not by accident.' His massive head rocked backwards and forwards. 'That's right.' It took a few seconds for Laura to grasp what he was implying, and when she did her heart seemed to balloon in her chest. She wanted to protest, but her lungs were unable to supply her voice box with sufficient air to accomplish speech. Before she had quite recovered, the inspector said, 'There was an Akai 4000DS tape recorder in your husband's studio. Do you know the model?' Laura shook her head. 'Your husband owned many tape recorders, but it was one of the smaller ones. He kept it on a stack of equipment on the right side of the main . . . consul.' The inspector created an imaginary floor plan in the air with his hands. 'One of my officers has one just like it at home. It was all set up and he managed to get it going. I have to say, what we heard was quite disturbing. Your husband seems to have recorded a child screaming, a child who must have been about the same age as your daughter. Can you tell us anything about it?'

When Laura had discovered Chris listening to Faye's cries and screams, he had been seated in front of a tape machine positioned above the mixing desk. Moreover, it was big, not small. Clearly, the inspector was referring to a different recording. How many recordings of Faye were there? She raised both hands to her head and massaged her temples. And what would the police conclude when they worked out how to operate the big machine above the mixing desk? What then?

She thought of the chains again, the chilling *clink-clink-clink* of their collision.

'Mrs Norton?' The assistant spoke in a hoarse whisper. 'It *was* your daughter we heard on the tape, wasn't it?'

The silence that followed was long and unforgiving. Suddenly, the task of concealing the truth felt impossibly arduous. Her distress was so profound, so prodigious in its extremity, that she was only dimly conscious of her surroundings. Why not tell them everything? If she told them the truth, they might release her and then she could book herself into a hotel and sleep. The prospect of oblivion seemed enormously attractive.

'I'm sorry,' said the inspector, 'but I really must press you for an answer.'

Laura closed her eyes. 'There's a lot I haven't told you, Inspector.' Her voice sounded distant and alien. The flickering light penetrated her eyelids and destabilized the darkness.

'Go on.'

'I was worried that you'd think me mad. But what you're thinking now is much, much worse.' Laura opened her eyes again. The two men – the bulky, misshapen inspector and his death's-head familiar – were hunched forward, eager to hear more. They reminded her of gargoyles perched on a cathedral.

'Please continue, Mrs Norton,' said the inspector, unable to hide his impatience. His expression was almost salacious. She watched as the red, pointed tip of his tongue appeared and travelled slowly from left to right, moistening his upper lip.

'Faye wasn't taken by a person, as such.'

'I'm sorry,' said the inspector, 'I don't understand what you're suggesting.'

'She was taken by a spirit – an evil spirit.'

Thirty minutes later the inspector and his assistant rose from their chairs and left the room. In the corridor the assistant asked, 'What are you going to do now, sir?'

'I'm going to call a psychiatrist,' the inspector replied. The rubber soles of his shoes made a high-pitched squeaking sound as he lumbered to his office. 'Make sure she doesn't go wandering off anywhere, will you? I won't be long.'

Laura guessed what was happening. When the assistant came back she said, 'I'm *not* mad.'

'No one's saying that you are.'

'But that's what you're thinking, isn't it?' The assistant swallowed and loosened the large tie knot below his prominent Adam's apple. 'I know what I just said sounds crazy. I'm perfectly aware of that.'

'Don't get agitated, Mrs Norton. There's no need.'

'Listen to my husband's tapes.'

'We intend to.'

'All of them. He had become obsessed with making recordings of the dead.'

'That must have been very upsetting for you.'

'Please don't patronize me.' Laura pulled her hair back with both hands. 'There's something bad in that house.'

The assistant bared his teeth in lieu of a smile. 'I understand.' He made a cigarette lighter revolve with his spidery fingers.

'No!' Laura stood up abruptly, slapped her palms on

the tabletop and shouted, 'You don't understand! You don't understand at all!'

Simon was working on a new piece: *Three Lamentations* for countertenor, strings, and celesta. He had completed the introduction to the second lamentation and was pencilling in the voice part when the telephone rang. He waited for Amanda to answer it, but when she didn't, he swore and dashed out of the music room and into the hallway, grumbling under his breath. He snatched the receiver up and said, rather brusquely, 'Yes.'

'Is that Mr Ogilvy speaking?' It was a woman's voice.

'Yes.'

'Good evening, Mr Ogilvy. My name is Dr Fiona Castle. I'm a consultant psychiatrist. I'm calling you on behalf of one of the patients in my care, Mrs Laura Norton. Have the police been in touch with you?'

'The police? No.'

'I see. Mr Ogilvy, I'm afraid I have some bad news. She's currently on remand in Holloway prison.'

The psychiatrist explained the circumstances surrounding Laura's incarceration with professional, telegraphic brevity. Christopher Norton was dead, having supposedly fallen down a flight of stairs; forensic evidence suggested foul play; Laura was under suspicion of murder and exhibiting first-rank symptoms of schizophrenia. When Dr Castle had finished speaking Simon could only say, 'Oh my God.'

'I'm sorry,' said the psychiatrist, modulating her voice to sound more sympathetic. 'It's a terrible, *terrible* tragedy. Particularly following so soon after the . . .' She paused before adding, 'disappearance of Faye Norton. Needless to say . . .' Again she paused, as if unsure whether to proceed. 'All of these events are very probably connected in some way.'

'Yes, yes,' Simon agreed. 'Very probably, but, with respect, why are you calling me?'

'Mrs Norton would like to see you.'

'Didn't you say she was suffering from schizophrenia?'

'She admits to hearing voices and has some very odd beliefs about the alleged abduction of her daughter.' *Why alleged?* Simon wondered, but he was too flustered to ask. 'That said,' Dr Castle continued, 'she's been medicated and her condition is stable.'

'But is there any point in me coming? I mean, will we be able to have a coherent conversation?'

'Yes, I think so.'

'What does she want to see me for?'

'I have no idea. You'll have to ask her that yourself.'

They talked for a few more minutes and the psychiatrist elaborated on her earlier summary, fleshing out a few details, and when Simon put the phone down he could do nothing but stand in stunned silence, listening to the ticking of a clock. He stared into the orange, vertical plane of the wall and somehow seemed to get lost in its featureless infinity. After surfacing from his trance, he went in search of his wife and found her sitting in the kitchen, smoking and reading a copy of the *Radio Times*. She looked up and said, 'Are you all right?'

'No.'

'Who was that on the phone? You haven't lost a commission, have you?'

'No.' He inhaled deeply and said, 'It was a psychiatrist.'

'What?'

Simon sat down at the kitchen table. 'I don't believe what's happened. I just don't believe it.'

He began telling Amanda about the telephone call, but found it difficult to find the right words. His account was stumbling and disjointed, full of syntactical errors. As he spoke, Amanda's hand floated off the table, as if suddenly weightless, and in due course it became attached to her mouth. She looked like a mime artist reproducing the studied intensity of slow-motion film.

Tragedy on this scale was something that touched the lives of other people, not them. They shared a common, defensive delusion that their circle of acquaintances was immune from real harm. The abduction of Faye Norton had left them feeling raw and exposed; however, they had just about managed to come to terms with its shocking irregularity. Now, the news of Christopher's death – or possible murder – and Laura's descent into madness proved too much. They were both rendered inarticulate and had to resort to a more primitive method of communication – a useless dumb show of exasperated signals and lengthy sighs. A period of mute bewilderment ensued.

'I don't believe it,' Simon repeated.

'I know,' said Amanda. 'It just doesn't seem possible.'

'I don't believe it.'

'I know, I know.'

They discussed scenarios. Simon paced around the kitchen table, gesticulating like a fictional detective reconstructing the scene of a crime in his imagination. 'Faye's abduction must have put them under so much pressure. Laura must have cracked up, snapped. They were quarrelling, apparently, on the first-floor landing. Although, really, they must have been fighting. The psychiatrist said it was a quarrel, but really it *must* have been a fight. Chris went over the banisters. That's some drop. He died instantly. God, how awful . . . Chris and Laura – it's unthinkable.'

'How could she have overpowered Chris?' Amanda asked.

'Perhaps she took him by surprise, caught him unawares.'

'But they were supposed to be fighting.'

'I don't know. Maybe he turned his back on her and . . .' Simon stopped pacing. 'Oh, I don't know.' He sat down again and said, 'When I go to see her, will you come with me?'

'No!' Amanda's response was so forceful that Simon flinched. Observing his reaction, she apologized. 'I'm sorry. It's just . . . I don't think I'm up to it.'

'OK,' said Simon.

'You're going then? You've already decided.'

'I don't have any choice.'

'Yes you do.'

'I don't think so. Not now. Not now that Laura's asked for me – *specifically.* It wouldn't look very good, would it? If I didn't go.'

'What does she want?'

He shook his head. 'God knows.'

They fell silent and bowed their heads, both withdrawing into private, inaccessible worlds of reflection. Suddenly, Amanda began to cry. 'Poor Chris.' Once again, Simon was discomfited by the rare spectacle of his wife's tears. Amanda, anticipating a maladroit attempt to provide consolation, stood up, made an uncontrolled fending-off gesture and departed from the kitchen in a hurry. Simon felt obliged to follow even though he supposed that her gesture (like a starlet thrusting the palm of her hand at a flashing camera) implied that she wanted to be alone. He waited for what he judged to be a respectful interval before mounting the stairs and entering their bedroom. Amanda was prostrate on the eiderdown, her head buried in a pillow. Simon crept across the rug, sat down by her side and rested a solicitous hand on her convulsing shoulder.

Later, he found Amanda sitting in the lounge reading a volume of Stevie Smith poetry. She had washed the spoiled make-up from her face and tied her hair back with a ribbon. There was a hint of renewal in her scrubbed appearance and it made her look unusually childlike. Simon went to the music room, sat at the piano, and tried to complete the vocal line he had been working on just before the telephone had rung.

Occasionally, he heard Amanda sniffing, and the sound of a paper tissue being pulled from a cardboard box. He was unhappy with the music he was composing because it was too derivative, too reminiscent of Benjamin Britten. He rubbed an arc of quavers and crochets from the score and tried to think of something more original. A door opened and closed. The stairs creaked as Amanda ascended them. He glanced at his wristwatch and guessed that she was going to bed. Simon wasn't tired and he persevered with his melody, repeatedly failing to find a satisfactory combination of notes. Frustration mounted, and he abandoned composition and drifted around the ground floor, eventually settling on the sofa in the lounge. Amanda had left the volume of Stevie Smith poetry on the coffee table. Without much thought, Simon picked up the book and flicked through its pages until he came to 'Not Waving but Drowning'. He began reading but couldn't get beyond the line about the poor chap who always loved 'larking' having died.

It was not merely the pertinence of the words that made Simon stop reading, but something less tangible, a marginal perception that made him uneasy without obvious cause. He became alert, his nostrils flared, and he raised the open book to his nose. Was he imagining it?

The pages smelt very faintly of Christopher's aftershave. His first thoughts were panicky and irrational: he was reminded of phantom fragrances in ghost stories, communications from beyond the grave. And hadn't Christopher become extremely interested in recording spirit messages? Simon lowered the book and gazed around the room, even straining to look behind the sofa. He studied Amanda's collection of Indian deities: Shiva dancing in a ring of fire, four-armed Vishnu, and a miniature elephant god. Gradually, his initial panic subsided and he began to think more rationally. Connections were made, memories were cross-referenced, and he found himself considering alternative possibilities.

He remembered the marks on Amanda's skin. *No,* he thought, *surely not*.

His mind travelled back in time: a holiday in the south of France with Chris and Laura. He hadn't known Amanda for very long and he had convinced himself that their relationship was going to work, that he had found a woman who would cure him of his public-school vices, the bad habits he had picked up as a boarder during his unhappy adolescence. Yet he had become uneasy towards the end of that holiday, mistrustful, suspicious. He had detected exquisitely subtle changes in the way Amanda and Chris related to each other. By that stage, Simon had already made a significant emotional investment in Amanda and he couldn't bring himself to challenge her. Besides, a simple denial on her part would have left him looking insecure and foolish. What evidence did he have? So, on their return to London he had dismissed his suspicions, chastised himself for being paranoid, and focused his energies on preserving Amanda's romantic perception of him as a 'serious artist'.

Simon raised the book to his nose again. The fragrance was faint but distinct.

'No,' he said aloud, 'surely not.'

A few days later Simon drove to Holloway prison. He was ushered into a room where he was made to wait for some time before a uniformed officer arrived with Laura. He folded his arms around Laura's frame and he was horrified to discover how thin she was: he could feel bones beneath her clothes. The officer, a plump woman with bad eczema, sat by the door watching them intently. It was obvious that Laura was heavily sedated. Her eyelids were droopy, her speech slurred, and her breath carried an unpleasant, metallic odour. Nevertheless, there was a curious urgency about her manner and she was clearly resisting the effects of her medication in order to remain lucid.

'Simon, I need to tell you what happened. It all sounds crazy but you must believe me. You knew about Christopher's project, didn't you? The new piece of music?' Simon had been warned about her odd beliefs, but hearing Laura talk about spirit voices coming out of the baby monitor and Faye's abduction by a supernatural entity was deeply upsetting. It filled him with unbearable sadness. Her eyes sustained a desperate, penetrating appeal for acceptance and vindication. Simon took her dry, papery hand and urged her to remain calm when she became agitated. 'No, Laura, don't – you're upsetting yourself. It's OK, I understand. I know what you're saying.' He rubbed his thumb along the ridge of her knuckles, trying to soothe her with slow oscillations.

'I didn't murder Chris,' she said, lowering her voice as if taking Simon into her confidence. 'We were arguing at the top of the stairs and he fell. It was an accident. The police say it couldn't have been an accident, but it was, I swear it.' She pressed on, forcing the words out, straining to overcome her chemical malaise. 'I need your help, Simon. You will help, won't you?'

'Of course I will. I'll do everything I can.'

'Thank you.'

The sound of heavy machinery could be heard outside. Simon had noticed that the prison grounds resembled a building site. Apparently, Holloway was in the process of being completely rebuilt.

'What do you want me to do?'

'I want you to arrange for the sale of the house and its contents. I'm never going to go back there – ever. My solicitor has the keys.'

'Sure. I can do that.'

'And there's something else . . .' She glanced at the plump officer. Boredom had made the woman's expression slack and vacant but Laura still lowered her voice. 'I want you to go up into the attic. There's a large blue hatbox up there. Inside it you'll find a hat, but underneath the hat is a can . . . you know, a film can. I want you to remove the reel and destroy it.'

'OK,' said Simon.

'Please don't try to view the reel.'

'I won't.'

'And don't hang around in the house – don't stay there any longer than is absolutely necessary.'

'I won't.'

'Thank you.' Her eyes began to moisten. 'There's going to be a trial, Simon.'

'Yes, I know.'

'They think we killed Faye.'

Inspector Barnes was sitting opposite Laura's GP. They had been drinking tea and the gentlemanly atmosphere was vaguely reminiscent of a club room. Even so, the policeman was aware that the gilt leather inlay of the large desk that stretched between him and the doctor represented a kind of social no-man's-land, an unbridgeable divide that discouraged overfamiliarity. The doctor dragged his half-moon spectacles down the slope of his nose in order to bring Laura Norton's medical notes into sharper focus.

'Yes, the last time she came here for an appointment her behaviour was quite hysterical. She was rude and stormed out of the surgery.'

'Did you ever consider referring her to a specialist?'

'It crossed my mind, but you see, Inspector, the NHS has limited resources, and as a GP one is expected to take this into consideration. If every GP in the country referred all of the anxious young mothers on his patient register to departments of psychological medicine, the system would soon break down. Hospitals simply wouldn't be able to cope with the numbers.'

'Yes, of course,' Inspector Barnes agreed.

The doctor pushed a plate of biscuits towards his guest. 'Thank you,' said the inspector, taking a sugared shortbread finger.

'Nowadays,' said the doctor, 'it's standard practice for GPs to treat mild anxiety and depression with drugs. There's usually no need to trouble the local hospital.'

The inspector bit into the shortbread and caught the crumbs with his free hand. Then, with great care, he tipped the crumbs into his saucer. 'The psychiatrist says that all this nonsense about ghosts is the way Mrs Norton's brain deals with guilt.'

'Indeed. My Freud is rather rusty but one must suppose that Mrs Norton's belief in the supernatural allows her to shift the blame for her abominable crimes onto another party, albeit an entirely imaginary party. As a consequence, the delusion alleviates a weight of guilt that would otherwise be intolerable.'

The inspector was momentarily awed by the fearsome complexity of the human mind. He swallowed his shortbread and said, 'Extraordinary.'

'Yes, it all begins to make sense when you think about it.' The doctor seemed to be talking to himself rather than addressing Inspector Barnes. 'The fact that she used to come here so often, expressing worries about the health of her child . . . that too must have been significant, psychologically.'

The inspector shifted position to attract the doctor's attention. 'I always thought there was something wrong with their story.'

'Oh?' The doctor raised his teacup.

'It just didn't add up. Baby-snatchers don't make life difficult for themselves. They're opportunists. You wouldn't get a baby-snatcher choosing to take a child from a first-floor bedroom in the middle of the night.'

'Quite.' The doctor coughed and appeared somewhat abashed. He put his teacup down and said, 'Forgive me, Inspector, but I'm curious about something. What did the Nortons do with the child's body?'

Barnes shrugged. 'We don't know. We just don't know.'

Henry Baylis arrived early at Le Gavroche. He ordered a bottle of wine, lit a cigar, unfolded his newspaper, and read some disturbing reports about the Notting Hill Carnival. Petty criminal activity had led to clashes between black youths and the constabulary; missiles had been thrown and a police van turned over and set alight. A pitched battle had ensued and by the time it was over more than a hundred officers had been taken to hospital.

When Bill Loxley appeared, Baylis dispensed with polite formalities. He tapped the sensational newspaper headline and said, 'What the hell is happening to this country?'

'Yes,' said Loxley. 'Law and order appear to be breaking down.'

'See. Enoch Powell was right.'

'Oh, I don't know,' said Loxley, taking his seat. 'The streets aren't flowing with blood yet, are they?'

'More than a hundred policemen injured. They might disagree.'

The two friends talked about the parlous state of the nation until a waiter came to their table and handed them menus. After they had ordered their starters and main courses, Loxley said, 'Have you heard any more about the Norton case?'

Baylis sighed and rubbed his forehead as if he had just experienced a sharp, lancing pain. 'Terrible business. Still can't take it all in really. No, I haven't heard anything more. The wife's in Holloway awaiting trial and the police haven't been in touch again.'

'Did you know her? The wife?'

'Yes. Not as well as I knew poor Christopher, of

course. She was a famous model once, a beautiful creature.' Baylis's gaze misted over. 'She had the most remarkable eyes – a kind of golden, amber colour.'

'Do you think she did it?'

'They say she's gone mad. If that's true, then . . .' His sentence trailed off and he produced a descending, musical sigh.

Loxley stroked his Van Dyck beard. 'He was such a nice chap.'

'Yes, I'll miss him awfully.'

'Tell me . . .' Loxley leaned forward, placing his elbows down on either side of his wine glass and linking his fingers. 'Did Christopher ever mention Maybury again?'

'Who?'

'The magician who used to live in his house – Edward Stokes Maybury.'

'No.' Baylis shook his head. 'Why do you ask?' He had detected a certain alertness in his friend's attitude.

'Well,' Loxley replied, 'after meeting Christopher, I was inspired to do a little research on Maybury myself. I'm still naive enough to believe that chance encounters can be provident.'

'O, I am fortune's fool!' said Baylis.

'*Romeo and Juliet*?'

'Yes.'

'Anyway, I tried to find out where Maybury was buried. He lived in Hampstead so I assumed I'd find his grave somewhere local, somewhere like Highgate Cemetery. Well, it turns out that he wasn't buried anywhere.'

'Oh?'

Loxley paused for a moment, unable to resist delaying his revelation to achieve a heightened sense of drama. 'Maybury disappeared. He didn't die in 1914, as we'd thought. That was the year he vanished.'

'Ha! How ironic – for a magician, I mean.'

Loxley's bald head glistened in the candlelight. 'The house – Christopher's house – was inherited by Maybury's next of kin. A niece called Dorothy Pritchard.'

'But when you say vanished—'

'There's hardly any detail, Henry.' Loxley's interruption was dismissive and employed more force than was strictly necessary. 'War had just broken out and the disappearance of a not-very-well-known retired stage magician didn't merit much coverage.'

'So, something of a mystery?'

'Indeed. I might report my discovery in a letter to *The Magic Circular* magazine. The editor, David Beckley, is very keen on history and arcane footnotes.'

'How did you find out about Maybury's disappearance?'

'Archives,' said Loxley, clearly not wishing to elaborate. The sudden waywardness of his eyes made him look untrustworthy, an effect that was augmented by the impishly tapering of his ears. 'Henry?'

'Yes.'

'You're quite sure Christopher didn't say anything else about Maybury?'

'Yes, quite sure.'

'It's just that . . . I came across something else . . . a letter actually, written by a Circle member back in 1908. Apparently Maybury had outbid him for a very rare sixteenth-century book of magic that was up for auction at Sotheby's: *The Devil's Troth*. It was never heard of again. God only knows how much it'd be worth now.'

'Sorry,' said Henry, shaking his head. 'I can't help you, old boy.'

The tension seemed to flow out of Loxley's body and his shoulders dropped. He smiled apologetically. 'Shall we order another bottle?'

September 1976

The start of the month was unsettled, and in the first week there were cool, north-westerly winds that felt refreshing and autumnal. Simon and Amanda attended the performance of *Nyx* at the Roundhouse and the reviews that followed were wholly positive. 'Distinctive string writing and subtle use of tape; a dark, lyrical piece that demonstrates, once again, Ogilvy's rare, expressive gift.' For a few days, they enjoyed the pretence of normality. They even made love – a brief, painfully desperate coupling initiated by Amanda.

Unfortunately, the cooler weather did not last. At the end of the third week temperatures began to climb again. A thunderstorm was needed, a storm of biblical proportions, like Noah's flood, a cathartic release that would cleanse the air and wash away the filth. Drains reeked. Exhaust fumes collected in the mouth. The heatwave had lasted too long; the sun was too large, its domination of the sky a foretaste of a final expansion that would one day consume the Earth. Every morning, the fiery disc returned, not to banish darkness, but to remind humanity of its ultimate doom.

When the brouhaha surrounding the premiere of *Nyx* had subsided, Simon recognized that the time had finally arrived for him to pay a visit to the Vale of Health. He was obliged to honour the promises he had made to Laura.

'I'm going this afternoon,' he said to his wife over breakfast.

'OK,' Amanda replied. He had hoped that she would offer to accompany him. Instead, she looked away to avoid the silent appeal in his shining eyes.

There was much to do. He would visit the house, check that everything was in order, and make a preliminary assessment of the contents. Choices needed to be made with respect to what should be sold and what might go into storage. There was the funeral to arrange. Christopher's parents were both dead and Laura had become estranged from her family in her teens. It would be a small gathering: a few friends, some professional associates and one or two of Christopher's cousins, perhaps. And then there was Laura's odd request to find and destroy a reel of film she had hidden in the attic. Did it really exist? He had his doubts. Even so, he was obliged to look: he had given his word.

Simon spent much of the day at the piano, reworking passages he'd written for the *Three Lamentations*. The cello and double bass parts were too busy and he removed some of the unnecessary ornamentation. He was satisfied with the result and felt a strong temptation to stay at home, but he was troubled by his conscience. The bar lines suggested imprisonment and he was reminded of Laura. The premiere of *Nyx* had already served as a justification for putting things off. Any further delay would represent a betrayal of trust.

As he drove down East Heath Road, Simon became aware of the changing light. Dark clouds were accumulating with remarkable speed. He glanced up through the dirty windscreen and felt an odd, primal emotion that combined excitement with fear. The trees became monochrome as an eldritch dusk intensified. Simon tapped his indicator, turned left into the Vale of Health, and drove through a tunnel of overhanging branches that dipped down to the hidden village with its faux gas lamps and old-world charm. He pulled up outside the house, got out of the car and inhaled deeply; he could smell the sharp, sweet pungency of ozone. Suspended six thousand feet above his head, the weight of the coming deluge was oppressive.

Simon checked that the key was still in his pocket.

He had collected it from Laura's solicitor the previous week.

The first claps of thunder, like the crump of distant ordnance, sounded as he stepped beneath the porch. He unlocked the front door and entered the hallway, where he stood for a few moments, arrested by a chalky outline on the floor that showed where Christopher's body had come to rest after his fall. Simon shivered. Death was too palpable here. He felt as if he had strayed within range of the grim reaper's scythe. Warily, Simon backed away from the chalk outline and turned to enter the drawing room. A flash of lightning transformed the garden into a vision of lurid brilliance and after a short interval a loud detonation shook the house. For a split second, Simon had seen what appeared to be a man standing by the gazebo. It had been a curious illusion, like a silhouette, but with the suggestion of a face beneath a top hat. Simon continued to stare through the glass until he was confident that there really was no one there.

Rain began to fall, the downpour quickly increasing in volume until the air resonated with its insistent rataplan.

Laura had told him that he would find a ladder in the side entrance, so he unlocked the French windows and went round the back of the house to collect it. As he crossed the terrace he cast a wary glance in the direction of the gazebo.

Carrying a cumbersome, heavy object proved extremely difficult for Simon; he wasn't particularly strong and his progress was clumsy and uncontrolled. He miscalculated the length of the ladder and, when he turned, the rails banged against the walls and banisters. On reaching the uppermost landing he tested the rungs with his weight (they didn't look very safe) before climbing towards the hatch in the ceiling. The door offered only minimal resistance and swung open on hinges. Simon poked his head into the attic and looked around. Heavy rain drummed loudly on the roof tiles and streamed over the skylight. There wasn't much to see in the flickering gloom: some plastic crates, some ruptured bin bags and a pyramid of wooden chairs; however, next to the piled furniture he thought he could make out something blue and cylindrical.

Simon clambered onto a beam and stood up. He advanced cautiously and dropped on one knee when he reached the chairs. The lid came off the hatbox easily and inside he found an extravagant creation made from folded white sails and exotic feathers. It made him think of Ascot and society weddings. Through the trembling plumage he saw a glint of silver. Simon raised the hat and discovered a film canister underneath. Subsequently, he put the hat back in its box and, gripping the canister tightly, he began retracing his steps along the beam.

He had not gone very far when he noticed something that he had previously overlooked. Between the beams was a toy monkey. Simon crouched down to take a closer look. A key sticking out of its back suggested that it was clockwork. The creature was dressed in a military jacket and clutched cymbals in its outstretched hands. Simon wondered whether it once belonged to Christopher – a memento of his childhood, perhaps? – but he very quickly rejected this idea. It looked far too old.

Suddenly the cymbals came together, and although the sound of their collision was not loud, the movement was so quick and unexpected that Simon, startled, lost his balance and found himself rocking backwards and forwards. He only just managed to stop himself from falling through the flimsy plasterboard panels that separated the beams.

'Jesus Christ!' He reprimanded himself for being so nervy.

Exercising extreme caution, he made his way back to the hatch, pausing only once to glance back at the toy. He was oddly relieved when the soles of his shoes made contact with the landing floor. Hoisting the ladder over his shoulder, he embarked on a slow descent that inflicted further damage to the walls and banisters. He returned the ladder to the side entrance, locked the French windows, and stopped by the sofa, where he brushed the rain from his hair. The silver canister, which he had deposited on the coffee table, caught his eye. He had already guessed what kind of film it contained and the prospect of seeing explicit, possibly humiliating images of Laura did little to excite his curiosity. He wasn't even tempted to hold a few frames up to the light.

Simon walked over to the bureau and looked inside. There were some letters and writing materials and it occurred to him that he would have to go through Christopher and Laura's personal papers. He wondered what he would find. Bank statements? Contracts? Love letters?

The police had already ransacked the bureau and they hadn't bothered to put things back in their proper place. He had been informed that he would find an address book in the bottom drawer, an item that he required in order to contact people who might want to attend the funeral. It wasn't there.

Simon closed the bureau and ascended the stairs to the bathroom, where he relieved himself in the toilet bowl. After flushing, he washed his hands at the sink and, as he was doing so, he found he could smell Christopher's aftershave. Simon opened the bathroom cabinet and he saw a red plastic bottle with a white screw top. He thought again about how the same fragrance had risen up from Amanda's book of Stevie Smith poetry. Placing his palm on the mirrored surface, he slammed the cabinet door shut. It was something he didn't want to think about.

In Christopher and Laura's bedroom he stared at the rumpled sheets and the partially exposed mattress. He felt uncomfortable, as though his friends were still in bed together and he had intruded on their intimacy. The baby monitor crackled. It caught his attention and he stared at the device, wondering whether it was a fire risk. He decided to turn it off at the wall socket; however, when he ran his fingers along the lead he discovered that the monitor was already unplugged. It crackled again, but this time the noise approximated speech. It sounded, to Simon, just like a distorted radio broadcast. Again, there was a burst of static and he thought that he could distinguish words: '. . . shall never . . . this trap of souls.' Something was said in German, but a rhythmic buzzing – which he recognized as interference produced by a passing vehicle – made it impossible to hazard a translation, and when the buzzing ceased, there was silence. Assuming that the monitor had a reserve power source, he shrugged and went out onto the landing, from where he glanced into the nursery.

Simon did not feel inclined to enter. He could just about accept that Laura, in a deranged state, might have been capable of murdering her husband. Wouldn't any woman if she was afflicted with a mental illness? But he could not accept that Christopher and Laura had killed Faye. That, to Simon, seemed patently absurd.

When he had gone to see Laura in prison, she had mentioned some misunderstanding about certain tapes that the police had found in Christopher's studio. She had subsequently become very inarticulate and the severity of her illness quickly became apparent. As far as Simon could ascertain from her garbled attempts at an explanation, she had managed to convince herself that poor Faye had been abducted by a supernatural agency and that the confiscated tapes were a form of spirit communication. 'You knew what Christopher was up to, didn't you?' She had gripped his arm tightly. 'He was meddling with things he didn't understand.' Her distress was so great it had been necessary to summon the prison GP.

Simon remembered the little girl's face, her strangely pensive expression and her curly blonde hair. What had happened to her? He prayed, pointlessly, to a God that he did not really believe in, that the child was alive and being cared for.

Another clap of thunder roused him from his distracted state. He climbed the remaining stairs to the top floor and entered Christopher's studio. The rain was particularly loud, like a herd of wild animals stampeding on the roof. There were tape boxes scattered everywhere, spools heaped on the mixing desk, and tangled cables crossing the floor. Simon scanned the room, registering the banks of equipment, the oscillators and filters, the synthesizers, the TV screen, the microphones, and the stringed metal frame that Christopher had removed from a piano. Eventually, Simon's gaze fell on the empty office chair and he felt the dark, hot flow of guilt passing through his gut.

Hasting-Bass had asked Simon if he knew of anyone writing 'conceptual' music and he had chosen to say nothing. He had known full well how much Christopher craved recognition, how much he wanted to be acknowledged as a composer of substance, and he, Simon, had spitefully denied his friend the perfect platform for his work. He had sat there, stealing surreptitious glances at Hasting-Bass's young assistant, gradually sinking into a state of self-pity.

Why hadn't he recommended Christopher? It would

have been so easy. *Well, as it happens, Hugo, Christopher Norton is working on something very suitable at the moment. He hasn't written any serious music for ten years or so, but he played me a new electronic composition recently and I have to say it's very interesting. It'd be something of a coup, Hugo. Imagine it: Christopher Norton's return to the cutting edge. Your programme would be the first to announce his come-back. They used to call him the 'English Stockhausen'. Do you remember?* Advocacy of this kind would have been very persuasive, yet Simon hadn't been minded to say such things, because, fundamentally, he did not believe Christopher deserved an introduction to Hasting-Bass. While Christopher had been attending glamorous parties in the 1960s and jetting around the world, Simon had been living an impecunious existence, refining his technique, poring over scores, finding his voice, night after night, year after year. Christopher would have to make comparable sacrifices if he expected to be given privileged access to the likes of Hasting-Bass. It was only right.

But now, looking at the empty office chair, Simon found his indignation vaguely embarrassing, even shameful. He had been petty and mean-spirited. His friend was dead. What did it matter anymore? The idea of belatedly assisting Christopher to realize his ambitions started to acquire a redemptive aura. Such an enterprise promised relief from the remorseful feelings that would otherwise trouble him in the hours when sleep did not come easily. Simon bent his knees and picked up a spool from the floor. He would listen to all of Christopher's tapes. The early works – many of them unfinished – were certainly of merit. Perhaps some of the more challenging film music could be edited into a form suitable for broadcast on Radio 3. And then there was the piece Christopher had played him, the piece that his friend had been so excited about. One didn't have to believe the sounds that Christopher had recorded and manipulated were spirit communications. The procedure that Christopher had employed was sufficiently novel and the overall idea sufficiently 'conceptual' to engage Hasting-Bass. Simon pictured himself being interviewed on a television arts programme, talking earnestly about his commitment to ensuring the survival of his friend's music. Such selfless dedication would undoubtedly raise his own profile and impress his peers.

Simon cleared the spools from the mixing desk and gathered the tape boxes together. The majority had been labelled with cryptic titles: *Phobos landing, Android Insurrection factory, Time Slip – Jurassic landscape 3, Motel (Isadora's secret)*. It was all film music. Simon pressed the 'on' switch of an Akai 4000DS but the VU meters didn't light up, so he walked around the room inserting plugs. The speakers popped and buzzed and the studio filled with a faint hum. When he returned to the mixing desk, he noticed that one of the cassette players was loaded. He pressed 'eject' and removed a C-60 cartridge. It was labelled *Speech of Shadows: third movement*. He pressed 'play', then traced the connecting leads to an amplifier and worked out how to direct the output through the speakers. Suddenly he heard a female voice saying something about an ocean. He continued listening. Complex chords were slowly constructed from oscillator pitches that entered one note at a time. The music evoked the ebb and flow of the sea, and in the brief interval that preceded each successive wave of sound, Simon heard the shimmering of electronic voices. Occasionally, single words or phrases stood out from the background murmur: 'eternity' . . . 'we have been called' . . . 'peace' . . . 'the dominion of angels' . . . This unusual composition, Simon supposed, must be Christopher's special piece, and he wondered whether Christopher had really recorded the dead, or whether his friend had simply shaped radio interference and random noise until it conformed to his expectations. That had certainly been his initial impression.

The music was strangely hypnotic. It drew Simon in, its soft undulations gradually dissolving thoughts, its continual unfolding encouraging the surrender of identity. He may even have fallen asleep once or twice – brief but perplexing absences. Amanda had been smoking a lot of cannabis lately, and over the last two weeks Simon had taken to sharing her perfectly rolled, compact reefers. Ordinarily this wasn't his custom. Smoking cannabis made him feel very sluggish and his faculties were often blunted the following day by episodes of torpor. The music came to an abrupt end. It was clearly unfinished.

Having established the title of Christopher's swan-song, Simon began rifling through the tape boxes. He remembered that he had seen several opening flaps inscribed with the words *Speech of Shadows*. When he had set these boxes aside, Simon counted sixteen in all. The sides were covered in writing that identified the contents. *Second movement – section 4, Tranquil; Fourth movement – We are many to The door is open. Female voices; First movement – introduction, spaced oscillators, all voices; Climax – I pray the Lord.*

Simon selected one of the sixteen boxes, removed the spool from inside, and pressed it onto the supply spindle of the Akai 4000DS. After he had threaded the tape through the head block and guides, he attached the laminated end to the take-up reel. He then wound the tape forward a little and experimented with the controls until he could hear music. This time there were many voices, with only a sparse accompaniment. A resonant gong-like effect sounded intermittently against a chorus of exclamations and cries. This din carried on for several minutes but faded as a man's voice declared, 'Their suffering has purpose,' and a woman replied, 'The summer shall return.'

Through the window, the livid sky was divided by a branching river of white light. Almost simultaneously, thunder boomed. The speakers emitted a crepitating blast of electrical interference and when it subsided there was nothing but tape hiss. Simon was about to turn one of the chunky switches to the 'fast forward' position when he was halted by a rhythmic sibilance. He tilted his head to one side and strained to locate the source. Standing up, he pressed his ear against the fabric cover of one of the speakers and heard what sounded like someone whispering. It was impossible to understand what was being said, but once or twice he thought he'd heard his own name. He drew back, somewhat unnerved. The pitch of the tape hiss changed, becoming lower, and the speech became more distinct. 'Simon. Simon.' Although enveloped by noise, Christopher's voice was clearly recognizable.

Simon looked at the revolving spool and then back again at the speaker. Why had Christopher recorded repetitions of his name? 'Simon.' The voice became clearer and was animated by a note of urgency. 'Simon. Get out of the house.' It was as though his dead friend were addressing him directly. 'Simon. Get out of the house.'

Confused and disturbed, Simon withdrew from the horseshoe of equipment. A spool that he had failed to pick up earlier crunched under his heel.

'Simon. Listen to me. Get out of the house.'

Again, it was as though the voice wasn't pre-recorded. Christopher sounded uncannily present. Simon's confusion curdled into fear and he found himself responding, 'Chris?'

The window became a featureless white oblong and another explosive thunderclap sent vibrations through the floor. Simon could hear water overflowing from the gutters and splashing on the flagstones below. There was something else, another sound, intruding on his senses, but it wasn't dramatic enough to draw Simon's attention away from the speakers.

'You must leave. You must leave now.'

There were more bright flashes and simultaneous claps of thunder and the lights on the electrical equipment began to blink. The studio had been unpleasantly humid, but now the temperature seemed to plummet. It was then that Simon identified the sound that, up until that point, had been fluttering in the background. He turned sharply and stared at the Akai. The recording had come to an end. One reel was empty, the other full, and the loose, untethered end of the magnetic tape was making a continuous noise. Yet he could still hear Christopher's voice: 'Run, Simon. Run.'

Simon's head jerked back to its original position. He stared at the speakers, his body becoming tense. Cords of muscle swelled on his neck and cold perspiration made his forehead as reflective as polished marble.

'Run, Simon. While you can.'

The impossibility of what he was experiencing created a momentary paralysis. His thoughts lost coherence and terror vacated his mind.

'Run.' The barked command emerged from a foamy littoral of static.

When Simon finally reacted, he did so instinctively. He wasn't aware of having made a decision to flee. A few seconds of time seemed to have been excised from his life. Suddenly, the studio door was coming towards him at high velocity. Then he was leaping down the stairs. As he made his descent he became aware of a curious perceptual distortion, a subtle disconnect between effort and accomplishment. It seemed that he was taking too long to reach the next landing, and when he arrived there, he was disorientated by double vision. There were two staircases leading down to the ground floor instead of one, and he couldn't choose between them. The house seemed to expand and he sensed a proliferation of invisible avenues extending in all directions, a multiplicity of alternative routes that might lead him astray. His rising panic, which had the quality of a harsh, sustained screech, filled his mind with preposterous, fantastic visions of entrapment in a building that had ceased to obey the laws of physics.

Simon took a deep breath and gripped the banister rail. The reassuring solidity of the wood helped him to reconnect with reality. He shut his eyes and when he opened them again, the two staircases drifted together until they were overlapping. As soon as their reunification was complete, Simon seized the opportunity and completed his descent. He skidded down the hallway, knocking over a consul table, and when he reached the front door, he didn't trouble to look back.

Outside, the rain was falling in sinuous sheets and the road had been transformed into a fast-flowing river. Simon pulled his jacket over his head and dashed to the car, where he made a fumbling entrance with keys that almost slipped from his wet hands. He sat behind the steering wheel of the Austin 1800, panting like an animal, watching the world blur behind a layer of opaque condensation. After turning the keys in the ignition, he activated the windscreen wipers. The swinging black blades removed a film of water and thumped loudly at the extremity of each synchronized oscillation.

What had happened?

Too much cannabis? Too much stress? An anxiety attack? An overspill of the contents of his unconscious? A psychoanalyst would say that he had experienced an auditory hallucination caused by excessive guilt. And he had once known a concert pianist who had had to abandon a promising career because stage fright gave her double vision. He glanced at his wristwatch, cleaned the inside of the windscreen with a paper tissue, and turned the car around.

By the time he got to Jack Straw's Castle it had stopped raining. Simon was one of the first customers. He sat in a corner drinking single malt whiskies until his hands stopped shaking. A young man entered and strolled up to the bar. While waiting for the barman to get his drink he looked over his shoulder and smiled at Simon. The boy's teeth were evenly spaced and somewhat luminous in the half-light. Simon did not respond. Terror had blinded him, even to a thing of sublime beauty.

When Laura received Sue's letter she couldn't quite believe it. She savoured each line, each heartfelt expression of sympathy, and every night, just before the lights were extinguished, she slipped the envelope beneath her pillow. Lying on a paper-thin mattress and immured in a variegated, swirling darkness, she pictured Sue working in the garden, as seen from the nursery window. The image had the brute simplicity of Soviet poster art.

On the day of Sue's visit, Laura was restless. She rehearsed conversations in her head incessantly. There was so much she wanted to say. Yet when Sue was finally sitting in front of her, something odd happened. The sense of urgency melted away and as they looked into each other's eyes they seemed to enter into a state of wordless communion. When the warden looked away their hands slid across the table and their fingertips touched.

Eventually, Laura spoke. 'I didn't kill Faye.'

'I know, love,' Sue responded.

'And I didn't kill Christopher.'

'Of course you didn't.' The phrase was spoken without a trace of condescension. 'You couldn't have. I know that.'

'They don't believe me. I told them what really happened, but they don't believe me.'

'I believe you.'

'That house . . .' Laura bit her lower lip and it became colourless.

Sue nodded. 'I could feel it too, as soon as I stepped through the front door. I was worried about you . . . and Faye. That's why I offered to do the rockery. I wanted to keep an eye on you. I should have said something. I'm sorry.'

'You did – and I wasn't very receptive. I remember.'

They talked softly while sustaining their surreptitious physical contact and Laura felt as if a healing energy was flowing from Sue's body directly into her own. Her fingertips had started to tingle.

When their time was up, Sue said: 'They can't keep you locked up in here forever. They'll have to let you out one day.'

For the first time since Faye's disappearance, Laura imagined a life – *her* life – extending into the future.

September 1979

Three years later

The preceding winter had been catastrophic: blizzards, deep snow, unspeakable cold; retail markets had collapsed and public sector strikes had produced widespread despondency. The streets of London had been littered with stinking refuse and hospitals had closed their doors. Yet none of this had affected Terry Vance. His business was booming; the new Tory government would surely reduce taxes; and he and his wife, Eileen, had just moved from nondescript Enfield to glamorous Hampstead. He sensed change. A better world coming, one in which a man like him – ambitious, practical, and hard-working – could expect to be rewarded.

The residents of the Vale of Health viewed their new neighbours with suspicion and muted disapproval. Vance owned two sports cars – one red, one blue – with personalized number plates, and every Sunday morning he would emerge from his Victorian villa carrying a bucket of soapy water and proceed to hand-wash both vehicles. He evidently enjoyed the task and when he was finished, he would stand on the kerb admiring the glossy bodywork and scintillant chrome. His wife (a short platinum blonde who was rarely seen without high heels, full make-up and encrustations of jewellery) usually brought him a mug of tea at the end of his labours. The sound of her immoderate laughter could be heard throughout the Vale.

In 1971, Vance had started an employment agency for computer-room personnel. It had become successful very quickly and he now rented offices overlooking Cambridge Circus. His achievement was substantial, given that he had started his working life as a humble punch-card operator.

One Sunday morning, shortly after moving to Hampstead, Vance was – as usual – washing his cars when he noticed a woman in dungarees standing on the opposite side of the road. She had arrived in a van spray-painted with stylized flowers and an advertisement: 'Gaia: Landscape and Design'. Vance assumed the woman was looking for work and called out, 'Sorry. I've already got someone to do the garden. They'll be starting in a few months.'

She crossed the road and stood by his side. 'How long have you been living here?'

'Not long,' Vance replied. He looked her up and down. She was quite attractive but definitely not his type. Her hair was untidy and he found her large, masculine boots almost offensive. Unfortunately, each stage of his negative appraisal was accompanied by a transparent change of expression.

'I hope you don't mind me asking,' said the woman, 'but when you bought this house, did they—'

'Like I said,' Vance snapped, 'I've already got someone coming.' He glanced at her van and then added with friendly malice, 'A *proper* company – professionals.'

The woman's expression hardened. 'Do you have any children?'

'What?'

'Do you have any children?'

'No. What's it to do with you?'

She seemed about to answer his question but she stopped, on the brink of speech, and then sighed. 'It doesn't matter.'

'What doesn't matter?'

'I was going to offer you some advice. But . . .' She hesitated again. 'I've decided against it.' She turned abruptly and clumped away. Vance chuckled to himself and set about removing some bird droppings from the soft-top of his TR6. 'Mad,' he muttered. When the woman drove off he didn't even bother to look up.

Vance had wanted a swimming pool, but the garden designer (a rangy man with a weathered, sage-like face) argued against it. A swimming pool would be costly and not in keeping with the character of the house. Subsequently, Vance had lost interest in the project and Eileen was left to make all the decisions. There would be a wide lawn, several water features (including a Gothic fountain) and a pergola leading to a timber-framed summer house.

By the end of August, the clearance of the back garden was almost complete. The gazebo had been demolished and the apple trees felled. Many of the bushes and shrubs had been uprooted and burned. Two close-standing stone cherubs were uncovered and the designer had been keen to incorporate both of them into his plan. Eileen had agreed because she thought they looked 'cute', especially the one reading the book.

A small digger was hired to make trenches that would eventually become ornamental pools, and the exposure of fat, writhing worms attracted flocks of hungry birds. The air smelt of moist clay and the unpleasant, faecal undertow of decomposition.

Vance had had an uneventful day in the office, which was just as well, because he needed to get away early. He had arranged to play tennis with a friend at five. The traffic, for once, wasn't too bad, and he managed to get home with plenty of time to spare. When he got out of the TR6, he could hear the digger at work. He found Eileen in the drawing room painting her nails. She was wearing a woollen dress that hugged her shapely figure, a belt made from large interlocking metal rings, and gold pendant earrings. The room was fragrant with her perfume.

'I've got all your things ready,' she said. 'Your sports bag's under the stairs.' Her accent betrayed origins from somewhere along the Thames Estuary.

'Thanks.'

'What time do you think you'll be back?'

'I don't know. We're going for a drink after . . . nine maybe.'

Eileen put the little brush she had been using back in its bottle, splayed her fingers and blew on her nails. 'Do you want me to put something in the oven for you?'

'Yeah, OK.'

'Stroganoff?'

'Yeah, all right.'

Eileen stood up and moved to the fireplace, where she lit a cigarette. The hem of her dress had ridden up her legs, revealing the black brocade trim of her stockings. Vance put his arm around her waist and kissed her on the mouth. She tasted of ash and mouthwash. When they separated, she smiled and raised her plucked eyebrows.

The sound of a knuckle tapping on glass made them both turn. One of the gardeners, a middle-aged man with a beard, was looking in at them, a hand held horizontally against his forehead. Eileen wriggled her hips and pulled the hem of her dress down. 'Come in, Jack.'

The man opened one of the French windows. He made an apologetic gesture, indicating that he couldn't enter on account of his dirty clothes. 'Mr Vance,' he said uneasily. 'Would you come with me, please? We've found something.'

'What?' Vance was irritated by the gardener's untimely intrusion and his response was brusque. Eileen rested a restraining hand on his sleeve.

Jack glanced from husband to wife and back again. 'I think you'd better come and see for yourself.'

'Hang on,' said Eileen. 'Wait for me. I'll put some mules on.'

'No, Mrs Vance,' said the gardener. 'Perhaps your

husband should . . . first . . . if you don't mind . . .' He winced, ashamed by his own inarticulacy.

The couple looked at each other and Eileen shrugged. Vance crossed the room and sashayed out onto the flagstone terrace. Another gardener, a teenager, was standing near the digger, some distance from the house, and he appeared to be looking into a hole.

'What's the problem?' Vance asked.

The gardener shook his head. 'I don't know what to say.' He seemed stunned, unable to speak properly. They proceeded along a temporary woodchip path. 'Be careful,' the gardener added. 'It's a little slippery just there.'

As Vance approached the digger he saw an opening in the ground surrounded by several mounds of freshly excavated earth. 'Blimey!' said Vance. They had uncovered an old stone staircase, the uppermost step of which was flanked by the two cherubs. It led down to a half-open metal door.

'What's in there then?' Vance addressed the younger gardener. The boy looked at the older man, unsure as to whether he should speak or not. Jack consented with a subtle inclination of his head. 'It's horrible,' said the boy. 'I've never seen anything like it.' He swallowed and the greenish pallor of his complexion suggested that he was about to be sick.

Vance descended the muddy stairs and when he reached the bottom he pushed the door open. The hinges creaked and some loose soil trickled down from above the lintel. Vance swore and brushed the dirt out of his hair. He peered into the gloom, before warily stepping over the threshold. The air was cold and damp.

For a few seconds, Vance was unable to interpret his surroundings. The experience was like looking at an abstract painting in which everyday objects are merely suggested and emerge only slowly from obscurity with sustained study. Vance was aware of vertical lines and shapes, but they stubbornly resisted resolution into forms that could be readily identified. Gradually, with attendant feelings of mounting horror, the world became comprehensible.

A number of chains hung from the ceiling, but his attention was drawn to the shrivelled thing that dangled in the air at eye level. The skull was small and covered with remnants of desiccated skin and flesh. Blonde curls still adhered to the crown and the eye sockets were empty. The remains of the dead infant – for that is what it appeared to be – were held together by its clothing: white cotton pyjamas decorated with pink flowers.

'Fuck.' Vance looked back over his shoulder. The two gardeners had followed him. They were standing close together, slightly hunched, as if they were about to be whipped or beaten.

'What's going on down there?' It was Eileen.

'No!' Vance shouted. 'Stay where you are, love.' Her heels sounded on the stairs. She pushed past the gardeners and before Vance could dissuade her from advancing any further she came to a sudden halt. He watched her mouth become a black oval rimmed with bright red lipstick. She pressed her palms against her cheeks and the scream that she produced threatened to continue without end.

Sources and Acknowledgements

I would like to thank Wayne Brookes, Catherine Richards, Clare Alexander, Steve Matthews and Nicola Fox for their comments on the first and subsequent drafts of *The Voices*. I would also like to thank Dr Heidi Hales for an enlightening discussion on the subjects of forensic psychiatry and prison procedure, and Jennie Muskett for explaining how film music composers go about their work.

I read many books while researching *The Voices*; however, the following deserve special mention. *Breakthrough: An Amazing Experiment in Electronic Communication With the Dead* by Konstantin Raudive; *Special Sound: The Creation and Legacy of the BBC Radiophonic Workshop* by Louis Niebur; *Seasons in the Sun: The Battle For Britain 1974–1979* by Dominic Sandbrook; *Hiding the Elephant: How Magicians Invented the Impossible* by Jim Steinmeyer; and *Circle Without End: The Magic Circle 1905–2005*, compiled and edited by Edwin A. Dawes and Michael Bailey. I found the penny-toy man verse on the childhood pages of Lee Jackson's superb Victorian London website (www.victorianlondon.org). I made one small change: 'dots' becoming 'tots'. The earliest version of the children's prayer 'Now I lay me down to sleep' was written by Joseph Addison and first appeared in an edition of the *Spectator* on 8 March 1711. I have used the version which appeared in *The New England Primer*, although there are many others. Sue's copy of Susan Brownmiller's *Against Our Will* (1975) had yet to be published in 1976; however, I describe this later Penguin edition because the cover design served my purposes.

The soundscapes I describe are imagined; however, listening to a double CD issued on the Chrome Dreams label called *Forbidden Planets: Music From the Pioneers of Electronic Sound* made the process less effortful.

I was seventeen in the summer of 1976. I wish I'd paid more attention to what was going on . . .

F. R. TALLIS

London, May 2013